"*You.*" Aristide

"What are you doing l

She peered up at the artist's twisted face and backed farther down the steps. A doorknob poked her in the back. Panicked, she twisted it open and dashed into an unlit basement storeroom.

She stumbled forward into the dark, tripped over a metallic cylindrical object, and landed on her stomach. All the air whooshed out of her. Rectangular objects with sharp corners tumbled around her, jabbing her in the arms and neck. Rough cloth scraped her skin.

On the staircase above her, the beast hovered in the doorway like a predator scenting his prey. For a second, he hesitated, then he dashed down the steps and moved toward her, huffing as he shoved objects out of the way. She pushed herself up on hands and knees and scuttled further into the dark.

"*Sto diávolo.* Where are you? If you destroy any of these paintings, I will have your hide, or at least my lawyer will." He came closer. "Busy man, my lawyer, and to think I almost didn't hire one."

She scrabbled back and touched torn canvas. Heavens, these were his paintings—the ones that sold for thousands of dollars.

She was in deep, deep trouble.

Kudos for Zara West

A member of RWA, Zara is an award-winning author of both fiction and non-fiction. Her short stories have appeared in several anthologies, and she has received awards from Women on Writing, Stone Thread Publishing, Tryst Literary Magazine, and Winning Writers. Her novels have placed first in the Romance Through the Ages contest, second in the Touch of Love Contest, fifth in the Fab5 Contest, and long listed in the Myslexia Novel Competition.

Beneath the Skin

by

Zara West

The Skin Quartet Series

Beneath the Skin

Cover Art by *Angela Anderson*

The Wild Rose Press, Inc.
PO Box 708
Adams Basin, NY 14410-0708
Visit us at www.thewildrosepress.com

Publishing History
First Crimson Rose Edition, 2016
Print ISBN 978-1-5092-0832-6
Digital ISBN 978-1-5092-0833-3

The Skin Quartet Series
Published in the United States of America

Dedication

To my husband
Always my hero

Acknowledgments

My love and thanks to Jeanne Rose, Lillian Krasner, and Kristin Nelson for their reading, critiquing, and enthusiasm for my first foray into romantic suspense, with especial thanks to my editor at The Wild Rose Press, Inc., Kinan Werdski, for her careful reading of my manuscript and many helpful suggestions.

The quote from Giorgos Seferis' speech at the Nobel Banquet at the City Hall in Stockholm, December 10, 1963 from *Nobel Lectures, Literature 1901-1967*, Editor Horst Frenz, Elsevier Publishing Company, Amsterdam, 1969 Copyright © The Nobel Foundation 1963 is reprinted by permission of the Nobel Foundation.

The selection from the poem "Mythistorema" by Giorgios Seferis from the volume *George Seferis, Collected Poems* by George Seferis, 1995, is reproduced with permission of Princeton University Press.

Chapter 1

"We have many monsters to destroy.
Let us think of the answer of Oedipus."

~Giorgios Seferis

Melissa Dermont stood on the tips of her toes and peered through the window of The Siren tattoo parlor. No sign of Bella. She checked the time on her cell phone again. Seven-thirty. Bella's shop should be open. The neon mermaid sign with the rainbow fish tail should be flashing. Customers should be jammed in the small waiting area, and Bella, crimson red hair pulled back into a braid, should be bent over muscular biceps, pale fleshy thighs, and quivering stomachs, plying her art.

"Looking for Bella?" A salesgirl stuck her fuchsia pink head out of the boutique next door. The diamond stud in her nose twinkled in the street light. "She's not been in at all today. She might have come in yesterday morning. But the Siren never opened so I may be wrong."

Melissa glanced over her shoulder. "Closed two days?"

The girl nodded. "Perhaps she took off on vacation?"

"Without leaving word?" Melissa frowned. "That's not like her. She knew I was coming tonight. She would

1

have called." Her stomach clenched. Without Bella's interview and the promised illustrations, her dissertation in anthropology wouldn't be completed in time to make the January graduation deadline, and paying the grad fees for another semester was out of the question. Her college loans were maxed out.

Worse, Iza was scheduled for a private session with Bella in the morning. The poor woman was desperate. If she didn't get the disfiguring tattoo of her pimp's name covered over soon, Melissa feared the distraught woman would take a knife and try to skin it off herself. Bella wouldn't renege on that appointment unless something serious got in the way.

She pulled out her cell and checked for messages. Nothing. She tapped in Bella's number and listened to it ring and ring and ring. One of those annoying canned voicemail ladies droned in her ear. She tapped her foot impatiently waiting for the beep.

The salesgirl called across. "No answer?"

Melissa shook her head, left Bella a brief "Where are you?" and disconnected.

The girl shrugged. "Know where she lives?"

"No. We've always met here. It's like she lives in her studio and never goes home." She hesitated, afraid to say more. Bella had secrets. She'd interviewed her three times, and there were things Bella wouldn't tell her. Basic things—where she'd been born, where she lived, where she'd learned tattooing. And many times the tattoo artist just blatantly lied. She hadn't even given her her real name. Bella Bell was her trade name.

Melissa bit her lip. People were entitled to their secrets. She had secrets, too.

Voices echoed down the street. A motley

assortment of would-be hipsters in skinny jeans, vintage pearl button cowboy shirts, and wildly striped socks strolled around the corner.

The salesgirl gave a wave. "Gotta go. Potential customers coming. Good luck finding her." She tugged down her skintight halter top and disappeared into the store.

Melissa pushed away from the window and tucked her cell in the pocket of her battered gray knapsack, shivering despite the lingering warmth emanating from the sun-heated pavement. Bella might be lying in pain on the floor of her apartment, and no one would know. New York City could be a frightening place for someone living alone.

She jiggled the doorknob. Bella's home address or a clue to where the tattoo artist had gone might be inside. She stepped out of the doorway and studied the row of stores. The Siren stood at the end of a line of quirky boutiques running along heavily trafficked Bedford Avenue, a few blocks from the Williamsburg Bridge. Way too public a place to stage an amateur break-in. With her luck, a patrol car would pass by, and the last thing she wanted was to deal with the police. Not after her previous run-in with New York City's finest.

She cupped her hands and peeked through the windowpane again. Inside, the tattoo parlor was long and narrow with a small storeroom at the rear next to the john. The red glow of the exit sign over the back door lit the hallway.

She peered up and down the block. If she found a side alley leading to the backyard, maybe she could open the rear door without anyone noticing and get inside. The Siren had no alarm. "No one'd steal from me," Bella had boasted with a laugh. That had been one of the few times when she knew Bella told her the truth.

Fingers crossed, Melissa headed down the street. Two stores down, she found a grilled iron gate ajar and an alley filled with overflowing trash cans. Wrapping her arms around her to protect her only decent sweater, she wiggled past the stinking garbage and then worked her way down the narrow passageway.

At first, the streetlight cast enough glow for her to glimpse the graffiti-covered walls rising on both sides and the broken up pavement beneath her feet. But the further in she went, the deeper the shadows. She trailed her hand along the wall and edged forward, the only sound the crunch of what she hoped was crumbling mortar beneath her feet and not something worse.

A screech pierced the air, followed by a skittering noise. Heart thundering in her chest, she pulled up short. A wise person would turn back. A cat yowled. Then another. She pressed her hand against her beating heart. That's right. Bella's cats. She was always bragging about the kitties she saved as a trained trap-neuter-release caretaker for the City Feral Cat Initiative. No surprise to find a resident cat colony behind her shop.

The tension in Melissa's shoulders eased, and she hurried forward. She hated that panicky feeling. It made her feel weak and stupid, like the day Laura disappeared. She pushed away the memory, wrinkled her nose against the increasing reek of cat, and entered the shadowy backyard.

High above, the faint light from an apartment window illuminated empty tins and plastic bowls overturned on the ground behind the tattoo parlor. A knot formed in her stomach. Bella wouldn't neglect feeding her strays. She'd have gotten someone to put out food and water for them before leaving for a vacation. The knot tightened. She'd have asked her.

She picked her way around the empty cat dishes and climbed the steps. Cats of all sizes and colors lay against the door. They scurried away from her feet in a clatter of tipped and knocked about pans, except for one, a shabby, orange tom with raggedy ears. The old fellow rubbed against her legs and purred.

"You hungry, Mr. Tom? Well, let's see if I can find your mistress for you." She patted his head and turned her attention to the back door. Despite the peeling paint and deep gouges from thousands of cat claws, the door was solid and securely locked. The only weakness was a painted-over glass window in the top half. Dare she break it?

She glanced around. The steps lay in the shadows, out of sight of the one lit window. All the others were dark. No one could see her, and hopefully, if the tenants heard anything behind their barred windows and their blaring TVs, they would blame the noise on the cats.

At the foot of the steps, she found a broken brick and picked it up. She'd once smashed a window pitching a softball. A well-aimed brick should work even better. Teeth gritted, she drew back her arm and hefted it at the glass. The resulting crash reverberated off the building walls. The tom cat huddled at her feet scurried away with a panicked cry.

Heart pounding, she huddled in the doorway and waited for the clatter to die away and the tenants to discover her. But nobody yelled or leaned out a window. Her heart slowed, and she studied the hole she'd made. Her arm would fit, but a ring of jagged splinters remained wedged in the sash. Better a torn sweater than a cut tendon. She reluctantly pulled off the angora sweater that had been Laura's and wrapped it around her hand.

She hesitated. Despite the chill evening, perspiration gathered on the back of her neck. She hated taking risks, and here she was in the act of breaking and entering. She scanned the yard. A posse of cats stared at her with unblinking eyes. Bella would forgive her. She wouldn't want her kitties to go hungry. Taking a deep breath, she reached in like a two-bit crook in *Law and Order*, shoved back the bolt, and then slipped inside.

Before her, the hallway to the studio lay dark and silent. She took a step. Beneath her feet, the floor boards creaked. The hairs on her arms rose. She'd spent many hours in The Siren interviewing Bella and observing customer behavior, trying to discover why women chose to brand the names of their men and worse on their skin. But without Bella's rich laughter and the excited voices of her clients, the tattoo parlor felt devoid of life. She hurried forward toward the front, peeked into the john and storeroom, and burst into the studio proper. The familiar aroma of ink and disinfectant swirled around her.

She switched on the overhead fluorescents and let out a sigh of relief. Nothing seemed to be disturbed in the tattooing area. To her left, the hydraulic tattoo chair was shiny and clean, ready for the next client. To the right, the rolling cabinet containing Bella's tools sat tucked underneath her work counter. On the golden yellow walls hung the city licenses and a mirror for satisfied clients to admire their new skin decorations. A bulletin board on the far wall was plastered with photographs of limbs and torsos and necks of all sizes, shapes, and colors wearing Bella's designs.

She moved to the waiting area. Along the window wall sat two plump black leather sofas. Faux, Bella liked to say, easier to clean. In front of them, stretched a long, low coffee table covered with binders of tattoo designs for potential customers to thumb through while waiting.

A wire rack held brochures. She ran her hand over the safety notices and glossy flyers featuring Bella's art and glanced out the plate glass window. Outside, cars whizzed past. A group of college-age girls in skin-tight denim stopped and peered in. Melissa pointed to the closed sign and held her breath until they moved on. She needed to hurry. If she stayed much longer with the lights on, some passerby who knew Bella might start questioning how a strange girl got inside the closed shop, and what she was doing there.

She took a breath and glanced around again, forcing herself to take her time. If she'd learned nothing else during her ethnographic work, it was that people's secrets lay in the details. This time, she noticed small things out of place: a half-full take-out cup of latte left on the counter, a binder knocked crooked on the coffee table, Bella's lucky eyeball paper weight—her *mati*, she called it—lying against the door molding as if accidently knocked off the little side table where it usually sat.

Behind the counter, she found a freshly pressed apron lying on the floor, and in the far corner, the bottom file drawer was pulled out, papers sticking up as if searched through in a hurry. Her heart beat ratcheted up. Miss Everything-In-Its Place Bella would never have left her files in disarray.

She bent down and shuffled through the papers in the file cabinet. Most were bills addressed to the store. One folder contained sketches of old-style sailor tattoos, the kind Bella mocked. "I could make a fortune on all these guys who come in here wanting to be dirty old pirates inked by a mermaid," she'd said. "But I hate to think of them walking round with that garbage on their arms. If they don't want one of my designs, I send them on to Silenco or Espana." Melissa reached for another folder and flipped it open. She stared at the sketch on top, unable to breathe. It couldn't be.

At that moment, the phone rang. She jumped up and put her hand on the receiver of Bella's quirky 1980s Aladdin's Lamp reproduction phone. It rang again. She hesitated. Bella liked her privacy. She'd be angry if she knew she'd broken into the shop and gone through her papers. But then it could be Bella, herself, on the line, desperate for help. Melissa lifted the receiver. "The Siren."

"*Sirena? Pos ise?*" a man with a rough voice said. She heard foreign speakers every day in the polyglot neighborhood, and this man sounded Balkan or Middle Eastern. He also sounded angry and frustrated. She made out the name *Sirena*. Was he asking for Bella? Was that her real first name or was he mispronouncing the name of the shop? She took a deep breath. "Bella isn't here. Do you speak English?" There was a short huff on the other end, and the line went dead. She squeezed the receiver in her hand. She'd detected a tone of concern underneath—was this someone who knew

Bella? A family member—or an enemy? She hit redial.

"*Oriste*." It was the same voice.

"What do you want with Bella? I'm a friend of hers."

A long silence, then the man spoke in accented but impeccable English. "Inform your boss he won't get away with this. I fly in tonight."

She slammed down the receiver. Whoever the man was, he sounded like trouble.

With trembling hands, she leaned over and swept up the sketch she'd dropped when the phone startled her. She crushed it between her fingers. The last time she'd seen that small blue mark it adorned the arm of a boy driving away with her sister, and five hours later, Laura had been found dead in an alley. She slumped against the counter. If Bella had anything to do with people wearing this tattoo, she was in serious trouble.

She stuffed the incriminating sketch into her knapsack. Then she dumped out the rest of the files and picked through the bills and receipts for some clue as to Bella's address or where she might have gone. Nothing.

The pink velvet jewelry case that served as Bella's cash box caught her eye. She pulled it out from beneath the counter top. Expecting it to be locked, she was surprised when it clicked open and revealed a set of keys resting on top of what appeared to be several hundred dollars in bills and coins. Her stomach sank. Bella had come in yesterday, and if she left her house keys and the day's petty cash, then she hadn't left on her own.

She picked up the keys. Nondescript, like all keys, the only thing to indicate they were Bella's was the gold mermaid dangling from the key ring. She turned them over in her hand. She was an anthropologist, one of those curious folk who brazenly asked anyone anything. If she could ask hundreds of women considering a tattoo, if they were having sexual relations with their partners, surely she could find out where Bella lived. With her wild scarlet hair reaching her tush, three nose piercings, and the siren tattoo running from her neck to her ankle, she couldn't hide easily.

She tucked the keys in her pocket. Bella walked to work. A few minutes away, she'd said. How many Bellas or Sirenas lived within walking distance of Bedford Street? The police would know.

Should she contact them? All the old memories boiled up—the police with their cold faces, the reporters with their sneers and constant harassment. What if Bella was murdered the way Laura was? Could she face that circus again?

Chapter 2

Ari Stavros dropped his suitcase onto the scuffed terrazzo floor and leaned on the battered counter. His head spun and his legs shook from the twenty-four-hour flight from Volos via London to New York. Plus, the taxi ride through rush hour to get here from Kennedy Airport would set a much calmer man to raving, and he'd lost his placid temperament long ago. "I want to report a missing person."

The desk officer shook her head. "I've already told you to sit down and wait. The lieutenant will see you shortly, Mr. Stavros."

He dragged the suitcase back to the waiting area and lowered himself into one of the hard plastic chairs designed to bend one's spine in the wrong direction. Bolted together, the entire row of chairs shook when he lowered his considerable weight into a narrow seat built for people with average size shoulders and arms. The woman with the black eye sitting in the next chair gave him a stony stare and pulled herself into a smaller ball.

"Sorry, ma'am." He tipped up his lip in the grimace that passed for his smile. The woman turned away. They always did. Her arms were bare, and he studied her skin, a creamy brown like the color of *sketo* coffee and thought about what colors he would mix to paint it. His fingers twitched. He should be painting, not wasting time in a Brooklyn police station. " *Sto diávolo,*

Sirena," he cursed under his breath. He corrected himself. Not Sirena. She was calling herself Bella Bell now according to Vernon, and Vernon would know. Dumb name—sounded like a porn star. No wonder he'd not been able to find her.

Not that he'd tried much. He shifted in the chair. Had she been so angry at him she officially changed her name or was it a stage name to cover the ludicrous way she'd decided to use her artistic talent? *A tattoo artist?* He tugged down his sleeves. He'd never understood the desire to permanently emblazon one's skin with odd symbols for a frivolity.

On the other side of him, a bored toddler squirmed in the seat while his mother bit the end of a pencil and stared at a form attached to a clipboard. Fortunately, the little one was on the unscarred side of his face. Women might avert their heads when they saw his ruined face, but babies usually screamed. He closed his eyes and concentrated on the composition for his next painting. Perhaps he'd try a storm-threatened sky, the clouds hanging low on the horizon…

A brain-splintering shriek jerked him back to the waiting room. He turned and saw the child's hand wedged in a crack in the plastic seating. The tiny fingers turned blue instantly. "Hold on, little man." He jumped up, seized the seat bottom and yanked, snapping the thick plastic like it were made of cardboard. The trapped fingers shot free, and the child screeched louder.

"*Ásto moró.*" He scooped up the boy and handed the wailing child to his mother. She glared at him, eyes wide in shock, more likely because of his face rather than his show of strength or the fact he was speaking

Greek. Not that it mattered. He didn't expect a thank you.

"We need ice," he yelled at the desk officer.

Another cop appeared and rushed forward. "We'll handle this." He eyed Ari's wrestler's build and battered face and put more force in his voice. "And don't leave. You'll need to complete an accident report and"—he glanced at the mangled chair—"one for the damage you caused to city property." He turned and shepherded the woman and child down the hall.

What next? Ari shook his head and sat back down. He peered at the clock. He'd wasted an hour here. New York police were no more efficient than Greek ones. He should have gone directly to the sublet, showered, and changed. At least, he'd be more comfortable, and it didn't help his credibility to be dead tired, unshaven, and dressed in the sweaty, crumpled suit he'd been traveling in for over a day.

He settled back against the hard plastic and took his passport out of his coat pocket. He tapped it on his thigh. Three weeks. He had three weeks to find Sirena. The American embassy refused to issue him a longer visa because of his *unfortunate background*, as they so politely put it. If he hadn't arranged to have a major retrospective of his paintings, they certainly wouldn't have issued one at all.

Loud voices and a curse echoed from the back corridor, and a protesting prisoner, escorted by two officers in NYPD blue, burst into the waiting area. The inmate, in an orange jumpsuit, arms in cuffs, leg chains scraping along the tile floor, was hustled past him by his guards. The wild-eyed man swerved in his direction, and Ari yanked his feet out of the way of the chains.

Zeús, but that brought back memories. The police officers gripped the man by the back of the head and pushed him hard, hurrying him out the door. Ari turned to watch them go.

Xristós. Ahh. A delicate Asian girl stood sidewise in the doorway, waiting for the group to pass by. Cropped raven-black hair, skull-sleek as a monk seal's fur, emphasized her perfect profile. Her creamy yellow skin glowed, the color of the sky seconds before the sun rose from the deep azure of the Mediterranean Sea. She reminded him of a sea nymph—a Nereida—like the one riding the dolphin on the fifth century red-figured vase that somehow, in the diaspora of Greece's artistic heritage, ended up in the Getty.

He imagined slipping down the tight little black sweater to reveal more of the glorious honey-colored skin covering her high perky breasts and cupping them in his palms. He grew hard and heated at the thought of running his fingers along the graceful curve of her hips, lowering his mouth to kiss the gently rounded stomach.

But no—he trailed a hand over his broken nose and scarred cheek and glanced away. A beauty like her wouldn't want him. They never did. He shifted again in the chair, the seatback creaking behind his shoulders.

Once upon a time, he'd been compared to a Greek god. Girls idolized him. Now all they wanted was his money. He swiveled toward the door and examined his sea nymph again. The girl stared at the police desk, dread on her face. He looked over his shoulder at the indifferent clerk. Right on, girl, they make you wait forever here.

Enough. He tucked away his passport and stood. Maybe for a generous fee she would be willing to pose for him after his painting supplies arrived. He'd need some local models.

"Mr. Stavros." A squinty-eyed officer holding a clipboard stepped in front of him twirling a pencil. "Lieutenant Dobbins will see you now."

He shook his head to clear it. This was no time to be dazzled by a stunningly beautiful girl. His sister had been kidnapped, and it was up to him to rescue her. With a last glance at the lovely Nereida, Ari turned and followed the cop down the hall.

Chapter 3

Melissa froze in the tiled entrance way to the station house. She'd forgotten the tinny echoes and rotten stench of the place. A prisoner, his face contorted into a mockery of humanity, shuffled by her, radiating anger. She pressed back against the wall to let him pass. Two officers gripped him by the arms and hurried him along with sharp jerks like a piece of worthless meat. As they came abreast of her, the man dragged his feet and pulled back, chains rattling. She pressed harder against the lobby wall, making herself as flat as possible. They scuffled and shoved. One of the officers trod on her toes. An elbow whacked her in the shoulder. Then they were gone without a word of apology or concern. They didn't care. They'd never cared.

Not when her sister went missing.

Not when they found her—an angel sprawled in a pool of blood.

Not when they'd stopped looking for the murderer.

The bastard still roamed free.

She turned to go and halted. A man in the waiting room was staring at her. Not an ordinary man—a beast of a man—with long black hair gathered in a ponytail and eyes dark as midnight on a starless night. He had the broadest shoulders she'd ever seen, with powerful arms she was sure could squeeze a man to death. Even his posture radiated tension, a coiled energy that could boil up like a sudden storm or trap an unwary enemy or make passionate love.

His pitch-black eyes met hers, and heat pooled in her stomach. It was like he could see right through her clothes and into her heart.

She gave herself a shake. The man was ugly as hell—a monster. His nose had been smashed and broken so severely, it formed an S-shape. A ridged scar slashed from the corner of his eye to his lip. The man might have the body of a god, but anyone with a smashed-in face such as his, had violence in his blood.

Still, for all that, she wanted to touch him, for him to touch her. She had no idea why; perhaps to discover if he was not some ancient god—a newly awakened Zeús—descended from Olympus to ravish her.

An officer toting a clipboard approached him, and the black woman next to him rose up and demanded something. The cop, with a curt bark, turned her away, and continued talking to the monster, leading him further into the station. The woman stared after them, then gathered up her bags, and stomped to the door.

She swung her hip on the panic bar and slammed the door open. "Sit there for over two hours, and then they bend all over for him, the ugly bastard." She readjusted her bundles. "Might as well go home and get beat up again. Next time he'll kill me, and the police might take some notice."

Melissa glanced back into the waiting room. She'd find no help inside, but she could help this woman. She jogged to catch up, and matching the woman's stride, pulled out a card for Mercy House. "I know where there is a safe place your husband will not be able to hurt you. Can I take you there?"

17

****

An hour later, Melissa watched Perlita, the woman with the black eye, disappear down the hall. She gave a sigh of relief. It had taken a cup of coffee, three walks around the block, and finally a welling of tears to convince her to enter the shelter.

Daniela Reyes, the angel of Mercy House, patted her on the shoulder. "We'll take good care of her. That slime of a husband won't find her here. You did the right thing."

"Took forever to get her to come without going back for her clothes or her dog."

"At least there are no children. I'll see what I can do about the dog." Daniela tipped her head. "What's wrong, Mel? You look like you have the world on your shoulders."

A co-worker passed by the open door. Melissa leaned over Daniela's desk and lowered her voice. "We need to find another tattoo artist for Iza. My friend Bella—isn't available right now."

"I'm getting worried about these girls you're hiding. Better if they came here," Daniela said.

It was an old argument. "You know they won't. They don't want to get trapped in the system. They just want the tattoos gone."

"It's not worth the risk, Mel. Sooner or later one of their keepers will come after you. It has to stop."

Melissa gave her friend a hug. "It's the least I can do. I wish I could do more."

Daniela fussed with the ruffled sleeves of her tropical flowered blouse. "I have never understood the appeal of tattooing. People change and grow, but the tattoo is a permanent reminder of some stupidity, an all-night drunk, or some bastard who once swore to love you forever."

"There's much more to it than that. Deep psychological and cultural reasons for marking one's body. People have done it for thousands of years." She picked up her backpack and slung it over her shoulder. "That's why I am doing this research."

"I'd be happier if you could convince every tattoo artist to refuse to engrave a man's name on some woman's skin."

"Hopefully, my work will make a difference. But I really gotta go. See you Friday."

Daniela nodded, and Melissa slunk out the side exit. It would not do for anyone to know she brought abused women here. With a quick check to make sure the sidewalk was clear, she left the safe house and hurried down the quiet residential street, Bella's keys heavy in her pocket. She'd have to find the tattoo artist's apartment on her own. Maybe the White Pages on the Internet would work. It was amazing what one could find with a little searching.

She glanced at her cell. Drat, late for work again, and she'd be lucky if her boss didn't carry out her constant threat to fire her. She sped up her pace as she rounded the corner and headed down Bedford toward Cary's Coffee.

Chapter 4

Ari stepped out of the precinct house and squinted against the sunlight, hoping to see his Asian beauty. Of course, she'd disappeared. Probably never came in. She'd appeared petrified. What business could she have with the police to terrify her so? He wheeled his suitcase to the curb and signaled for a cab. Not his problem. He was here to rescue Sirena.

A cab pulled out of traffic, and he slipped inside with a grunt. He barked out the address and let the cool artificial lemon-scented breeze from the air conditioning waft over him as the cab lurched back into the line of cars.

"New to New York?" the cabby asked in a thick accent.

Ari glanced up at the string of beads dangling from the visor and glanced at the cabby's name on the license. Something Turkish. He shook his head. He tapped the glass privacy panel. "I'm no tourist. I know where I'm going. Cut the chitchat and get me there." He leaned back on the seat and rubbed the puckered skin of his left cheek.

The cops had grilled him as if he were the reason his sister was missing. What could be sinister about a business letter concerning deeding over an island, they'd insisted. But a foreigner with his history and with his face must be up to no good. They'd be watching closely all right—watching him, not Vernon Newell. He'd have to save Sirena on his own.

Idiot. What had he expected—to be treated like a successful multimillionaire who owned his own island, flew a private helicopter, and was a major name in the art world? He caught the taxi driver staring at him in the mirror and gave him a scowl. The man jerked his concentration back to the traffic. It's what people expected. If you looked like a monster on the outside, you must be one on the inside. It made life uncomfortable for someone who had been an overly sensitive boy.

He flexed his muscles beneath his suit jacket. He couldn't wait to get the monkey suit off and wash the sweat away. As far as he was concerned, a hot shower was the only thing civilization had to offer, and the studio loft he'd sublet through the Internet had better have working plumbing. He'd do Bella no good in the state he was in.

This afternoon he would go to her apartment and search for clues to where she'd gone to escape Vernon—a knot of acid rose up his throat—if she had escaped the bastard and found a place to hide.

He sat up. *Zeús*, he couldn't start searching yet. He had an appointment at the gallery with Ms. Este Keeler, the uptight manager. He'd gotten the text when he'd arrived at the airport baggage carrel. After the excitement of planning a grand showing in New York, selecting his best work, and overseeing the meticulous packaging, he had no taste for it now. He should have thrown everything to the wind and rushed to New York. He might have saved Bella. But he'd put his work first, and let her down *again*.

The taxi stopped.

"Here's the place, sir." The taxi driver studiously kept his face averted, his hands gripping the wheel, knuckles tight.

Ari shook his head. One scowl and he was master. What a joke. He reached into his pocket, extracted a wad of bills, and without counting them stuffed them into the cabby's hand. "For your trouble." He gripped his suitcase and jumped out, shutting out the man's gape of surprise and eruption into profuse thanks.

He rolled his shoulders and searched for an opening in the graffiti-covered plywood fence surrounding the two-story cement building. Money was magic. It could paper over every defect. And he had plenty. So what if he lost the pretty little sea nymph. There were plenty of others. He had a list of potential models from his agent. One of them was sure to have perfect skin and be willing to close her eyes and warm his bed—for the right price.

Chapter 5

Melissa swallowed a spoonful of soup and listened as the clatter of high heels turned the corner and headed up the third flight. She wasn't ready to face her roommate. Living with Jana was like being trapped in the middle of a tornado with a psychoanalyst. She couldn't keep anything hidden from her. Still, she shouldn't complain. At least Jana had given her a place to stay. She moved over to the wobbly kitchen stool Jana disdained and waited for Volcano Mouth to arrive.

The door flew open, and Jana, her curly blonde Angelina Jolie locks out of control as usual, burst into the apartment. She threw her briefcase on the floor and stopped to catch her breath. "Soon as an apartment opens on the first floor I'm going to scoop it up."

Melissa peered up from her bowl of soup. "Three flights aren't bad. Keeps us in shape. Besides, it's much quieter up here with no one walking above our heads."

"My job keeps me in shape. Oww." Jana kicked off her strappy heels and fought her way out of her electric yellow suit jacket. She tossed it on the chair. "Stupid Patels wanted to see every two-bedroom apartment between here and Meeker Avenue. In and out. Up and down. Want a river or park view, but don't want to pay for it. I'll fix them good though. Tomorrow I will show them that flea-bitten place in among the warehouses on South Third. It's got a view, and it's in their price range. I just won't mention the stain on the bedroom floor was where the former tenant bled to death from a knife stick to the belly." She sidled up to the counter. "What smells so good?"

"I bought myself soup and a sub at the deli," Melissa said, putting down her spoon. "Thought you were eating out."

Jana wrinkled her nose, opened the refrigerator door, and searched through the contents. "Nah. The last client canceled. How'd the meeting with your advisor go?"

Melissa unfolded the paper around the sub and stared at it, hunger gone. "It didn't."

Yogurt in hand, Jana jerked up, hitting her head on the top of the door. "What?" She pulled the lid off and snagged a spoon from the dishrack.

"I couldn't finish the last section. I went to The Siren last night, and Bella wasn't there."

"I don't believe it. You skipped meeting your advisor? He's going to be furious." Jana thumped down on the sagging futon that sat against the wall of their tiny living room. "You've spent hours with the tattooed lady. Couldn't you make it up? Who'd ever know?"

"That's not ethical." Melissa shifted on her stool. She, of all people, shouldn't be touting morality to anyone. "I think something's happened to Bella. No one on the block has seen her since yesterday morning. I almost went to the police."

"The police?" Jana glared at her. "Because a hoity-toity skin artist doesn't open shop? Gad. She's probably sleeping off a drunk or spreading her legs for some sailor guy."

"Bella's not like that."

"The skin prickers are all like that. Druggies and whores, the lot of them."

"They're creative artists."

"Creative cons is what they are. They steal money from idiot teens."

Melissa sat beside Jana on the couch and took a bite of her sandwich. She swallowed. "I told you I could get that horrid tattoo Mike put on you with his ball point pen removed. I know someone."

Jana stiffened. "No, I'm keeping it. As a reminder never to trust a man."

"You were just kids fooling around."

"Fooling is right." Jana lay back on the pillows and closed her eyes. "I almost forgot. Nancie texted me. I don't know what happened with her high fashion job, but she'll be coming back early from Cannes. You'll have to leave by the end of the month."

Melissa choked on her sandwich. "That's three weeks from now."

"Won't Colin be back from that health conference by then? Do the nice. Get him to marry you. Handsome, clean-cut, kind to women." She swallowed a spoonful of yogurt, turned it around, and licked the back clean. "Family has plenty of money. He can pay off your college loans, fund your research."

"He's *too* kind to women." Melissa pushed herself up and tossed her uneaten sandwich into the trash. She took a can of beer from the fridge and traipsed across the tiny room they affectionately called the salon. There was barely room for the purple futon and a small white wicker chair. Vintage India cotton prints draped the windows, creating curled shadows on the walls. Melissa lifted a corner of the cloth and peered out into the

25

slanting light of the setting sun. "The whole time we were together and he was professing undying love, he was sleeping with his teaching assistant. Took her with him."

"Oh you poor thing. Come here." Jana tossed the empty yogurt container to the floor and opened her arms.

Melissa slid into them and pressed her head against the cool silk of Jana's blouse. She curled closer. "I saw a man today. At the police station."

"Gad, you actually went to the station?" Jana slid her hand under the back of Melissa's tank top and massaged her back.

"I never made it in. He was grotesque. His face all flattened in like a cement block dropped on him or something."

"Egad, a veritable monster. Bet he doesn't need a mask at Halloween." Jana rested her head on top of hers. "So who was he?"

"I have no idea. There was a battered woman sitting next to him. She left in a hurry. Could have been her husband. Looked the type, if you know what I mean."

"Too many of that type as far as I'm concerned. Sure you won't reconsider my offer and come to my bed? I'd make you forget all about men." She slipped her hand around her and snugged her closer.

"I can't, Jana. You've been a terrific friend, but I don't feel that kind of attraction, not to you. Not to anyone." Jana's hand brushed across her breast. She pushed the exploring fingers down. "Colin called me stone-cold."

"Dash Colin. You're not cold, Mel. You've just

never done it with the right person. Try me."

"You don't really know me." Melissa stood and picked up the yogurt container. Nobody did. She wondered which was worse—to look like a monster or be a monster on the inside. She tossed the cup in the recycle bin and snatched up her jacket. "I have to go out."

Jana rolled over onto her belly. "You're obsessive about everything. Tattoo parlors again?"

Melissa fingered the address in her pocket. Her computer search turned up a Sirena Patras living on Grand. She needed to check it out. "Without Bella's data, I have to start all that research over." She swept her satchel off the counter. "I'll be in late."

"Well. Stay alert out there." Jana tipped one side of her mouth up. "You might meet a monster."

Chapter 6

Melissa stopped in front of the five-story apartment house sitting on the corner of Grand and Bedford and took out Bella's keys. The ornate white stone building was old, probably from the beginning of the twentieth century, but had been updated with modern black framed windows. Four steps led up to a freshly painted turquoise door. She hesitated. The rents in a building like this would be incredibly high. It seemed an unlikely place for the outrageous tattoo artist she knew as Bella to reside.

Still, everyone she'd asked in the neighborhood affirmed that this was where someone who looked a lot like her friend lived. Nobody forgot a tall, generously bosomed woman with crimson hair and extensive tattoos. And her line that she needed to feed Bella's cat and had forgotten the building number worked like a charm, along with the fact that at five foot two and one hundred pounds, she looked as innocuous as she was.

Everyone from the vagrant on the corner to the hot dog man knew about Bella's crusade to spay the strays. The last person she'd asked, a foxy-faced teen with a beat up, paint-stained gym bag slung over his shoulder, told a convoluted story of helping her catch a particularly fecund tabby after a merry chase in and out of the aisles of a green grocer's. He'd been the most helpful too. Taken her right to the door.

She ran her finger down the names on the bell plate and stopped on Cat Lover, Apartment 4. That must be Bella. Now to get inside. She put the key in the lock and turned it. The door opened.

****

Ari pressed back into the stairwell and watched the girl shift her bag to the other shoulder, take out a set of keys, and open Bella's door. She turned as she pushed the door open, and he caught a glimpse of thick-lashed, tilted-up eyes, and a wide, full-lipped mouth. *Zeús*, it was his Nereida from the station house—the one with all that glorious golden skin. What was she doing here?

He took a step toward her and stopped. This was too much of a coincidence. She had to be one of Vernon's minions. The pint-sized pixie didn't seem Vernon's type, but then he hadn't seen the man in years. He shrugged. What did he know of the man now, other than that he'd kidnapped his sister?

The girl jumped as an orange cat streaked out and ran up the stairs. Ari laughed under his breath. Stupid cat did the same thing to him. It had taken him forever to catch it. He waited to see what his pixie would do.

The cat stopped on the top step and peered down through the railing. The girl put her hands on her hips and stared up at it, smiling. Ari's heart clenched. She was even more beautiful when she smiled.

"I bet your name is Pussyballs, and I bet you're hungry too." The girl spoke with a lighter version of the nasal Brooklyn accent that rubbed his ears the wrong way every time he heard it, as if she'd grown up on the edge of Brooklyn instead of in it. She slipped inside the apartment, leaving the door wide open behind her.

From his shadowy perch, Ari could see straight in.

He watched her stumble around in the dark until she found a light switch and then disappear into the kitchen alcove. Cabinet doors snapped open and closed. Dishes clattered. She reappeared with a bowl of dry cat food.

"Psst...Pussyballs." She put the food down inside the doorway and stepped back. "Come and get it."

The cat waited a long minute, and then it bounded down, curled around her ankles, and gobbled down the kibbles. Ari laughed under his breath. Just like a woman to know the way to a male's heart was through his belly. The girl knelt and ran her hand along the cat's back in long, even strokes. "You poor dear."

Ah—Ari watched her elegant fingers glide smoothly over the cat's fur, imagined that same small hand touching his skin, and all the blood fled his brain for lower regions. He shook himself. Think. Surely, this was Vernon's strategy—throw a beautiful girl at him so his blood pooled in his groin and stopped his brain from functioning. *Zeús*. He needed to figure out who she was and what her agenda was, not picture her underneath him begging for more.

Nevertheless, he couldn't take his gaze off her. She wore a faded red, form-fitting bolero jacket over a plain white tank top, skinny jeans rolled up to mid-calf and strappy Roman-style sandals that would be perfect on Eudokia's beach, but seemed too thin-soled for city pavement. One thing was for sure, she wasn't rich. Everything was off the rack and well-worn. The fingers petting the cat were long with plain, sensible nails, not the painted glitz of the manicurist. A working girl, then. Except for that dawn-colored Asian skin, she resembled every waitress who'd ever served him tea and biscuits with her head averted, or the salesgirls who rang up his order while avoiding staring at his face.

The cat finished and sat back to lick its paws and wipe its whiskers.

"Come along, puss." She picked it up and cuddled it against her breast, crooning an off-note version of Michael Jackson's *Man in the Mirror*. "Let's see if we can discover your mistress's secrets."

The hair on the back of his neck rose. No ordinary miss, this one. Still singing, she moved out of sight beyond the kitchen and into the living room. He needed to find out what she was seeking. He had turned the place upside down minutes ago and found not a single hint as to Bella's whereabouts. He put his hand on the door and pushed it further ajar, relying on the darkness of the hall to keep him hidden.

The golden girl had turned on all the lights, revealing the wild colors of Bella's living space, and the mess he'd made in his desperate search. He cringed. Bella's décor had been richly exotic and tasteful. Now swathes of silk and Indian shawls woven in luscious hues of gold and green and maroon lay puddled on the floor where he'd dropped them. Huge pillows with tiny sparkling mirrors embroidered on them, tossed in frustration, lay scattered about the room. Above the chestnut brown leather sofa, the picture of the village Sirena had painted as a child hung crooked. He must have bumped it digging behind the cushions. Worst, all her beautiful art books lay upended, the pages crushed and torn from his last ditch effort to find a scrap of paper or anything that would lead him to his sister's kidnapper.

Anyone could tell the apartment had been ransacked. He waited for the girl to scream or dial 911.

Instead, with infinite care, his Nereida picked up each of the pillows, fluffed it, and put it back in place on the divan. She kneeled on the sofa and straightened the painting. She gently rearranged the scarves and throws and wiped the dust from the table top with her sleeve. Finally, she sat down on the floor and with the cat in her lap, examined each book, smoothed the damaged pages and piled them in a neat stack. He pinched his lips together. Maybe she was just what she appeared to be—a friend of Bella's—come to feed the cat and clean the apartment. Then again, perhaps Vernon had sent a housekeeper as a spy. She reached out to pick up the last book, and her T-shirt tightened across her breasts. Ari closed his eyes and fought for control. Some spy.

When he opened them again, she had finished with the cleaning and moved on to wandering from one section of the small living room to the next, peering high and low, checking under and behind the furniture. By the divan, she knelt and reached underneath, snagging a framed photograph. She examined it a moment and then stood it upright on the end table.

He stared at the old black and white of him that had once graced his mother's bureau. He'd wondered what happened to it. He shook his head at that boy with his cocky smile and large sensitive eyes. Both gone now. Inside, he softened. Bella still thought about him even though he'd chased her away.

There was a clang from the kitchen and water started running. The pixie spy was doing the dishes. What secrets lay in Bella's dirty pots and pans? Who was this girl? He needed to find out. He grasped the doorknob and stepped inside.

****

The apartment door squealed and flew open. Melissa dropped the dish she'd been scrubbing and whirled about. Her heart rose into her throat. It was the monster from the precinct house. With his wild black hair, smashed nose, and the scar cutting through his upper lip, he belonged in a Stephen King novel, not standing in Bella's doorway facing her. He must have followed her to get revenge for his wife. Heavens, she'd thought she'd covered her tracks. Furious husbands were always a danger in the work she did for Mercy House.

She gripped the edge of the counter, barely breathing, and weighed her options. Her phone was an arm's length away. She'd never reach it before he attacked. From the corner of her eye, she spied a knife in the dish drain. She'd just washed it. It was dull, but still a knife—a weapon.

She edged her hand toward the strainer, her knees weak, her whole body trembling. The monster's dark gaze dropped to her inching fingers. He'd seen the knife too. She'd have to distract him. How?

Talk. Didn't her research subjects say she could talk a person to death? She forced her mouth open, but no words came out. She sucked in a breath of air, her lungs tight, and tried again. "Uh, your wife, she isn't here."

His eyebrows rose. "Wife? I have no wife."

"Your girlfriend, then. The one you battered and threatened."

"I don't threaten women." He tilted his head and advanced a step. "Who are you? Are you working for them?"

"What do you mean you don't threaten women?"

33

She slid a little more to the left. The knife was a fingertip away. She pictured herself coming at him with it and shook her head at the irony. She didn't have strength enough to take down this man. He wasn't extraordinarily tall, but he was broad as a wrestler, all upper body and narrow hips. Still, she'd taken a self-defense course. She knew to go for the eyes and the groin. She stretched for the knife.

He tipped his chin and took a step toward her. "I don't suggest you try using that on me. I've killed men for less with these bare hands alone." He lifted his hands from his sides and held out them out toward her. She backed up hard against the counter—the knife forgotten—and stared. His fingers were long and thick and on his left hand—the last two digits were missing.

Throwing logic aside, she seized her phone from the counter, and ran straight for the door, hoping she was faster. But for a big man, he moved at lightning speed. Encircling her waist with his hands, he pulled her against a body that was all hard, lean muscle. For a moment, she stilled against his warmth, those powerful hands embracing her snuggly, but gently. She breathed in the faint hint of some exotic spice that set her blood buzzing through her veins. Then, the hardness of his erection pressed against her, and she had a new fear.

"No!" She beat on his chest. "No. Let me go."

His arms fell away, releasing her. He held his hands out to the side, palms up. "I can explain—"

She didn't want an explanation, not from him. She turned, dashed down the stairs, and out into the street. Then she took off running like a rabbit escaping a fox.

****

Sto diávolo. He'd lost her. Ari leaped after her,

slamming the door behind him. Outside, he looked both ways, but the girl moved fast. The street was empty. He stood, fists clenched at his sides, and cursed in five languages. For the briefest of moments, he'd held her, inhaled her heady scent of honey and spice, and all he wanted to do was to bury himself inside her, claim her—whoever she was. He turned to go back into the apartment.

A youth in his late teens or early twenties, a Mets baseball cap drawn low over his face, grinned at him from his perch on a low-hanging fire escape. "Lost the lady, *hombre*?"

Ari squinted up. The boy was dark-skinned, his limbs thin and limber as a gypsy acrobat's, but he appeared harmless enough. "What business of yours?"

Baseball Cap tucked a can in his bag, jumped down, and took a loose-legged stance well back from him. Ari recognized the heady scent of benzene from spray paint.

"For a twenty," the youth said with a broad smile, "I'll tell you where she's gone."

Ari raised one eyebrow. "You know her? Where she lives?"

Baseball Cap scuffed his sneaker along the crack in the pavement. "No, but I know where she hangs out. She's a tattoo groupie."

Ari pulled out his wallet and searched for a twenty, but found only a few dollars. *Sto diávolo,* he should have taken out more cash at the ATM at JFK or given less to the taxi driver. He rubbed a hand over his scarred lip. "How about you guide me there, and I'll not tell the landlord about your little artistic work up there on the side of the building." He tipped his head in the direction of the bright orange Aztec style bull, spray painted on the bricks.

"Tell who ya will. Nobody catch El Toro, *hombre*."

"Budding artist, are you?" He peered up at the work. "Some real talent there, but you need to take into consideration the point of view of the pedestrian, not just yours. It's the people on the street who you truly want to appreciate your work." He pointed up. "If you made the bull's head larger and the eyes bigger, it would be more threatening to us folks down here."

"You some artistic guru from the museums, like?" The boy backed away. "Don't want nothing to do with them. They feed you lies about making it big and then drop you back in the mud after they get their raves from the money pockets."

"I know what you mean. Happened to me."

The boy tipped his hat back and leered at him. "No way, you just another big mouth hipster."

Ari reached inside his coat pocket, pulled out his business card, and flicked it toward him.

Baseball Cap snatched it from the air with the grace of a bird and studied it. He tossed the card in his satchel. "You a real artist? You make money at it?"

"Yes, and I did it on my own. After my first 'patron' stole everything, including my best work." He tipped his head. "I arrived in the city yesterday, and I don't happen to have a twenty. How about El Toro comes around to my place? My studio's on River Street. And we talk a bit about art and graffiti—might like to try my hand at that—*and* that tattoo groupie. And let's say I'll find you a fifty for your trouble?"

Baseball Cap licked his lips, considering. From down the street came the blare of sirens. He adjusted his cap. "Ho, *hombre*. Time to make like Spiderman."

Ari watched the only contact he had to the girl scramble back up the fire escape. *Zeús.* He tore off his suit jacket, tossed it in a cellar well, and swung up after the boy, balanced on the railing, and with a leap, grasped the cornice and hauled himself up onto the roof. He stood for a moment, peering down at the pavement five stories below, glad he'd kept his body in shape rappelling up Eudokia's cliffs after he'd stopped wrestling.

From the opposite rooftop, the boy peered down at him. "What you up to, *hombre*? Not ya turf. You follow me—you break something, or better yet, someone will break it for you."

"The fifty dollar offer stands. If I get rid of the police, will you meet with me?"

The boy glanced down at the street where a patrol car sat in front of the building, lights flashing. "Deal. But not your place. El Toro's not that dumb. I find you. And no money. I want a duffle bag of spray paint. Krylon. You pick the colors. We'll see if you can make a better bull. And if you can't, you owe me a lot more than fifty bucks, Señor Ugly Man."

"Deal." Ari nodded at the cocksure street artist, wondering what he'd gotten himself into, and then worked his way back down the fire escape, enjoying the stretch to his muscles. He'd been cooped up too long all by himself on the island. Scrambling up and down buildings trailing after a graffiti artist would keep him in shape, and if it helped him keep tabs on the girl too, so much the better. He swung off the end of the ladder and retrieved his jacket. Time to play the wealthy businessman lost in Brooklyn.

Once the police were gone, he would search Bella's again. The girl had barely done more than plump up some pillows. Surely there was something they both had missed.

Chapter 7

Orange Man's tat shop, Paradisio Tattoos, was cramped and overheated and buzzing with activity. Melissa leaned on the counter and smoothed out the printout. "I'm looking for a man who looks like this. He threatened me, and I think he may have something to do with Bella's disappearance." She looked up into the wildly tattooed face of Orange Man. With dreadlocks to his shoulders and piercings circling his mouth and eyes, he looked like someone you wouldn't want to meet on a dark night. But Bella had told her that of all the tattoo artists in Williamsburg, Orange Man was the kindest. Right now, she needed all the kindness she could get.

"Let's see what you have, darling." Orange Man came around the counter and wrapped his muscular arm with its intricate cuff of Celtic art around Melissa and gave her a hug. "We take care of our own here." He spun the paper around so it faced them and studied the Rodin sculpture of the 'Man with the Broken Nose' she'd downloaded from the web. "If he's this ugly, he'll have a hard time hiding. And we'll send out word on the Grinders' grapevine to keep our eyes and ears open for news of Bella. Four days now, you say? Let's hope she's kicking up sand in the Bahamas. That's where I'd be." He released her and smiled. "You go, girl. Thought your research would interfere with business. But you've done a great job with the tenderfoots. And the bit of your stuff you gave me to read has given me some new insights into ways I might approach these half-drunk babes dragged in by their he-men. You've got friends here, Melissa." He poked her in the arm. "And if you ever want a tat or two on that lovely body, stop in. I'll do it at half-price."

Melissa left Paradisio Tattoos and headed up Berry Street, a surprising lightness in her steps. The skin artists, like Orange Man, had taken her under their wings the minute she said she was in trouble. Orange Man would do the illustrations she needed. His buddy, Red Rage, agreed not only to submit to the in-depth interviews required to complete the section on the artists' perspectives, but was willing to rework Iza's tattoo. She couldn't wait to tell Daniela at lunch. She checked the time on her cell. Luck was surely with her today—she was even going to be on time for their weekly picnic in McCarren Park.

For so long, she'd thought of herself as an outsider peeking in at the lives of these tattoo artists, poking and prodding the indices of their culture like a surgeon probing for the cancerous tissue. She hurried down the street. Her advisor assured her that feeling alone and separate wasn't unusual for anthropologists out in the field. Still, she hadn't expected to feel that way when her research site was an ordinary Brooklyn neighborhood and not some far flung exotic tribal village.

She crossed North 12th and headed into the park. It was one of those rare fall days, the air fresh, the grass brilliant green. The ordinary sounds of thumping basketballs and children's shouts filled the park. Melissa's spirits lifted for the first time since Bella went missing.

She scanned the area near the gate where Daniela usually sat. There. Daniela was impossible to miss. Today, she wore a blouse covered in a pattern of huge red peppers on a turquoise background that clashed with the reds and golds of the maple leaves fluttering down around her.

Melissa hurried over. The busy social worker rarely took more than a half hour for lunch. She waved.

"Glad you're early." Daniela took a sip of *Jarritos* soda in her favorite flavor—Jamaican hibiscus—and gestured around her. "Glorious day. Sun shining. Sky blue."

"Yeah, but fall's a-coming and they're predicting frost tonight." Melissa swept away the leaves on the bench. "The trees know."

"Hope you're hungry. I baked *pambacitos* for you. Mama's recipe." She peeled away the foil wrapping and held out an orangey-red sandwich piled high with filling.

Melissa took a big bite. The spicy heat of chorizo, beans, peppers, and sour cream filled her mouth. She swallowed and licked her lips. "*Muy bueno.* You're a terrific cook, Dani."

Daniela patted her ample belly. "Too *bueno* for my own good. But you're a skinny thing. So you eat up as much as you want. There's lots more. And if you eat them, I won't be tempted to snack on the leftovers all afternoon." She took a bite of her own sandwich. "So have you found your friend Bella yet?"

"No. I went to her apartment last night, and I was—well—attacked."

"*What?*" Daniela grasped her arm and pulled her

41

closer. "Tell me what happened."

Melissa put down her sandwich. "The husband of Perlita from the police station showed up while I was searching the place. Looked like it had been tossed. He grabbed me, but I got away." She bit her lower lip. "Actually, that's unfair. He did grab me, but he didn't act like he'd actually hurt me." She remembered how his hands encompassed her waist gently, not like someone who intended harm. And he'd dropped them like stones the moment she'd protested. It was almost as if he were as surprised at his attraction to her as she was frightened by it. And his scent—a mix of salty sea, herb-covered mountain, and him. She'd never forget it. But damn, he shouldn't have been there at all, threatening her.

Daniela took another sip of her soda. "He followed you?"

"Must have." She took another bite of her *pambacito*. All the spicy flavor seemed to have leached away. "Though how a man who looks like he's posed for Wes Naman's scotch tape art could have done so, I have no idea."

"Tape art?"

"You know that photographer who wraps scotch tape and rubber bands around faces to make them grotesque. Saw an article in Huffington about him."

Daniela flipped her hand. "Eh. So what does this tape art character look like?"

"His nose is smashed in and his cheek is scarred. Must have been a fighter or something."

"Smashed face?" Daniela licked a dab of bean filling off her fingers. "That's not Perlita's husband."

Melissa dropped her sandwich. Beans and sour

cream smeared the front of her blouse. She scrubbed at the drips. "What do you mean?"

"Perlita had a photo of her batterer in her wallet. We were able to post it for all our employees and volunteers. In fact, I have a copy for you right here." She pulled a folder out of the giant striped tote she used as a briefcase and removed a computer printout.

Melissa stared down at the young crewcut guy wearing a smile and military uniform. "It can't be."

Daniela nodded. "Same old, same old. Ex-Marine. Post Traumatic Stress Disorder."

Melissa fingered the picture. Her stomach tightened into a knot. She laid her sandwich down on the foil. "Then who's the monster who followed me to Bella's?"

Daniela squeezed her hand. "You have to go to the cops."

"You know I can't."

"I know you have a hard time believing this"— Daniela patted her knee—"but the police are your friends." She sat back and shook her head. "You must have missed that lesson in kindergarten or something."

Melissa shuddered. "But how could I explain why I was there? How I got the keys to the apartment."

Daniela frowned. "The keys? Didn't Bella give them to you?"

"Nooo. I—I—broke in her shop."

"*Cielios*." Daniela slapped the side of her head. "You're worse than my clients. You could go to jail for that."

Melissa picked at the stain on her blouse. "I panicked. I thought Bella might be sick. Need help."

Daniela clasped her hands together. "You'll just

have to talk nicely to the police. Explain. You meant well."

"There's something else."

Daniela closed her eyes. "I don't think I want to know."

Melissa ran her hands down her face. "I've been thinking. What if Bella is in trouble because she's been helping my street girls cover over their pimps' tattoos? And that guy who followed me is involved in some way? Oh, Dani—what if she's *dead*?"

Daniela pursed her lips. "I know you went through a really tough thing with your sister. But as much as I love you, *chica*, you're talking crazy now. I'm sure there's a simple explanation for everything." She stood. "If you're scared—*go* to the police. Otherwise, trust that things will work themselves out and concentrate on getting your dissertation done so you can get away from here and all your bad memories and have a life."

Melissa folded her sandwich up in the foil. "You're right. It's just—I can't help myself—the way that beast of a man showed up at Bella's. I'm glad he's not Perlita's batterer." She jumped up. "Heavens, his voice. He had this accent. I think he might be the same man who called The Siren when I was searching the place." She went rigid. "What if he's a detective checking up on me, or worse, had something to do with Bella's going missing? Dani, my fingerprints are everywhere."

"Look. I thought putting up those girls at Lenny's was risky enough. Now you're scaring me to death. If you're involved in criminal acts, I could be seen as a co-conspirator or something. *Dios mío*, I could *lose my job*." She gathered up the leftover sandwiches and smashed them into her bag. "Right now, I've got to get back to work. If I were you, I'd hole up somewhere and try to calm down. Let's hope you're just letting your nerves get to you. And stay away from Mercy House—from me—for a while. Please."

Melissa picked up a stray napkin and crumpled it into a ball. "I did have some good news. Red Rage will take care of Iza's tattoo, and I can make up the research I need to finish the dissertation."

Daniela hefted herself up. "Iza will be thrilled. I'll let her know. Now get to work on the big D. I'll try to find places for your two girls at Lenny's. And don't pick up anymore. I gotta think of my kids."

Melissa threw the napkin in the trash. "I won't. I promise." She waved goodbye and set out for Jana's. It was time to stop fooling around. With Red Rage and Orange Man's input and a lot of hard work, she could have the last section written and all her stats and tables finalized and ready for her advisor in a week. Fortunately, she'd already organized her notes last night and put them in her knapsack.

Her knapsack. She halted mid-street. It wasn't on her shoulder. The spicy sandwich she'd eaten turned sour in her stomach. If she'd lost her notes, she wouldn't have to worry about meeting any deadlines. She wouldn't be getting a dissertation at all.

A car horn blew, and she raced to the curb, Bella's keys clinking in her pocket. *Bella's.* Holy heavens, she'd set the bag down when she fed the cat, and must have left it behind when she fled the monster in a panic.

She jangled the keys in her pocket. She'd have to go back and see if it was still there. Daniela would think she'd lost her mind, insist she call the police. But all they'd do was laugh at her. She had no proof of foul play.

She crossed over to 12th Street. And if Bella were murdered—a chill slithered down her spine—they'd treat her as a suspect. Her face would be splashed across the dailies again, the reporters crowded around her door.

For now, the police didn't know she had any connection to Bella. Better to keep it that way.

She hurried along the sidewalk. Then again, maybe they were already on her trail. Her stomach tightened into a hard little ball. *Monster Man*. He'd been at the police station. He could be working for law enforcement.

She glanced around and willed her stomach to settle. Everything looked normal, an ordinary day, ordinary people doing ordinary things. Tourists and hipsters, school kids and factory workers headed to lunch. Mothers pushed baby strollers along the pavement. A pizza delivery boy hurried past, boxes stacked high in his arms. Daniela was right, she was overreacting. She would go back to Bella's and retrieve her bag. And if the beast followed her, well—she'd have to take that risk.

Chapter 8

Ari thumped the duffle bag full of spray paint on the floor and threw the well-worn baggy jeans, faded black sweatshirt, and floppy hat he'd picked up at the thrift store on the bed. He must be crazy. His sister was missing, a beautiful girl who made his heart beat too fast was somehow involved, he had an art show to mount, and he was having a graffiti contest—an illegal one at that—with some smart-mouthed street artist named El Toro. He rummaged in his suitcase and pulled out the very expensive fake beard he carried around for public appearances. Black and curly, it didn't hide his nose, but it did cover the scar that gave him a permanent sneer. He tossed it to the side. It would take too long to glue it on. The kids would just have to stand looking at his mug.

Time to show his young prodigy a thing or two about painting. He pulled the sweatshirt over his head, holding his breath against the musty smell that always accompanied charitable discards, and glanced out the window. Dusk. His favorite time of day. The sun slipped behind the Manhattan skyline, leaving that golden afterglow that only a city's pollution could create. *Zeús,* he wished he were home at his villa, walking on the beach below the terrace walls with the whole sky open to him and the sea air filling his lungs. But he wasn't in Eudokia, and if Vernon got his way, he never would feel that white sand beneath his feet ever again.

He sat down on the bed to put on the light Puma hiking boots he'd splurged on at Paragon after he'd finished at the gallery. He'd also purchased rappelling ropes, building anchors, strapping, carabineers, and a Swiss army knife at Galaxy Army Navy. No way would he be left marooned on the rooftops by a bunch of streetwise art criminals.

He hefted the satchel over his shoulders, tipped the hat down low, and stalked through the shadow-filled studio with its gray cement-block walls and pseudo-industrial exposed piping and air vent tubes. The Foundry, as it was called, turned out to be well worth the exorbitant rent.

He stomped down the open metal stairs, an iron worker's fancy, the narrow steps suspended from cables attached to the ceiling, and looked up. Yes, a very fine investment, indeed.

The apartment area was a suspended cage over what used to be a machine shop of some kind, now converted for welding supersize metal sculptures. The living area, consisting of a substantial workspace, a galley kitchen, a huge bath, and equally spacious bedroom, hugged the west wall of the building with windows facing the New York skyline. But the best thing was the plumbing worked, and he had the whole building to himself.

As he opened the door to leave, his cell phone dinged. He jerked it out of his pocket and checked the text message. The gallery director managing his art show was getting nervous, she'd never dealt with a Biennale finalist, wanted to meet for dinner. He tossed the phone on the metal work table and strode out the door, slamming it behind him. Este Keeler would have to wait. He was in search of a wall to paint.

****

Twenty some odd blocks south, he found himself in graffiti wonderland. Plywood fences covered in Full Monty murals stretched block after block. He stopped and reread the note El Toro stuck to his door.

"Right place, *hombre*," El Toro said, slipping up beside him. He waved his hand. "Meet the judges."

Ari stared at the bunch of young men wearing baggy pants, sweatshirts, and multi-pocketed vests. There were four of them. A tall black kid, skinny as a lamp post, with a shaved head, called Fur Tree; two mixed-race twins with Hispanic accents and matching black T-shirts reading "If You're Reading This It's Too Late" who went by Neto and Solo; and someone's hyperactive teenage brother. The kid, introduced as Hanger On, swung back and forth from a stair railing, his too-large pants threatening to slip off at any second.

Ari gave them his best scowl, and when they didn't flinch, turned it to a smile. "So where's the wall?"

"Show him, T-Crew," El Toro yelled.

They took off, racing ahead of him in an attempt to lose him in the shadowy streets. But despite elbows in his ribs and the occasional foot stuck out to trip him, he had no trouble keeping up. He looked back at the last twelve-foot chain link fence they'd scaled and smiled. He'd run a lot harder obstacle courses when he'd been in training, but he was glad he still ran daily on Eudokia. When a man looked like a prize fighter, he'd better have the muscle power and stamina to match, even if he was afraid to let it free.

"Over here." El Toro pointed up to a cement block wall covered in fading gang marks and tags. "Our canvas." He unzipped his duffle and pulled out a can of paint. Then he signaled to his friends. "Up, *mis amigos*."

Ah, that was the game. Ari watched as El Toro climbed up onto the shoulders of Fur Tree and set to work, calling down to his buddies Solo and Neto for a new color or a new can.

The young Van Gogh flipped back his cap. "Too high for you, Señor Ugly Man? You gonna have to grow longer legs to beat me." The crew below him grinned and stamped their feet.

Ari glanced around the demolition zone. A large block of cement about five feet by five feet with a broken pipe sticking out of it rested ten feet away. He looked up at his challenger and nodded. El Toro needed a little lesson in physics.

He strolled over to the block. "Hey, El Toro. Did you like school? Listen to your teachers?" The whole group broke out in laughter. The twins slapped each other on the back. He took hold of the pipe and wiggled it back and forth. "Ever hear how they built the pyramids?"

"Yeah, Ugly Man, with slaves," Solo said.

The pipe slipped free. He picked up a large piece of granite and wedged the pipe beneath the cement block. "*Smart* slaves. This, my friends"—he placed the granite under the pipe, leaned down on the end, and slowly raised the block—"is a lever." He grinned at their astonished faces as he tipped and turned the block, maneuvering it closer and closer to the wall with the finesse born from years of working in his father's marble quarry. He stopped to judge the distance.

Hanger On circled around him, sticking out his tongue. "You tired, Ugly Man?"

"Just marking the spot where this *oikólithos*—that's big rock in English—needs to go." He narrowed his eyes at the imp and drew a rectangle in the dirt. "Tell you what. How about you put it in that spot?"

The kid stopped and stared at him. "You kidding?"

"Archimedes—ever hear of him?"

"No."

Ari wiped his hands on his jeans. What were they teaching in the schools here? "Well, Archimedes said, 'Give me a lever long enough and I can lift the world.' I promise you, you can lift this block. It's only about seven hundred pounds."

"Go on, Hang Toe," one of the twins shouted. "I dare you."

The kid spun around and gave the speaker a swift kick in the shins. "*Idiota.* That's not my name." Then he spun back. "So show me what I gotta do, Señor Ugly Man."

Ari showed him where to put the pressure and stepped away. The kid grinned as the huge block lifted. Ari put his hand on it and tipped it into the spot.

Hanger scrunched up his nose. "You some Incredible Hulk?"

Ari's stomach twisted. He didn't need a starry-eyed hero worshipper trailing after him. "No." He gently shoved him aside. "Stay out of my way, now. That bull up there is going down in defeat." He slung his satchel over his shoulder, heaved himself up on the block, and picking up the first spray can to come to hand, furiously sprayed away the demons poking up their ugly heads.

Chapter 9

Bella's apartment house looked innocuous during the daytime. Melissa peered down the row of nameplates and pressed the one labeled "Wilson, Super." This time she would speak to the building's superintendent first. She jingled Apartment 4's keys in her pocket, and when she got buzzed in, made sure the door locked behind her. She shivered again at the memory of the monster's hands on her.

The Super in Apartment 1 was a hunched-over Asian woman in her late sixties, her hair still black. The sepia skin of her face was lined with millions of fine wrinkles. But age was not enough to disguise the faint traces of dotted lines that swirled from brow to chin. The old woman looked Melissa over and put down the baseball bat she'd been holding. She shrugged and opened the door wider. "Never can be too careful, Missy. The strangest people show up on people's doorsteps." She had an unusual accent with a rising and falling tonal quality similar to Chinese, but rougher and more nasal. She turned and beckoned Melissa into her apartment. It smelled of bleach and polish. Starched doilies covered the arms of the sofa and the top of the TV. On the wall hung black and white photographs of a lean British soldier and a diminutive Asian woman with a sunny smile, standing in front of scenes full of rice paddies, elephants, and conical temples.

She pointed to the sofa. "Sit, girl." She plopped down next to her, pulled her feet under her long cotton batik skirt and rested her hands in her lap. "So you say you're here to feed that cat of Sirena's?" she asked. The wrinkles around her eyes deepened.

"Uh, yes. I bought food and"—Melissa shifted the plastic grocery bag of cat food to one hand and pulled the keys from her pocket—"she left me the keys." She exhaled a breath of air to cover her lie.

The old lady squinted at her with one eye. "You're not planning to flop in her place, are you? Or meet up with anyone? No sublets or visitors allowed in this building w'out the owner's say so. Likes to know who's coming and going. So do I."

"No. No. I live over on North 7th." Melissa placed the bag on her lap and reached into her pocket. "Here, I will write down my cell number and address for you." She pulled out a pen and a scrap of paper, jotted down the information and handed it to her.

The woman glanced at it and then at her. "Well, you look and sound innocent enough, but it's not like Miss Patras to fly off without a word to me like that and ask a stranger to do her business. Sirena is a *very* private person."

Melissa fiddled with the keys. "But she has lots of friends among her fellow artists."

"Does she now? But none that come here, I think." The woman muttered something to herself in what must have been her native tongue and picked a piece of lint off the velvet cushion. "And now there's you hanging around."

Melissa's stomach sank lower. Super Wilson must have seen her in the building last night.

53

The woman bobbed her head back and forth. "So—you say she's gone on vacation?"

"Uh, yes. I'm not sure how long. But I'll see to the cat."

The woman tipped her head this way and that. "I guess you'll do." She rested her hand on the sofa cushion and moved to rise.

Light from the window struck her face making the blue tattoo designs stand out. Melissa let out a breath and laid her hand on the old woman's arm. "I couldn't help noticing your tattoos. Mrs. Wilson."

The woman jerked away. "Not Wilson. Call me Zeya Aung. No last names in Burma."

"Zeya Aung, tattooing is a special interest of mine. And yours are—unique."

"*Unique?*" The lines around the woman's mouth tightened, and she fell back onto the sofa with a huff. She ran her arthritis-twisted fingers down her face. "See them? The lines? Sirena, she says they are art, but they are not. They are bad memories, Miss"—she looked down at the paper scrap—"Dermont." Her accent thickened. "You want to know about these lines? *Payae.* They are called *payae* by my people—the K'Cho Chin. My people live in the rainforests of South Burma—Myanmar, they call it now. It is a place of warmth, and light. So different from this cold walled-in place my husband brought me to. Sirena understood. She too comes from a warmer place." She leaned forward, her eyes glassy, and touched her chin. "It is beautiful where I come from to do this to girls. But not here. People stare or look away. Make fun." She glanced at the photos. "My husband was a diplomat. He loved me, but he was ashamed of this face and hid me away like a dirty secret. I still hide." She curled her fingers over her mouth. "But I say too much."

She stood. "Now you go. Take care of Sirena's cat. Keep it quiet and clean." She wagged her finger. "No stinky smells."

Melissa seized her hand. "I will. And I will stop in to see you, too. My mother—my real mother before I was adopted when I was three—was from somewhere in Southeast Asia. In my memory I see blue lines running down her cheeks."

Zeya yanked her hand free. "I have only a boy child."

"Of course, of course. That's not what I meant. It's just I grew up feeling misplaced. Like I was a cuckoo in someone else's nest. I never understood why they adopted me from that orphanage in the Philippines. My adoptive mother said they saw it on TV and wanted a sister for their little girl." The ache that always accompanied her memory of Laura shot through her. "But they didn't—not really—not a girl that looked like me." The woman was holding the door open and staring at her. Melissa bowed her head. "Sorry to have upset you."

The woman stepped out of the way to let her pass by. Her melodic voice followed. "I, too, am sorry—but I can be no mother for you."

****

The door clicked closed, and Melissa found herself alone in the stairwell. Memories of the monster's hands on her came flooding back. She gave herself a shake and crept up the staircase, checking behind her with each step. No one would sneak up on her this time.

Outside Bella's door she halted, shoved the key in

the lock, and pushed inside. With a strong shove, she bolted the door behind her and flicked on the lights. Her heart sank.

Her knapsack was not where she'd dropped it. She stepped further inside and peered around. Nor was it in the kitchen or the living room.

She sank down on the divan. The monster had taken her bag. A thump and a rattle emanated from behind her. She jumped up. Heavens. What if he were still here, despite Zeya's vigilance? After all, she hadn't stopped either of them sneaking in last night.

There was no place to hide in the kitchen and living area, but he could be in one of the bedrooms. Clutching a heavy wooden bowl, the first thing she could lay her hands on, she sidled around the living room and opened the guest room door. No one. The sparsely furnished room lay empty. The bed neatly made. The blinds drawn.

The next door led to Bella's bedroom. Holding the bowl tighter, she slowly pushed it open and came face to face with Bella's cat sitting on top of a chest of drawers. She glanced around. No monster.

The cat batted at her with its paw. "So it was you making that racket." Melissa dropped the bowl and picked up the cat. His purr rumbled in her ears. "Poor thing. Did that mean man lock you in here last night?" She ran her hand down the cat's sleek fur and glanced around again.

The room was in perfect order. The bed made. The blinds drawn. Sunlight flickered through the yellow leaves of the ash tree that fronted the building and gave the room a soft glow. A stray ray illuminated Bella's closet. The door stood open, the tattoo artist's outrageous outfits hanging neatly from hangers, her signature spike-heeled shoes in orderly pairs on a shoe rack. On the shelf above sat a brilliant orange suitcase and carry-on bag.

Melissa stared at the luggage with its dangling mermaid-shaped luggage tags. "Oh, Pussyballs. If your mistress hasn't taken her luggage, then she isn't sunning on some beach." She hugged the cat tighter to her body and rocked back and forth. Her missing dissertation notes were a miniscule problem compared to her friend's disappearance.

She buried her face in the cat's fur. "Oh, Bella, where are you?"

Chapter 10

The unmarked envelope must have been slipped under his door during the night. Still heavy with sleep, Ari scooped the letter off the cement floor. He rubbed his aching back with his blistered fingers. Who knew spray painting graffiti was so wearing on the body? Definitely an art form for the young. He laughed. He'd thought himself in shape. Twenty-seven, and after a night with T-Crew, he felt a hundred years old.

Right. He gazed down at the sealed blank envelope, turned it over and over, willing it to be a note for the owner of the loft, an advertising circular, or something that didn't have anything to do with him. But he knew better. He strode over to his work table, tore it open and read the news he dreaded. His sister hadn't escaped in time.

She was merely on an extended stay at Vernon's penthouse—redecorating. He reread the note delicately formatted as a business deal. Not a word about kidnapping or ransom. Nothing he could take to the police. He would just deed over the island to make peace between old friends.

He smashed his fist against the oak table top. Vernon Newell could wrap it up in any packaging he chose. The bastard had kidnapped his sister, and this was a ransom demand, not a business deal. Venomous Vernon wanted the villa, the beach, the island. The man wanted everything that was his. It was what caused all his problems with his sister from the beginning—Vernon's greed.

Sto diávolo. He spat out the curse that used to earn him a switch on the bottom from his mama. Now the bastard had the nerve to ask him to deed over the island for his sister's sake. For a moment, he considered giving in. He fingered one of the paint brushes lying on the table. He had his art. A source of income.

He pictured the villagers' faces. He'd promised them he'd protect their bit of paradise. They had been supported by the Stavros family for centuries. They'd seen what happened to other villages invaded by modern tourism.

No. He tossed the letter on the worktable. There must be a way to get his sister back and still protect the island from commercial development. Because that is what Vernon really wanted. To build a casino and resort on Eudokia and destroy one of the few untouched places in the Mediterranean.

That lawyer he'd hired would know. He searched his pants pocket for his cell and pulled it out. Vernon would fill the harbor with tour ships and fancy yachts. Loud-mouthed tourists and small-time hucksters would mob the winding street and crisscross the hills on motor bikes. Modern cement and glass hotels would replace the red-tile-roofed houses dotting the hillside. Without protection, the caves and underwater lagoons that provided sanctuary for the endangered monk seals would be overrun with sightseers. The seals would leave, taking the spirit of the island with them.

He couldn't let that happen. He stared at the blank screen on his cell. *Zéus*, he'd forgotten to charge it last night after his escapade with the street artists. He looked over at El Toro and Hanger On asleep in the corner of the studio. Toro was an extraordinarily gifted artist for one so young. Hanger On was his younger brother. And both homeless. He'd been astounded when they finally told him. How did bright, talented young people living in one of the world's richest cities end up sleeping in a homeless shelter?

He hadn't the will to send them away last night. He walked over and looked down at the dirt-smudged faces sleeping in the mess of blankets he'd spread out on the floor after they'd drunk all his soda, gobbled down two cans of soup, and wiped him out of bread and butter. El Toro might be nineteen, but he looked so defenseless, his body curled protectively around his little brother, like a mother bear protecting its cub. Ari understood that feeling.

Still, they couldn't stay. He'd a lawyer to see, an irate gallery director to cool down, and three possible models coming to be viewed later in the day. Nude models and a thirteen-year-old boy—he rubbed his chin—a bad mix. And then there was that enticing Asian girl to track down.

He glanced over at the ratty knapsack sitting on the sofa. He'd searched inside for a clue to her identity, but all it contained were handwritten notes about tattooing, barely legible, and a variety of checklists with times, and coded numbers. It looked like research of some kind, but he could make neither head nor tail of it in the quick glance he'd given it. He would have to study it more tonight. Somewhere in all that paper he'd find her name.

He stared down at his unwelcome guests. The best

he could do was get the kids clean, find something for them to eat from the remnants left from last night, and send them on their way, hopefully to school, at worst back to the shelter. How bad could it be? He gave El Toro a light tap on the foot.

El Toro hissed, pulled Hanger On against him, and scudded back against the wall. He glared up at him, his eyes wide, his breathing fast. His shoulders dropped. "Oh. It's you, Ugly Man."

Something tightened in Ari's chest. He suspected the claim they stayed in a shelter was a lie. He gave himself a shake. Not his problem. "Time to move along. Shower's that way." He looked back at the pair. Hanger's eyes were open, dark pools of brown, studying him like he was a creature from another planet. The boy turned slightly and yawned, revealing a set of decayed teeth. He made a mental note to find toothbrushes and toothpaste and a patient dentist, and then glanced away. What was he thinking? They'd be gone in an hour.

Hanger sat up and grinned. "Morning, Ugly Man." He pulled up his knees, wrapped his arms around them, and stared up at him. "Were you a soldier? One of those guys in Iraq who got bombed in the face?"

It had been a long time since anyone had asked him about his scars. He stretched his lip to one side to emphasize the scowl. "No. I ran into someone's fist." Actually, several fists wearing brass knuckles, but he wasn't going to share those details.

"Oh." Hanger sucked his bottom lip, for a moment. "Why were you fighting?"

El Toro gave his brother a nudge. "Leave Ugly Man alone, Hanger. You stink. Go take a shower or

61

something."

Hanger cocked one eyebrow as if to say it didn't matter to him what he smelled like and headed to the bathroom.

El Toro rolled over, rose to his feet, and wandered over to the worktable. He ran his palms over the canvas Ari had laid out for priming in some mistaken notion that he'd actually have time to paint while in New York. The youth had slept in his clothes. The baggy pants and oversized sweatshirt hid his body. Only his bare feet showed, long toed, high arched, the elegant feet of a dancer or an acrobat. The boy's spray-painted fingers, as fine-boned as a girl's, inched toward the oil paint sticks.

"Go ahead. Use whatever you want."

The boy's head jerked up, his mouth hanging open.

Ari laughed and swept his hand toward the art materials. "Let's see what you can do with real paint."

El Toro pulled out the stool, picked up an oil paint stick and bent over the canvas, his tongue protruding slightly, a straight line of concentration marring his brow.

His new shadows occupied for the moment, Ari headed to the kitchen to see what he could rustle up for breakfast. There wasn't much left. He'd only had time for quick shopping last night and hadn't expected guests. Luckily, he'd bought a dozen eggs and some juice. He fumbled around in the unfamiliar cupboard, found a frying pan, and placed it on the burner to heat.

He plugged his phone in to charge, set the table for three, and went to search his jacket for the business card for the New York lawyer he'd retained in the context of his show. He glanced again at El Toro's thin back. He needed to get him off the streets and creating art legally. Despite his small size, El Toro claimed he was almost twenty, too old for juvenile detention, if American law was anything like Greek law. If he continued defacing private property, he would end up in jail. And the boy was too pretty to survive long there. Surely, there was a way he could fund his art studies without making it seem like charity—set up a scholarship of some kind.

He peered over at the youth's drawing. The tightness in his chest increased. Ari had expected graffiti—another bull or the cartoon letters of his graffiti gang's tag. But instead, the canvas was filled with the faces of T-Crew, as he called his team—the twins, Fur Tree, his brother with his cap shoved back, and in the middle, himself, the Williamsburg Bridge in the background. The young faces were looking up at something—perhaps the sky or a graffiti bull—with awe.

Zeús. The street artist had captured each individual expression with an elegance of line and knowledge of foreshortening that many successful artists would envy. Ari couldn't let that talent be snuffed. And the little brother would need support. Surely, he still belonged in school? Ari shuffled through the receipts and pinched out the lawyer's card. Something else he needed to talk to this—he glanced at the card—Walter Hanlin about.

The scent of hot metal and overheated oil attacked his nostrils. He dropped the card.

"Oh ho, Ugly Man, didn't that Archy guy teach you about fire safety? Leave a pan on the stove, expect to burn your toes." Hanger, his long hair dripping from the shower, expertly finessed the pan to the side with one hand, and broke the eggs into the bowl with the other. He had left off the oversized sweatshirt and baggy pants and now wore one of Ari's white dress shirts. He shuffled his feet and hummed as he beat the eggs into a froth with a fork.

Ari ran his fingers through his hair. No one had been comfortable around him in a long time. But these scamps were. Their monsters were empty stomachs, freezing nights, and police sirens. A mashed-in face was little more that another blip in life. For a moment, he wondered how two city brats would like living in a Greek village.

Zeús. He shook himself. He stood to lose the village, to lose his sister, to lose everything. Unless he and this lawyer could do some major financial maneuvering, these kids were hitching their spray paint to the wrong star.

Chapter 11

The wall behind Melissa's bed thumped.

"Wakey. Wakey. You must see this, Mel," Jana called from her own bedroom.

"Stop it." Melissa jerked herself out of bed. She glanced through the broken blind slats. Heavens, it was still dark out. "Do you know what time it is?" She stumbled the short distance to Jana's threshold.

Jana sat in the middle of her queen-size bed thumbing through a magazine. She gave her a smug look. "You're not going to believe this." She patted the spot beside her. "Sit."

Melissa rubbed her eyes and tried to flatten her sleep-spiked hair. "This isn't a trick to get me in your bed, is it?"

"No, idiot. Would that you were that easy." Jana, clad only in a thong and skinny tank top, threw herself back on the bed and kicked her feet in the air. "I thought you might sleep better if I showed this to you." She sat up again and grabbed the magazine. "Now I know you said no before, but things change, so if you want to be snuggled after seeing this, I won't turn you away. On the other hand"—she rolled the magazine into a tube and tapped the bed authoritatively—"if you've a mind to slap me up afterward, I won't reject that either." She winked. "See, I win either way."

"Oh, cut it out." Melissa crawled across the queen-sized bed and settled next to her scantily-clad roommate. Jana might be the only one of her high school acquaintances who believed her innocent of wrongdoing in her sister's murder, but she didn't trust the outrageous woman.

But that wasn't surprising. Jana had been Laura's friend, not hers. All through high school, Jana and her sister had been inseparable. Laura hung on Jana's every word and copied whatever idiotic fashion she wore, from skin-tight black leggings with tears in the knees to matching Napoleon Dynamite T-shirts. Arm in arm, they'd prance off to school, pods in their ears, yellow jelly wristbands on their wrists, leaving the ching-chong sister with her straight black hair and half-moon eyes to trail behind. And Jana could be cruel. Back then, she'd stomped on every ant or worm or injured butterfly she saw—useless things, she said—just to make her cry.

Now she stamped on clients.

Jana rubbed against her, and she stiffened. "So what's so all important in—what is that—*People Magazine*?" She reached for it only to have Jana whip it behind her back. Melissa groaned. "Enough. I'm back to bed." She slid over to the edge of the mattress. "I'm not in the mood for your teasing."

"That's because you haven't slept in days since you saw that *monster.*" Jana put her hands over Melissa's shoulders, then pulled her down. "Here, look." She opened the magazine and held up a page spread.

"I don't get it. It's about some art show." Melissa flicked her eyes over the headline. "World-renowned artist? What's he got to do with anything?"

"Here." Jana twisted around and pointed to a photo

near the bottom of the page. "The guy's a recluse, but he appeared at the Biennale last year for some award. That's him. He's Greek. Recognize the nose?"

Melissa squinted. "This guy with all the black hair and beard. Looks like a Neanderthal."

"Yeah, put your finger over the lower half of his face." She smiled. "See."

Melissa shot to her feet. "You're right, that's the nose." She sank down. "But it can't be him. What would a world-renowned artist be doing at the 90th Precinct?"

"Look, it says here he's in New York for a major exhibition of his work. So maybe he was mugged or pickpocketed or cheated by a cabbie or something. There's a thousand reasons for a foreigner who looks vaguely like an Arab terrorist to end up at a police station." Jana rolled onto her back. "In fact, I bet he's renting a studio somewhere around here. It would make sense."

Melissa bit her lip. What didn't make sense was why—if the monster was this Stavros artist character— he'd followed her and attacked her at Bella's apartment. She looked closer at the photo. It would be hard to find two men with the same grotesque bend to their nose. Any normal person would have had reconstructive surgery. She ran a finger over the photo.

"You agree then?" Jana was looking at her intently. "That's him?"

"It has to be." She leaned back. The monster was a serious artist, then, with work in some gallery in SoHo. Not a policeman. A photo showed white and glass rooms hung with rectangles covered with smooth, undulating landscapes. According to the article, his work sold for tens of thousands of dollars.

"So see, he's not a monster. He's fabulously wealthy." Jana laid her cheek against Melissa's neck. "I think we should go see his show. I want to meet this man who's keeping you from sleeping."

"What?"

"I looked it up. There's a grand opening next Friday." Jana poked her in the ribs. "Did you even look at the paintings?" She pointed to another picture on the page.

Melissa shrugged. "Nothing special. Just wavering slashes of colors like they all paint nowadays. Something that looks good over a dentist's chair."

Jana laughed. "Mel, I'm surprised at you. I thought you were a trained observer. Look again. I believe his art is more likely hung in penthouse bathrooms."

"Oh." She slapped a hand over her mouth. "Is that what I think it is?"

"Yep. He paints nude women, turns their skin into erotic landscapes." She flipped the page. "It says here he actually paints on the women. And then makes paintings of the painted women. I think the one they are showing here is one of the tamer ones." She swiped her iPad off the nightstand. "Let's see." She typed in his name. Melissa leaned in to watch. "Ah, there. Here's the gallery page. Ooo. Look at this one called *Tunnel*." Jana spun the tablet around to show her. "I'll leave it to your imagination to figure out what part of a woman's anatomy that is. Must be some sexy man." She licked her fingers and smoothed her hair back. "Wouldn't it be delicious to model for him? I wonder if he expects a little 'dividend' on the side."

Melissa squeezed her eyes closed, remembering the

man's exotic scent of sea salt and wild herbs, his strong arms holding her. Goosebumps crawled up her arms. "What woman would let him touch them? He has the face of a monster."

Jana slapped her on the back. "That's what I love about you. For an anthropologist you can be so parochial. For months, you watch people mutilating themselves on purpose, getting noses, tongues, and nipples pierced, but now you can't stomach some guy who ran into a fist. I hate to tell you this, Mel, but if you think sex is about looking at a guy's face, you got it ass-backwards."

Melissa stared up at the crack in the ceiling. If this artist was the man she'd met at Bella's, then she owed Bella to at least find out what he wanted. She tapped her fingers together. And what could he do to her at such a public event? She glanced at Jana. "I think you're right. I do want to meet this Aristides Stavros. Let's go to the opening."

Chapter 12

Melissa halted on the pavement and waited for Jana to catch up. Across the street, the gallery lights cast a soft glow. Only a few people wandered about inside, probably the workers putting finishing touches on the displays. Jana pulled up next to her.

"Damn shoes. They're like wearing stilts."

Melissa glanced down at Jana's red spiky heels and held out her own foot shod in her favorite wedge-heeled sandals. "I told you we had to walk from the station."

Jana sniffed. "Sensible footwear is for wimps." She flipped her silver-striped plissé Armani scarf around her neck and strode across the street.

Just as they stepped up on the curb, a catering truck pulled up and offloaded trays of hors d'oeuvres. Perfect timing. Melissa slipped in among them. She wanted to get a good look at Mr. Stavros before confronting him. After all—she clasped her hands together—he might not be the right monster.

Inside the gallery, huge paintings hung on walls so white they looked blue. Others were suspended from the ceiling by thin, nearly invisible wires. Across every canvas sprawled naked bodies. Only at first, they didn't look like bodies at all. They looked like idyllic landscapes—blue sky, low hills, pink-white sand beaches, and aqua sea. Only after serious study did the vegetation convert into hairy patches under arms, behind necks, and between fleshy thighs, and the sand soften into sweeps of skin in tones of salmon and cocoa and honey.

The ethereal tones of a flute floated around her ears. Mesmerized, Melissa wandered from painting to painting as if in some maze of fleshly delight. They were beautiful—Aristides Stavros's women—more beautiful than any living creature on earth. She wanted to reach up and touch them, memorize them, understand the meaning of the faint green and blue symbols flickering across their skin.

She studied the paintings, licked her lips, and swallowed. Only a man who truly loved women could paint like this. She thought of Bella. Could he also murder them?

From somewhere behind her, a tray crashed, and someone cursed in a foreign language. The familiar guttural voice plowed through her. Heart thumping, she spun around to tell Jana she'd found her monster. But Jana wasn't there.

She pressed her palm against her chest, the oversized bangles Jana insisted she wear to dress up her simple black sheath slipping against each other in a tinkle of cheap base metal. That's right—she pushed the bangles back down to her wrist—Jana had said something about freshening her lipstick.

The man's voice rose, full of anger, and came closer. Her heart beat faster. Her shoulders tightened. This was the monster who'd touched her with his huge hands, who'd sent swirls of desire through her, who'd frightened her to death at Bella's. She couldn't face him alone.

A door stood ajar at the back of the gallery, and she

dashed for it and slipped inside. Chill air wrapped around her, crept beneath her thin linen dress, and set her shivering. She crossed her arms in front of her and glanced around. A poorly-lit hallway led off to a row of offices to her right and a stairwell to her left. She leaned back to close the door all the way. Now was the perfect opportunity to unearth the monster's secrets.

Three offices and six file drawers later she knew a lot more about the financial and strategic problems of running a major gallery, but nothing more about Mr. Stavros than that his paintings sold. Sold for more money than she could imagine.

If he'd done something to Bella, it hadn't been for money.

A rising cacophony of voices and the tinkling of champagne glasses drew her back to the hall. The show must be in full swing by now. She'd better get back before Jana raised a hue and cry.

She took a step in the direction of the gallery and froze as the doorknob turned. The door opened, sweeping in the champagne-bubble voices, and the one man she didn't want to meet. Not here. Not now. She dove for the shadow-filled stairwell and hunched down on the first step.

Aristides Stavros strode into the corridor, cell phone in hand. He glanced over his shoulder. "Yes, Miss Keeler. I understand. I am sure we can work something out with the Nesbitts. Back in a minute. I need to check this text message." The door closed with a click.

He walked toward her hiding place. She lowered herself down another step and held her breath, praying he wouldn't see her.

He glanced at the phone. "I just knew it." He punched in a number. "Hanlin, sorry to call you at home. That young man I told you about—that's right—Fur Tree. He's been picked up by the police. Yes, I know you're not a criminal lawyer. Just get one over there—90th Precinct. And find the girl while you at it. Yes. Yes. I know it will cost money. Just do it. And that other issue about Sirena. Did you take care of it? Good. Good."

Melissa's heartbeat pounded in her ears. Sirena? This monster did have something to do with Bella's disappearance.

He turned in her direction and came closer. Heavens, didn't he need to be out front selling his paintings? Trembling, she stepped back, missed the step, and reached for the railing. Jana's stupid bracelets jingled. She smothered the sound against her hip, but it was too late.

"*You*." Aristides Stavros loomed over her. "What are you doing here?"

She peered up at the artist's twisted face and backed further down the steps. A doorknob poked her in the back. Panicked, she twisted it open and dashed into an unlit basement storeroom.

She stumbled forward into the dark, tripped over a metallic cylindrical object, and landed on her stomach. All the air whooshed out of her. Rectangular objects with sharp corners tumbled around her, jabbing her in the arms and neck. Rough cloth scraped her skin.

On the staircase above her, the beast hovered in the doorway like a hawk scenting a rabbit. For a second, he hesitated, then he dashed down the steps and moved toward her, huffing as he shoved objects out of the way.

She pushed herself up on hands and knees and scuttled further into the dark.

"*Sto diávolo.* Where are you? If you destroy any of these paintings, I will have your hide or at least my lawyer will." He came closer. "Busy man, my lawyer, and to think I almost didn't hire one."

She scrabbled back and touched torn canvas. Heavens, these were his paintings—the ones that sold for thousands of dollars.

She was in deep, deep trouble.

A grunt. The monster hefted a painting and pushed it aside. Another grunt. He was coming closer. She wanted to cover her head with her hands and curl up into a ball as she had done as a child to protect herself from the monster under the bed. But this monster was real.

For a moment, his powerful body was silhouetted against the faint illumination of the doorway as he picked up another painting, then disappeared as he stacked it to his right. He was clearing a path directly toward her. She could see the slash of light coming down the stairwell, her only escape to safety. But one furious artist blocked the way.

He'd be on top of her in seconds.

But not if she distracted him. She sat up and reached behind her for the hard object she'd landed on. She ran her fingers over it, found the plastic nub at one end. A spray paint can. She gripped it in her right hand, took a squatting position, and waited. The next time he passed in front of the light, she tossed the can with all her strength, aiming for where she thought his head should be. But for a big man, he moved fast. The can whizzed past him, landed on the steps with a clank and then clattered down to the floor.

The monster gave a short laugh. "Missed." He moved forward, his expensive suit swishing closer and closer.

She had to stop him. Desperate, she wiggled her hand around under the fallen artwork and found another can, pried off the cap. Then she put her finger on the spray nozzle and waited.

His enticing scent reached her before he did. The hairs on her neck rose, and she trembled. Heat gathered in her core and set her skin afire. She shook herself. She barely thought about sex—it's what had annoyed Colin so much—and now her body was turned on by a monster who made her cringe.

She held her finger on the nozzle. "Stay away."

His shadow rose over her. "I would never hurt you, Miss. But I do need you to stop flailing around my paintings. Let me help you up. We need to talk." She could see his outstretched hand, but not his face. She pressed the nozzle all the way down. Nothing happened.

"Can's empty." He reached toward her again. *"Your hand."*

She rose to her feet, pushed past him, and took off for the stairs. But her foot landed on the errant can, and she flailed backward, knowing she was going to fall, and praying she did not ruin another canvas. But she didn't. Strong arms swept her up and cradled her in a warm embrace.

She banged her fist on his chest, his very hard chest. "Let me go. I'm sorry about your paintings. You frightened me."

"Ah. Then I must apologize." He shifted her in his

arms and brushed his lips lightly across hers. The barest of touches, tentative, an asking for permission she hadn't expected from this brute of a man.

Her breath caught in her throat. His lips were soft and spicy, unlike any lips she'd kissed before. Her head demanded she pull away, kick and scream and insist he let her go. But her body wanted to taste more.

She slid one hand into his long wavy hair and ran the other down his finely woven lapel, found his silk tie, and clasped on. Heat radiated from his body and seeped through the clothing separating them, warming her to the core. Brazenly, she tugged his head down to hers. He licked the seam of her lips, slowly deepening the kiss, drew her closer with huge hands that cocooned her head and supported her body.

Her mouth opened, and she welcomed him in. He tasted of champagne and the salt of the sea. He brushed his thumb over her nipple. Fire spiraled through her and ignited between her thighs. She had never felt this alive, every cell ablaze, need throbbing through every vein and nerve ending. She twisted her fingers in his hair and demanded more.

In the dark, he was all glorious man, hard, male, and delicious. Jana was right. What he looked like didn't matter. She wanted the kiss to go on and on. She wanted him to keep touching her so she could not think of anything else. Time stopped. For the first time, in a long while, she felt safe.

Chapter 13

Ari clung to the girl like she was a lifeline to heaven. *Zeús*. He'd never been kissed so deeply. He wanted to tear off her skinny little dress and drive into her, claim her as his own.

Heels clicked in the hall above. Someone called his name. He gently pulled his lips away and rested his cheek against hers, regretting that he was wearing the false beard. He ran his tongue over his lower lip and savored the taste of her. He kissed her chin and along her neck, sucking and licking. He whispered in her ear, "Oh, Nereida, my beautiful sea nymph. I have not the time to pleasure you the way you deserve. This will not do, you know. Strangers kissing in the dark."

He knew the moment she became aware of him as something other than a shadow lover. Her breathing sped up. Her fingers slipped from his hair. Her lovely arm fell away from his neck. Her hand came up and scrubbed at her mouth.

Reluctantly, he swung her around and set her down, steadying her on her feet, every part of his body protesting the sudden chill of separation. He clasped her arm tightly, making sure she could not run away a second time and leaned across to flip on the light switch, fearing the dread he would see in her eyes the minute she remembered what he looked like.

The single bulb did little to light the temperature-controlled storeroom, but it was enough. Huge, slightly tipped-up eyes the color of dark amber peered up at him. Lips glistened, red and swollen from his kiss. Her neat little cap of hair framed the most beautiful face he'd ever seen.

He bit his lip and savored the lingering trace of her. "Your name, Nereida." His English slashed out harsher than intended, and her arm muscles tensed beneath his hand. He grasped her tighter, desperate. "Don't leave. There is heat between us—passion. All I need do is touch you"—he licked his thumb and ran it across her lips—"here, and you melt for me." Her glance flicked toward the door. He gave it a last try. "Please, your name—so we can meet again?"

The girl gave a soft squeak like a mouse in a trap. Her pulse pattered in her neck. It was no use. She was petrified of him, like all the rest. He dropped his hand. "*Fige.* Get out of here."

She froze like a rabbit freed from one of the villagers' snares, her nose scrunched up in disbelief, her mouth gaping open. "Go," he repeated. He stepped back and made an elegant bow. "You may go." Her beautiful mouth snapped closed, and she turned, flew up the stairs and out the door.

He sank down on the steps and listened to the door bang closed, the sound whipping his heart. He scanned the pile of twisted and torn canvases spread across the floor and assessed the damage. Three had already been sold. One had been a commission. He did the mental calculations. At least fifty thousand dollars in lost sales. Months of work lost. Money he needed to stymie Vernon and set up the conservation trust his lawyer had cleverly devised to save the village and the seals. He rubbed the back of his neck. *Ilithíos,* he was an idiot. He'd let her go, and he hadn't even learned her name or what she had to do with Sirena's disappearance.

He licked his lips again and tasted the fading sweetness of her. Then he stood, straightened his tie, and tugged down his sleeves. *Zeús,* that had been one very expensive kiss. He kicked a torn painting to the side. But fool that he was, he would taste those lips again in a minute. No matter the cost.

****

Melissa found Jana staring at a painting of a stretched out woman with skin pink as the inside of baby's ear. She tapped her on the shoulder. "Sorry I abandoned you."

Jana snapped a brochure in her face. "I was about to leave. You left me here staring at these breasts and cunts. Damn, but now I'm horny as hell. What do you say we take off and go clubbing in the Village?"

She looped her arm into Jana's. "Sounds great." She glanced back at the door to the offices. "Let's get a move on."

Jana gave her a quizzical look. "What? I thought you hated clubbing?"

Someone called Stavros's name and a murmur went through the crowd. Drat, he must be behind her. She pulled Jana around the corner and herded her toward the door. "Tonight I feel like letting go."

"Wait a minute." Jana planted her feet and stopped in front of her. "We haven't met the artist yet. Isn't that why we came?"

"Oh, I did. When you were in the ladies' room."

"So did you ask him why he was at the station-house?"

"No. Doesn't matter. He's a milquetoast type of guy. Can't even speak English." She gave a little shimmy and steered Jana past the row of nudes with the astronomical price tags. If he asked her in public for her name, she would have to tell him—and be sued. Her heart speeded up. She destroyed thousands of dollars' worth of paintings.

Out. She had to get out. She pulled Jana toward the door. "So where would you like to go? The Village Underground is a couple of blocks to the east." Melissa opened the exterior door. "Or we could try Café Wa."

"Give me a minute, will ya?" Jana flung back her hair and glanced around the gallery. "I told a colleague we'd meet him here." She frowned down at her feet. "I was hoping he'd drive us home. My feet are killing me."

Melissa pinched her lips together. "Well, I'm roasting hot. Let's wait outside."

Jana peered at her face. "I thought you looked quite flushed." She leaned in closer and touched her neck. "Wow. Is that a hickey?"

Melissa slapped her hand on the spot. "No, a tray—a waiter—with a tray—ran into me."

A tall blond man opened the gallery door. "Why, Jana Firth. Waiting for me, were you?"

"There you are, Theo." She tilted her head toward Melissa. "Melissa Dermont, meet Theo Tuccio, one of the up-and-ups at the office."

Melissa stared into the bluest eyes she'd ever seen. Over six feet tall with a finely sculpted nose and a cupid bow mouth that curled just the right amount when he smiled, Theo Tuccio was a woman's dream. He looked strong, competent, and nothing at all like a real

80

estate agent. He had on a black leather jacket, a gray turtleneck, and black trousers. The only touch of color was the ruby in the ring he wore on his left pinky finger. He lifted her hand and brushed his lips across. "My pleasure." Even his voice hummed with confidence and sexual appeal. Jana playfully slapped him on the arm. "So what do you think? Is she a beauty like I told you?"

Melissa clapped her hands over her face. "Jana."

"Welcome to my show."

Melissa turned around slowly. Aristides Stavros stood behind her, his hand held out, his hard gaze burning into her. In the white fluorescent light, her monster, in what had to be a fake beard, looked rougher than he had in the storeroom. She involuntarily stepped back, right into Tuccio, who draped an arm over her shoulder as if they'd been lovers forever, and drew her against a surprisingly muscular body.

The artist's black eyes narrowed into pinpricks. "Can I give you a tour of my work? There are some smaller pieces you might be interested in on the back wall." He flicked his hand in that direction and gave a half bow as if he expected them to follow.

"That would be delightful." Jana stepped forward as if to go.

Melissa clutched Tuccio's leather-clad arm like a lifeline. "Forgive me, I can't. I feel unwell."

The artist's hand dropped to his side. "May I get you some water or a chair while your friends tour the show?"

She shook her head. "No, I need to leave, now." She squeezed Tuccio's hand and gave him what she hoped was her most flirtatious smile. "Please take me home."

Tuccio's mouth winked up. "Home it will be." He glared at the artist. "I am sorry, Mr. Stavros. I will come back another time to enjoy your work."

Ari stepped to the side. "Of course. The show will be up until the end of the month."

Melissa's rescuer patted her hand. "Come, my dear. Some fresh air will help." Then he spun her around and whisked her out the door.

Behind them, Jana cursed as she hopped along pulling off one shoe and then the other. "Wait. Wait up, Melissa, damn it. Wait up."

Chapter 14

Ari stood in the doorway and watched his Nereida cling to Tuccio under the street light. *Melissa.* Her name was Melissa. He licked his lips—*mélissa*—honey bee was the perfect name for someone whose kiss tasted as richly sweet as honey. Blood pounded in his ears. *Zeús,* but he wanted her. And she'd wanted him— in the dark. He would have sworn to it.

Ari slammed his fists into his pockets and turned back to the gallery. Get over it. Melissa Whoever was one of Vernon's tools. If he'd had any doubts, her acquaintance with Theo Tuccio confirmed it. She was a spy. Although what she expected to find in the offices puzzled him. It was just a gallery contracted for the show. He'd be stupid to have anything Vernon would want here. And she was totally incompetent. He'd had no trouble seeing her slip through the door and following after her. What had Vernon done, hired some co-ed off the street?

Of course. He slapped his head. Spying wasn't why she'd been sent. Vernon knew his weaknesses all too well. The bastard knew he was a sucker for a nymph who kissed like heaven, actually, any girl willing to kiss him. And this one got high marks for weaseling under his skin. Oh, yes, very high marks. He could still smell her and taste her, and it would be a long time before he got rid of the image of her kissable mouth open beneath his. He took a glass of champagne off a proffered tray, wordlessly toasted the East Hampton Guilders who were considering the largest of his canvases, and gulped it down.

But Tuccio. Why had Vernon sent him for the girl? Did the bastard think he wouldn't remember the man who'd smashed his face in? Sure, Theo Tuccio looked different with his plastic nose job and dyed hair. He'd had work done to his cheeks and lips, too. But he still had that little tell-tale tattoo on his wrist, the one a wise person got in prison to survive. He pulled up his sleeve and stared down at the faded mark. He'd kept it to remember hell. He wondered why Tuccio kept his.

"There you are." The officious gallery director in her red Versace suit glided up to him, her eyes focused firmly on his lapels. "We've made a sale. The Guilders love the painting and are hot to sign the contract." She fingered her clipboard. "If you'll come this way, we can finalize the deal." With barely disguised revulsion, she stepped aside to let him proceed.

"This one, *Poppies on the Beach*?" He moved in front of the canvas and studied the painting with its cool pink sweeps of flesh set against a stark blue Mediterranean sea. What did people like the Guilders see in his work? Poppy had modeled for that one. She'd been one of his more adventuresome models, one of the few who'd been brave enough to join him in bed as well as lie still for hours while he painted her. He'd found her wandering the streets of Piraeus looking lost. Swedish student on holiday, she'd said, run out of money. She'd spent a summer at the villa. She'd seemed happy enough sharing crusty bread and sweet goat butter on the veranda. Letting the little fish nibble her toes in the sea pools. He'd thought he'd found a life companion.

And then one morning after making long slow love, while he lay on the bed fingering her hair, he'd told her he'd loved her, wanted to marry her. The next morning, she was gone, along with all the cash and gold he'd had in the house and a note saying she'd never marry a monster. He'd painted furiously for weeks afterward, wild emotional rips of colors that showed the truth of her and stained the terrazzo floor. And then he'd burned them, all but the first one he'd done before he'd loved her—the Venezia Biennale centerpiece, the one the Guilders wanted.

The painting on the wall was a clinical study in shading and contrast with a clever name. That's what sold. People with money enough to pay the price didn't want an artist's emotional guts nailed to the wall above their Bugatti sofa. They wanted it to match the color of the rug. They wanted it to be a good financial investment.

He looked back toward the door at Vernon's investment. The trio was still milling around out front waiting for their lift. Tuccio had his hand on the small of the nymph's back, his plastic plumped mouth mere inches from her ear, whispering something amusing. She was smiling up at him with that same innocent look she'd given him. The other girl was barefoot, rubbing one foot along her calf, her red lipstick mouth twisted to the side as if waiting for Tuccio to notice her. Did either of them know Tuccio was Vernon's procurer for an international prostitution ring? Theo Tuccio would suck all passion out of them, then throw them to his dogs. He pinched the hard lump where his nose had broken. It didn't matter. The nymph was Vernon's pawn, doing his dirty work. What did his *yaya* always say? *"Ena koráki para koráki ménei mazí"* A crow is always found near a crow.

A limo pulled up. Tuccio and Melissa got inside. Then it pulled away, leaving the dark-haired girl behind. For a moment, she stood there, and then she spun around, looked directly at him and threw him a kiss. After a long look back, she headed down the street, her hips swaying, her arms pumping, her head thrown back, laughing.

Ari's skin grew icy cold. There was no mistaking the message. He'd been had.

"Mr. Stavros?" Miss Officious was tapping on the clipboard. "The Guilders? They're waiting. And then there's the Congressman. He asked to meet you."

Ari gave her his nastiest scowl, and she took a step back. "I've had it for tonight. Set up an appointment with the Guilders' for tomorrow and give the guests my regrets."

"But you just can't leave."

He leaned toward her. "But I can. You need me. I don't need you."

Little beads of sweat gathered on her brow. "The cream of the New York art scene is here tonight. You've not been introduced to everyone yet."

Ari laughed. "They are here to invest in the art, not me. It's your job to take the money."

Chapter 15

Twenty minutes later, Ari was in the private town car he'd hired, heading over the Williamsburg Bridge, wearing his Ugly Man rags, with his baseball cap pulled low over his face, false beard gone, and his satchel of spray paint on his lap. He had to get out and do something wild to block out the image of Tuccio's hand on his Nereida's back. The idea of that bastard touching her made him want to smash something hard. He tapped the hired driver on the shoulder. The man was a huge ex-cop who looked like a linebacker, yet he flinched at his touch. "Here, Delaney. Drop me here. No need to wait."

"Whatever you say, sir." The Irishman glanced around at the factories silhouetted against the twinkling skyline of lower Manhattan. "Not my cup of tea. But you're the boss."

"Go home and spend time with your family. See you Monday morning." Ari climbed out and headed for the last place he'd seen El Toro's crew. From the wall to the right, the pair of bulls from the first night stared down at him. He moved further into the maze of rubble and concrete. A row of tags ran along a long, smooth concrete retaining wall. He took out a spray can and made his first tag. He'd been practicing it for days, his initials in the form of a Minotaur. It seemed suitable. That's what he was—would always be—a feared beast in a labyrinth.

He stood back and admired his work, and then moved on. That was one thing El Tori's crew had drilled into him. Keep moving. Watch your back. Especially when out on your own without your crew behind you.

Night watchmen had bludgeons and were known to toss unconscious punks into the river. And the NYPD Vandal Squad patrolled the area relentlessly. It was a lot easier arresting kids for making art than big underground criminals like Vernon and Tuccio for destroying lives.

****

It took a while before they found him.

Solo planted himself in front of him. "What's up, Ugly Man?"

Ari shook his satchel. "I've brought a supply of new Rusto cannons in your favorite colors."

Solo grinned. "*Perfecto*. We're to the heavens tonight. Got a run going on that needs touching up. Celebrating Fur Tree's release from the can. Come along. You can do the fill."

"The fill?"

"Yeah, Ugly Man. Fill. You're still a toy."

Ari couldn't stop laughing. Somewhere across the river the cream of New York were paying thousands of dollars for his paintings, and these kids barely trusted him to color inside the lines.

"So where's this heaven?"

Solo pointed toward the bridge. "Up there."

****

Ari sat on the railing and looked down at the streets below the Williamsburg Bridge. Several people walked their dogs. Young lovers strolled along the water's edge so close together they looked like contestants in a three-legged race.

"Get to work," Neto called up to him.

"*Endáxi*, boss." Ari twisted his legs around the railing and hung over the side of a girder spanning the pedestrian way. Ignoring the worrisome thought that if he fell, he would leave behind a lot of loose ends and let his sister down one very final last time, he adjusted the spray and concentrated on getting the paint inside the lines of T-Crew's red and silver tag. It was having a historic run, they'd said. Been up almost a year.

Down below, Neto was making funny faces at him, and Solo tossed pebbles while yelling at him to hurry up—people were coming.

He sprayed the final loop, pulled himself upright, and shook his head to get the blood flowing in the right direction.

Hanger cupped his hands and called up, "Get down, now, Ugly Man. It's been two minutes. You're gonna get caught. Then they'll kick you out of the country for sure."

He waved at the boy. It tickled him to have someone worried about him. Then he shook his head. Yeah, sure. More likely the kid wanted to make sure his food source stayed out of trouble. Ari put a hand on the girder, but couldn't resist one last look at the isle of Manhattan, so different from his own island.

He shifted slightly and gazed out across the inky flow of the East River. Across the river, the long glittering city hugged the shoreline like a languid lady spangled in lights, the jagged blocks of buildings smoothed over in night vapor. His fingers twitched as he imagined stroking ultramarine blue and ivory black and Payne's gray across a blank canvas, brush stroke by brush stroke, caressing into being the shadow woman, her nude body rising from the river, her luscious mouth—Melissa's mouth—calling to him.

He swayed, suddenly dizzy, and gripped the iron beam for support, the metal cold beneath his fingers. *Sto diávolo.* What was it about this Melissa that attracted him so? She was in league with Vernon and Tuccio. He'd caught her spying on him. She'd destroyed thousands of dollars' worth of his paintings. Ah, but she kissed like a siren. He ignored the heat that surged through him at the thought of her mouth pressed against his, swung over the railing, and dropped to the walkway with a thump.

"Move, fool." Solo seized him by the sleeve and jerked him back toward the Brooklyn end of the bridge. "Here come the cops."

El Toro nudged him in the side. "Toss the damn can."

"And waste a full load?" Ari shoved the can under his jacket and dropped well behind the rest. Two cops sauntered up, their eyes narrowed, hands on their holsters. They halted in front of them. "Deco boys," the taller one said. "Let's see your hands."

Ari smiled. They'd find no paint on T-Crew's hands. It was all on his. He walked up behind the group. "Trouble, officers?"

The shorter patrolman turned sharply. "Who are you?"

"Aristides Stavros. I am an artist visiting this fine country, and these gentlemen are giving me a tour of this art form." He deepened his accent. "How you say it—gráfoto?"

"Graffiti," Hanger corrected, his eyes alight.

"Ah, yes," Ari said with a tip of his chin. "That is it—*graffiti*—so like the Greek verb *to write*." He waved his hand, the one with the paint. "The bridge is quite— um—decorated. But yes?" The officer looked suspiciously from him to the kids. "Ah so, yes, we meet at my gallery, a—how you say—school trip for artists with talents—I think?" He held out a business card. "My card. Please come. See my show at Gallery Four in SoHo. The mayor and Congressman Flint were there tonight."

Oops. That might have been layering it on a bit much. From the puzzled looks on the cops' faces, he knew that they were beginning to think they were being bamboozled.

Then the taller one laughed and tipped his cap. "My God, begging your pardon, sir, but you're the guy who reported that woman missing. The man with the crushed face. Memorable, Detective Louis said. And he was right. Said you were an Olympic athlete. Competed eight years ago in—what was the sport?"

A chill ran through him. It wasn't something he wanted to remember. "Greco-Roman wrestling."

The cop pulled out his notepad. "Could I have your autograph, sir. For my son."

"Of course." Ari scrawled his name across the paper and handed it back.

The cop pocketed the notebook and waved them on. "Well, enjoy your tour." They turned and continued down the promenade.

Ari was instantly surrounded. Neto squeezed his bicep. "You were in the *Olympics?* The real one with the flame and all?"

He looked around at their open-mouthed faces. They'd grunted when he told them he was an artist—a really fine artist whose work was world renowned—and made him prove it. But just mention he'd been a sports star, and they fell onto the pavement and worshiped him. It didn't matter what sport.

They were just like his father who'd never acknowledged or encouraged his artistic side, but had driven him to perform on the wrestling mat, even though he hated it with a vengeance. He squeezed his hands into tight fists, his fury barely contained. And look where his father's obsession had led. The family destroyed. Sirena ruined. His joy of life stolen.

Hanger bounced in front of him. "So did you win?"

He pushed out of the group and strode ahead, the kids fanned out around him like a spray of paint. "No. It was a long time ago. When I was young and stupid."

"You have to be good to be in the Olympics," Neto said.

Ari avoided looking at the boy's face. He couldn't stand the look of betrayal, as if he'd hidden some golden crown.

Hanger On circled around him. "An Olympic hero. Who'd believe it?

"No hero."

"But you didn't hesitate to hang over the railing." The kid smiled shyly. "We thought you'd back out for sure when you saw it. Old man like you."

It was Ari's turn to grunt.

"Which Olympics?" Solo asked.

"Greece 2004."

El Toro pushed back his cap. "Twelve years ago?

How old are you, Ugly Man?"

"Old enough to know we'd better keep moving before those cops start thinking about how the spray paint on my hands matched that brightened-up tag." He looked back down the promenade. "They're just about there."

Hanger tilted his head. "No really, how old are you?"

"Twenty-seven. See, ancient."

Neto nudged El Toro. "Hey King Man, I think with Ugly Man here on our side we should put out a Whole Car challenge. We got to do something to protest those paid ads made to look like graffiti art they've stuck on the subway cars. It's not right. Graffiti is a crime when it's done by real artists, and just fine when some big company uses it for an advert."

El Toro frowned and then slowly a grin spread across his face. "Yeah, *hombre*, let's do it. They'll pull the car off after a few stops, but at least we'll have sent them a message." The others slapped him on the back.

Ari fell back and listened to the crew break into excited discussion about the when and the where. A Whole Car challenge, it seemed, was to paint an entire subway car in two minutes flat as it sat in the Bedford Street station. Sounded utterly impossible and entirely illegal. His chances of sweet-talking a patrol officer again would be sorely tested if they were caught. Not that he need worry. He had his high-priced lawyer, and at the worst, they'd kick him out of the country. He looked at T-Crew high fiving and laughing as they bounded from one railing to another. But if they got caught, they were risking jail time. And he didn't wish that on anyone.

Chapter 16

"This is delicious, but I really can't eat any more." Melissa folded her napkin, matching the edges precisely, and laid it down next to her fork. The Peter Luger Steak House was renowned for its prime rib, but she had barely been able to swallow a few bites.

Tuccio glanced at her plate. "I'm sure they can provide a doggy bag." He leaned in. "Can I tempt you with dessert? Their homemade *Schlag* on top of chocolate mousse, I have been told, is a whipped confection worthy of the angels."

"I don't think—"

"Do order a dessert." He reached across and swept a finger across her hand. "I am looking forward to licking it off your lips."

She stared at his perfect face and heat crept up her neck. "Really. I don't think—we just met." Still, he *was* handsome as a god and those luscious plump lips, that should look too feminine but instead just looked sinful, tempted her.

She put her fingers to her mouth. Maybe kissing him would wipe away the memory of that monster's mouth on hers. She dropped her hand. What was she thinking? After Colin, she had wanted nothing to do with men. Now she was considering kissing a second man on the same night? Idiot.

He smiled and signaled the waiter. "You are

thinking about it. That's good." He ordered a chocolate mousse and sat back in his chair. "So did you enjoy the art show tonight?"

"Stavros's paintings are very unique." Melissa shifted in her chair. "I regret you had to miss seeing them because of me."

"Don't be concerned. I've seen his work." He licked his lips. "I prefer women in my bed, not on the wall."

Melissa focused on those lips. "Still, I *am* sorry."

"So was the artist whom you expected?"

"Expected?"

"Jana said that you thought he had something to do with a friend of yours going missing."

"Jana talked to you about me?" She uncrossed her legs.

"I'm relatively new at the Brooklyn office, but we've shared lunch several times. She's worried about you. Says you're obsessed with finding this *friend*." He looked up. "Ah, here's your mousse."

The waiter placed the dish of chocolate and whipped cream in front of her. Her stomach tightened. "Oh dear, I never eat rich desserts. I fear this will be wasted."

One side of Tuccio's mouth curved up in a half-smile as he picked up the spoon and swirled it through the mixture. "I am sure you are wrong. Please take a taste."

She opened her mouth and let him feed her the spoonful. A dab of cream stuck to her lower lip, and she licked it up.

His eyes darkened to indigo. "Ah yes, my sweet Melissa. Not wasted at all." He put the spoon down.

"Come, it is a lovely evening, shall we take a stroll along the esplanade?" He rose and took her by the hand. She followed, wondering what his kiss would feel like.

****

It was a night for lovers. The city air had that clean, fresh Sunday-night taste. The factory emissions from the weekdays had blown away at last. Overhead the stars twinkled like the children's rhyme. Melissa slipped her arm into Tuccio's and dreamed of romance and kisses and a future with this man as they walked along the river's edge. He was everything a girl could want.

She couldn't keep from turning her head and gazing at him every other minute. Tall, broad-shouldered, with perfectly symmetrical features, Theo Tuccio looked like every famous movie idol she'd ever mooned over all wrapped up in one, and he reeked of money. Living with status-hungry Jana, she'd had a quick education in the lives of the rich and famous. The designer leather jacket that fit him like a glove was a Burberry or a Bailey and must have cost over a thousand dollars. His feet were shod in custom-made wing tips. His fingernails were perfectly manicured, and every time he moved, his Italian citrus bergamot cologne wafted over her.

But it wasn't his wealth that attracted her. It was when he looked at her with that movie star face. Every smile sent little tremors running up and down her spine. Every soft-spoken word and gentle caress made her feel cherished and desirable. Her heart sped up when she looked at him. He was not a monster—he was perfect.

She slipped her hand into his. "So tell me about

yourself. Jana said you're in real estate. I imagine sales, like her?"

Tuccio snuggled her closer. "And purchases. You might say—I am an acquisitions agent—among other things. And you, I understand from Jana, are completing a doctorate in anthropology?"

"Yes. Well, I'm trying to. I'm just about done. I am researching the reasons why women get tattoos, especially ones that—well, that they later regret."

He stopped and turned to face her. "Regret?"

"Like the name of their abusive husbands."

"A man who has to have his name engraved on a beautiful woman's body is a man without imagination." He took her hand in his and brought it to his lips. "There are far better ways to claim a woman."

Melissa tugged her hand free. "Mr. Tuccio, be serious, I've only known you a few hours."

"Ah, but don't you feel the attraction between us, even now? You have been searching for me. And I, for you." He lowered his voice to a husky whisper. "You are the most beautiful creature I have ever seen. So delicious I want to eat you up."

His gaze sizzled like oil in a frying pan. Heat suffused her. Melissa pressed her teeth into her lower lip. The man was tempting as sin, but he was rushing her to a precipice. She needed to cool down, keep her wits. They were on a public street after all. She dropped his arm and moved slightly away.

"You are thinking of him."

Melissa's bubble burst. "Who?"

"That artist at the gallery. He made you uncomfortable. You were desperate to get away." He took her hand in his and patted it. "Did the bastard hurt you in some way?"

"No, it's just—just." She hesitated. Should she tell him? The two men had seemed to know each other. Maybe Tuccio could help her. "I think he has something to do with my friend Bella. She's the missing woman."

"Ah, I can understand you being worried." He squeezed her hand. "But I'm confused. Why do you think some foreigner like Ari Stavros has anything to do with this Bella?"

"He was at her apartment when I went there to—to feed her cat."

"At her apartment? He came upon you there? Oh, my Melissa. You were lucky to escape."

"Escape?"

"You are, I am sure, unfamiliar with the man's history." He lowered his voice. "Look I shouldn't tell you this, but I'm not what I seem." He reached into his jacket pocket and whipped out a badge. "I am a special agent working undercover for Immigration. This Stavros, he's unstable, violent. In Greece, he killed a man with his bare hands. Went to jail for it. He's lived in seclusion ever since they let him out. This New York expedition is quite out of character. I am surprised the US government let him in, a cold-blooded killer. That's why I have been asked to keep my eye on him."

Bile rose in her throat. She'd been kissed by a murderer, had been physically attracted to him. "His face?"

"Retribution, I believe. Delivered in prison. The man he killed—he was an important sports figure, much admired." He looked behind and then guided her around the corner. "So how did you get into Bella's place?"

"You will think me terrible, but I found her keys and I thought—" Melissa bit her lip. "It was good I did. Her cat would have starved."

"You are all kindness, my Melissa." He stopped and drew her to him. He rested his forehead against hers. "I can see the fear in your eyes. I am so sorry you have gotten mixed up with that murderous criminal. Let me"—he lowered his voice to a whisper—"protect you."

Nobody had ever offered to protect her. He worked for the government. All her worries fled. She wanted to be kissed by this Adonis of a man until all memory of the monster's lips on hers was wiped away. Melissa threw her arms around his neck and drew him down to her hungry mouth.

He ran a hand over her hair and lowered his lips to hers. "So eager, my Mellie. So very, very eager."

He wrapped his arms around her and pressed down relentlessly, sucking, and licking, forcing her mouth open, and shoving his tongue deep inside. The hard bulge of his erection pressed against her thigh. His mouth against hers was cold and hard as a marble. This was no tender kiss, no gentle god of love.

She gagged and gave him a little push. He grasped her face with one hand, clamping her in place, and pulled her tighter to him.

She slid her mouth off his. "No," she whimpered in protest. "Stop."

He pulled back, his eyes narrowed. "What's wrong?"

She put her hand between them to separate them. "I am sorry. This is all too fast. Too much. You've overwhelmed me with your assistance at the gallery and the lovely dinner. "But I'm not ready for—" She hesitated. "Please, let's get to know each other better."

He stepped back and tugged down his sleeves. In the harsh glare of the street light, the beautiful face showed not a flicker of emotion, his pale blue eyes colorless as glass marbles, his full lips bloodless. A shiver trickled down Melissa's spine. It was as if he wore one of those clear plastic masks kids sported at Halloween, the kind that turned your face into a store mannequin's.

He adjusted his collar and straightened his tie. "Of course, my sweet Mellie. Shall we continue our walk?" He crooked his elbow and offered her his arm. Just then a gang of young men carrying duffle bags swirled around the corner and headed down the street. For an instant, they surrounded her, trailing a cloud of paint fumes and sudden laughter, and then all but one was past.

The last one, the biggest of them all, enshrouded in a dirty trench coat, pulled out a spray can and sidestepped around her with a tip of his floppy hat. Then in one smooth motion he let loose a spray of orange at the back of that very expensive leather jacket.

With a yell, Tuccio pushed past her and gave chase. Ahead of him, the group zigzagged down the street thumbing their noses and making farting noises before disappearing down a dark alley and reappearing on a rooftop. Tuccio stopped and shook his fist at them, letting loose a string of curses in some foreign language she'd never heard.

Melissa wrapped her arms around herself and stared at Tuccio. Under all that elegant beauty lay a storehouse of fury. Mr. Prince Charming might be perfect on the outside, but underneath he was a scary man. Heavens, she never wanted to see that anger directed at her.

He walked back up the street to her. "Damn hoodlums. No respect. Wait till I find a cop." He looked over his shoulder trying to see his back. "Destroyed my jacket. Tell me—what did he write? Here, take a look." He turned his back to her.

"Write?"

"Damn spray bomber tags. The police keep files on them."

Melissa looked at the fluorescent spray painted lines. "It looks like a twisted S with a triangle in the center. No words."

Tuccio turned around huffing. "The police will be able to read it. No way that paint ape will get away with this. I *will* find him." His eyes narrowed to reptilian slits. "And when I do I'll break every finger and every toe and *then*—I'll break his *neck*."

Melissa froze, her whole body trembling. "They're just kids."

Tuccio pressed his lips together. The smooth mask reappeared. "But I forget myself. You are cold. Shall I call my car?"

Melissa hesitated. No way she wanted to sit beside him in that soundproof Lincoln. Better to stay on the street. "Can you walk me home? We can get to know each other better on the way."

The corner of his mouth curled up. "Knowing each other better is high on my list."

Chapter 17

"What the hell did you do, Ugly Man? You can't tag people. Every cop in the borough will be on our tails." El Toro stood spread-legged, stiff with anger and fear.

Solo whacked Ari on the back with his fist. "Yeah, man. He goes to the police and all they have to do is match us up with the cops' memory of us on the bridge. They'll remember us—you gave them your card. Your real name. *Idiota.*"

Ari leaned out over the rooftop and watched Tuccio take Melissa by the arm. "He won't turn you in. He knows who tagged him."

Hanger bit his lip. "You know the guy?"

"You could say that."

Solo narrowed his eyes. "He a friend?"

"Can't say that." Ari watched Melissa pull her hand free and gesture up the street. Could he be so lucky? Would they lead him to her home? He stood. "I need to follow her."

"Her?" Hanger On tugged his sleeve. "You hot for her—that skinny Asian girl with no hair?"

El Toro frowned. "Don't want that one, Ugly Man. Sticking her nose in everything."

Ari froze. "What do you mean?"

"I heard on the street she makes women disappear," El Toro said, rolling his hands around in his pockets. "They go—just gone—poof-like, leaving their clothes behind. What woman leaves clothes behind if she gonna run off?"

Like Sirena. Ari's heart skipped a beat. How could this girl with all her innocence be crooked? It twisted him to the core. He swallowed and forced his voice to stay level. "Then that sounds like just the woman I want to meet. *Hasta la vista, amigos.*" He leaped down to the lower roof and then swung over the side.

"Wait up for us." El Toro landed beside him. The little gypsy gave him a hard look, his eyes narrowed to slits. "I think we'd better come along. I'm not sure you are a very good judge of women."

****

Tuccio gone, her wits scattered, Melissa climbed the steps to Jana's apartment with leaden feet. What was wrong with her? The monster kissed like an angel, and the angel kissed like death. A pox on men. Jana's invitation to her bed was looking better and better. She pushed open the door and prayed Jana was still out. Her stomach sank. No such luck.

Jana sat on the good kitchen stool, drinking a tall cup of joe. "So how was your dinner with Tuccio? No complaints about his face, I bet." She grinned like a Cheshire Cat. "I did good introducing you, didn't I? So what happened? Did you get to lap up any cream?" She patted the rickety bar stool. "Tell Auntie Jana all about it. I'm all ears."

Melissa slipped onto the stool. "We ate at Lugers. Walked a bit down by the bridge and then he walked me home."

"No limo? God, I could have killed the two of you leaving me to hoof it alone."

"But you said—"

Jana waved her hand. "No biggy. I called Floria, and we did a round of the clubs. Nothing much doing. Took a taxi home." She took a sip of coffee. "So Tuccio loosened those under-kissed lips, did he?"

"Does it show?" Melissa scrubbed her lips with her sleeve.

"Oh, like that, was it?" Jana got up and tossed her cup in the trash. "You're a lost cause, girl. I don't know why I keep trying to make you happy." She looked at her long and hard. "Laura—she had such dreams of you finding the perfect man."

Melissa blinked and examined her bitten down fingernails. "Laura's dead and her dreams were not mine."

Jana stood, her lip quivering. "I didn't mean—"

Melissa rushed over and hugged her. "Drat. I'm sorry. You've been wonderful to me. It's just—well, Tuccio—he's way beyond anyone I ever dated. He's rolling in money."

"So roll," Jana said, pulling away and leaning back against the counter.

"I don't know. His touch—it doesn't make me *feel* anything."

"Really? Adonis personified?" Jana reached out and ran a finger down her cheek. "Why, I think you prefer that creepy Stavros character." Her eyes widened. "Gad, Mel. You do."

Melissa's face heated. "No. Not how you're thinking. He's—oh—it's all so complicated. He has something to do with Bella disappearing, and Tuccio says—he says Stavros is a murderer. Done prison time. But I'm not sure."

"Not sure he's a murderer?" Jana pushed away from the counter and headed for her bedroom. "I'll show you how creepy he is." She came back with a thrice-folded *Williamsburg News* and slapped it down on the table. "Read this."

Melissa skimmed the quarter-page ad. "He's paying women five hundred dollars an hour to model for him? So what—he's fabulously wealthy, too."

Jana tapped the ad with her index finger. "When a guy looks like that, he has to pay a fortune for it.

"It?"

"*Sex,* you idiot. Those are call girl wages."

Melissa studied the ad. "Hmm, the address is over on N 7th and River. I wonder—"

"Don't be a fool, girl. There's nothing to wonder about. He preys on women. He's a sexual predator for sure. Scared you to death at the gallery somehow. Seems to me like a good man to avoid." She came around the counter and ran a hand over Melissa's cropped hair. "Unless you like your men rough."

Melissa looked at the ad again. Somewhere at that address were her notes and maybe answers to where Bella might be. "You're probably right." She handed the paper back to Jana and leaving her standing there headed for her bedroom.

She shucked her dress and sandals, turned out the lamp on her nightstand, and crawled under the covers. Outside, traffic rumbled by, the sound of a city that never rested. Overhead, the street light shining through her blinds created a crisscross pattern as tangled as her thoughts. She ran a finger over her lips. It was foolish to want to have anything to do with Aristides Stavros again, but if she could figure out a way to get into his studio and search the place, she'd do it in a minute.

****

On the street below, Ari leaned back against the wall and watched the lights flick out in the top floor apartment.

"The girl's off to noddy noddy," El Toro said with a shrug. He took his hand out of his pocket and flipped a coin between his fingers. There was a smudge of silver paint on the sleeve of the sweatshirt Ari had lent him and a corresponding one on his hat brim.

Ari shook his head, still amazed the cops on the bridge had bought his story about a graffiti tour. Sports-blind idiots like most of the male species.

Still, a graffiti art tour did sound plausible. There were tags and Full Monties all over the place. He looked again at El Toro, his mind whirring. With a little bit of promo and endorsement from a few major artists and art patrons, he could establish El Toro and his crew in business and see that they were set for life. The kid might take the money that way when he wouldn't accept charity. Ari glanced at Hanger On. He'd do it for his little brother, surely.

"Okay, you've seen her home. Time to move on." El Toro scuffed the side of his sneaker on the concrete wall. "Hanger has school tomorrow."

"School." Hanger stuck out his tongue. "I won't go back to that cesspit."

"You'll do what I say. You promised Mama you'd obey."

"It's hell. They treat me like a piece of dirt. Say I smell. No way to get clean at the stinky shelter."

Ari looked up at the dark window and then back at the boy in his oversized sweats that he'd probably slept in for the last year. He threw up a hand. "Oh, come back to my place. You can take a shower and steal something else from my suitcase." Hanger smiled and set off at a lope, El Toro racing behind.

With a quick glance, he took in the row of bicycles outside Joe's Gourmet Deli on the corner, the realtor across the street, the Italian Restaurant with the plasticized Mediterranean décor on the opposite corner. At least he knew where the underhanded bitch lived. Ari rolled his shoulders and broke into a jog, enjoying the physical activity. Hanging out with T-Crew definitely kept him in shape.

He glanced back. Confrontation with Melissa would have to wait. But he'd be on her case as soon as he'd taken care of the paperwork. He had to find out what her role was in Sirena's disappearance. El Toro said she made women disappear. His hands curled into fists. She was evil in a beautiful package. He would stop her anyway he could.

Chapter 18

Clutching her new second-hand portfolio to her chest, Melissa pushed open the door of the Sea of Ink tattoo parlor, and strode out into the late afternoon sunshine. Another dead end. It had been almost two weeks since Bella's disappearance, and Melissa still hadn't found a single clue to where she might be.

Neither had she found anyone who recognized the tattoo design she'd found in Bella's files. That surprised her. Local artists made it their business to know each other's work. More and more she was sure Ari Stavros held the key information along with her notes.

She crossed the street and pushed through a throng of tourists wandering along at the pace of a snail. It was early yet, but already the hip offspring of the Upper East Side moguls were slumming in their thrift store cast offs. A bicycle bell dinged. Startled, she swerved out of the way of a Hassidic man on a bike, his black top hat precariously balanced on his head, his long side curls flapping in the breeze, and stumbled.

Someone caught her by the arm and steadied her. She turned to thank her rescuer and caught a glimpse of a floppy hat and a black sweatshirt before he disappeared back into the crowd. The short hairs at the nape of her neck rose as if she'd seen a ghost. She glanced back. It had to be her imagination and too many horror flicks, but she'd swear she'd seen that man before loitering across the street from Jana's apartment and again outside the coffee shop. Had he been following her?

She shoved her hand into her pocket and wrapped her fingers around her can of pepper spray. She remembered Laura's bruised body lying on the slab in the morgue, her father's hand on the back of her head making her look. The city was a dangerous place. Murder happened.

Besides, who would follow her? Not the artist. Aristides Stavros had no idea who she was, and if he did, she expected a big lawsuit to arrive for damaging his paintings, not him.

It certainly was not Tuccio. She had a date to see him tonight. Jana had made her accept.

So she'd give Tuccio another chance. He was taking her into Manhattan for dinner and a play. She needed to relax. Besides, maybe he could tell her more about Ari Stavros. She patted the clipping in her pocket. She knew where he lived, but she needed a way to get into his apartment unseen.

Hmm. Maybe Tuccio could help. He was a real estate mogul after all.

She stopped on the corner and waited for the next bus. Once safely inside, she took out her cell, and her heart beating loudly, entered Tuccio's number. He picked up on the third ring.

"Melissa, my dear. We still on for tonight?"

"Oh, yes. I'm looking forward to it. I was just wondering if you could do me a small favor?"

"Anything for my delicious lady."

"Could you get me a key to the studio Stavros has sublet? He has all my field notes. I need to get them back so I can finish my dissertation."

There was a long silence. "The key is no problem, but can't you just knock on the door and ask?"

"No, the man gives me creeps. You said he's a murderer."

"Then let me get them for you."

"You wouldn't know what to look for. If he's like other artists I know, the place will be a mess. No, I have thought this out. If you call him and get him to leave for an hour or two, I can slip in and find my papers and be out in a wink with no one the wiser."

"You *have* given this thought. Look I'll have to check on which realtor has the key. Let me get back to you in an hour or two."

"I'll be seeing you at six. If you get the key, then bring it to our date."

****

Melissa avoided looking at Tuccio as they stood waiting for his limo. Hard as she tried, the desire wasn't there. The play had been well-acted, but surprisingly silly—one man talking to his hand. The dinner had been expensive, but overly rich—Lobster Thermidor in white wine cream sauce. The dessert had been elegant, but sickeningly sweet—chocolate caramel tarts. The cloying taste still clung to her lips. The man, however, had worn a self-satisfied smile as if he knew something she did not. The barely tipped-up lips in that smooth, perfect face made her skin crawl. If she let her emotions overcome her, she'd run from him as fast as she could.

But she wouldn't. Tuccio was everything a girl should want and more. She'd give him another chance. Besides, she wasn't dressed for running. Jana had decked her up in the skimpiest skirt she owned. "Gotta show your legs, girl, they're your best feature," she'd insisted. And the black tank top and thin white silk jacket that completed the outfit were better suited to a warm summer evening than a chill late September night.

She pulled the jacket closed and rested her fingers on Tuccio's arm. He smiled down at her with his swoon-worthy lips. She tightened her grip. He was so handsome—high-cheeked, square-jawed, his arrow-straight nose so different from Aristides Stavros's. If his kiss felt cold, the problem must be her. Like Jana said, she just needed to get to know him better.

"Come, my dear." He handed her into the car, slipping in next to her, bringing with him the scent of leather, expensive cologne, and potent male.

She inhaled the rich aroma and snuggled closer, hoping he wouldn't think her too forward. "Thank you for the lovely evening."

"My pleasure." He signaled the driver, and the limo headed for the river.

So far, so good. Melissa rested her hand on his thigh and smiled up at him. "I know nothing about you. Tell me about yourself."

"So curious. So much to teach you." He put his hand over hers and played with her fingers. "I was born in Macedonia. Rocks. Mountains. More rocks. Came to the States as a child and grew up in New Jersey. My father was in the import-export business. So we traveled a lot. Especially the Far East." He looped his other hand around her shoulders and ran a fingernail down her cheek, under her neck, and then lower, to the slight indentation between her clavicles. He pressed his nail in slightly. "You carry yourself with that secret silence the women in Southeast Asia have. That natural submission. It is very attractive." His nail cut across the top edge of her tank top, slipped underneath.

The minute his finger moved, every muscle in her body tensed. He was wrong about her being submissive. If Jana knew, she'd be laughing. She looked up into his handsome face, took a deep breath, and kept talking. "Macedonia is part of Greece, isn't it?"

"Bah." Tuccio's fingernail dug in sharply and she froze like a mouse under the paw of a leopard. "No part of Macedonia belongs to Greece."

She sought a safer subject. "So now you work for Immigration."

"On and off." His finger moved lower between her breasts and crept inside her bra. "I take special assignments like this one." He flicked her nipple. "I like the side benefits."

She controlled her breathing. "So you work undercover?"

"You might say that."

"Did you get the key?"

"The key?" He removed his wandering hand and sat back, one eyebrow cocked. "You are quite unexpected, my dear. May I ask how your—what did you lose again—that's right—*notes*, ended up in Mr. Stavros's sublet?

She swallowed. "I left them at a friend's apartment and he took them."

"Ah. Does this have something to do with your missing tattoo artist?"

"Not exactly."

"I take that to mean it does. And what do I get in return for this key?"

She rubbed his thigh and lowered her voice. "Well, I thought—"

He glanced out the side window. "A minute." He pushed a button on the console. The chauffeur nodded and pulled off on a quiet residential street, parked by a hydrant, and got out of the car.

She straightened up. "Why are we stopping?"

"Ah, I thought you wished to negotiate for the key." He pressed a latch on the console, and a panel slid open to reveal a mini-bar. He poured an amber liquid into a glass and held it out to her. You're too tense for me, China Doll. I thought a little privacy might help."

"I don't drink."

"I noticed. You only took a taste of wine at dinner." He held out the glass. "Try this. You'll like it." He held it to her lips, and she took a sip.

She rolled it around on her tongue. "I do like it. It tastes like honey with overtones of something else. An herb?"

"It's a honey mead from my home village in Macedonia. It goes down smooth but has a kick. You'll feel much more relaxed in a minute." He put the glass to her lips again. "Drink the rest."

The mead flowed down her throat and warmed her all the way through. Her vision blurred and her breathing slowed. "What's happening?"

"You're relaxing. Getting ready for me." He placed a hand around her waist and drew her close so that the whole side of her body touched his. The silky fabric of his expensive suit was cool against the skin of her thigh. His spicy cologne filled her nostrils. She could hear Jana cheering. She was going to do it with Prince Charming. She slipped her hand over his chest, exploring. He was all muscle and heat, her prince.

His hands slid up under her tank top, unhooked her bra, and closed around her breasts. His palms were smooth and warm. Her breath quickened.

Yes. He wanted her. Her head fell back, heat swirling through her, gathering between her legs. Yes, this was how it was supposed to feel. He squeezed her breasts and whispered in her ear. "China Doll, such tiny little things. We'll have to have them enhanced. They do amazing work, plastic surgeons today. You will be so beautiful." He touched her hair. "And no more of this buzz cut, I want your hair so long it sweeps that tight little ass of yours."

His words penetrated the fogginess in her head. They were not the words of a Prince Charming, but someone examining merchandise. He wanted to change her. "What?" She tried to twist away, but she seemed to have no strength. His fingers closed on her nipples and pinched. She squirmed, and his fingers clamped tighter.

"Small, but oh so tender." He pinched again. "We need to put piercings on these." He bent his head and sucked hard on one, then the other.

What was wrong with her? The monster had barely touched her, and she'd melted. But even with her head swirling and her body lax under the effects of whatever he'd given her to drink, Prince Charming's pinches and touches hurt. And his proprietary "love" talk was scaring her. She struggled to pull away. "I think—"

He brought his mouth up to hers. "Enough thinking. Remember that key. We're negotiating." He licked her lips. "Chocolate and caramel. You don't know what watching you eat those tarts did to me." He pulled her hand over and pressed it against his erection.

His tongue nudged the seam of her lips. "Open for me, China Doll. Open."

She put her free hand on his shoulder. Light from the street lamp illuminated Tuccio's face, silvering his skin and highlighting his sinfully full lips. A lock of his white-blond hair fell across his brow, gentling the intensity in his eyes. This was better. This was her Prince Charming, a glorious god-of-a-man, not a monster in the dark, and he desired her. She opened her mouth to invite him in.

Tuccio's pale eyes flickered beneath lids half closed. His tongue slipped inside, explored, tasted. He let out a low groan, rearranged himself so he could get a better angle and drove his tongue in deeper, pulled out and pushed in again. Over and over. Harder and harder. Driving her against the seatback. Beating her into submission.

No. She stiffened, unable to breath, every muscle tense. "Slow down." She pushed the flat of her hand against his shoulder.

He released her mouth and ran his tongue down the side of her neck, whispered in her ear. "As the lady wishes." He kissed her behind her earlobe. "You. Are. Delicious." He nuzzled the base of her neck, gently sucked and nibbled.

Better. Melissa closed her eyes and turned her neck toward him, offering more. Any minute now, she'd surely feel that spark of heat shoot through her. He wrapped his hand behind her head, gripped her hard, and bit deep into the tender skin above her collar bone.

She batted at him with her hands. "Wait. Stop. That hurts."

"Hush." His tongue laved the bite. He leaned back

and examined the mark. "Perfect."

Melissa slapped her hand over the raw skin and struggled through the fogginess enveloping her brain to make sense of what had just happened. Prince Charming had bitten her. It was like something out of a vampire story, except he didn't have fangs, and this was no fairy tale. If she let him manhandle her this way, she'd end up like the girls she struggled so hard to save. She took a deep breath to clear her head and pushed away from him. "Why did you do that?"

He flashed her the kind of grin boys gave after dropping a frog down your back. "Some girls like it." He reached inside his suit pocket and pulled out a key attached to what looked like a safety pin. He dangled it in front of her. "Consider it payment for this."

She blinked at the sudden change of tone. "What's that pin thing?"

"A little something for Mr. Stavros from Immigration. It's a tracking device. Might help lead us to your missing friend. I want you to attach it to something he wears regularly. A coat. A hat. A shirt. A wallet. You'll figure it out." He tucked it into the pocket of her jacket. "You're a smart girl, working on that doctorate and all."

Melissa fisted her hands. She wasn't smart at all. Tuccio might be all glittery on the outside, but inside he was cold and calculating, willing to send her into a murderer's lair to hide a tracking device. She slid back, putting some space between them. "I just want to find my note bag."

"And so you will." He patted her hand. "Don't worry, I'll keep an eye on you."

Chapter 19

Hurry up and wait. Ari pulled the cell from his pocket and checked the time. His appointment with the lawyer should have happened twenty minutes ago. Meanwhile, he had to trust El Toro to stay focused. The boy thought following a tattoo groupie around boring. But he'd agreed to do it in return for a cell phone of his own.

Ari glanced at the closed door to Hanlin's office. Might as well make use of the gift while he was stuck here. He pulled out his cell and entered the number. "Toro, do you still see her?"

El Toro snorted on the other end. "She's visited every tattoo parlor in Billyburg carrying a portfolio. Probably checking out girls to be abducted. Bunch of fribbit brainers down here every weekend with their boyfriends getting tats."

Ari squeezed his eyes closed and prayed she was not searching for a tattoo for herself. Her skin was too beautiful for someone to mark up with crude cultural stereotypes. "Any sign of the silver-eyed devil?"

"The guy you tagged? Nope. Hey, she's just come out. Got to go. *Caspita*. She's hopping a frigging bus."

"Don't lose her." The line went dead. He uncrossed his legs and shoved the phone back in his front pocket. This Melissa was a veritable whirlwind of energy. He'd learned a lot about her in the last few days of trailing her. She got up in the wee hours of the dawn and worked the morning rush hour crowd at some tiny coffee shop, whipping up lattes like a super storm. Then she went to Sirena's place to feed the cat and chat up the landlady. The rest of the day she hustled from one tattoo parlor to another. If she had been sent by Vernon to seduce him, she was doing a terrible job. And where did Tuccio fit in all this?

The receptionist interrupted his thoughts. "Mr. Hanlin will see you now, Mr. Stavros."

Ari turned off his cell and picked up his briefcase. After this wait, Hanlin had better have come up with a way to stop Vernon from destroying paradise.

****

It was late afternoon by the time Ari finished his business in Manhattan and arrived back at the Foundry. His best new buddies sat at his work table finishing off the last box of cereal. He looked across at El Toro. "What do you mean you lost her?" Ari tapped the table with his three fingers.

El Toro scooped a heaping spoonful of cereal into his mouth and spoke as he chewed. "She got on a bus, and I didn't have the fare."

"What did you do with the money I gave you this morning?"

"I bought a friend or two breakfast."

Hanger On wiped the milk off his mouth with his sleeve. "We fed the guys panhandling in McCarren. They used to share their blankets with us when Momma died, and we were hiding from Social Services because Toro was only seventeen."

Ari stopped tapping, then started again. Where did such good hearts come from out the hell of these kids' lives? It didn't bear thinking about it. "So she was on Metropolitan Avenue. Which direction did the bus go?"

"Toward the river—" Toro slapped his head. "Hey, she could have been coming here."

Ari stopped tapping. Of course, she would come here. He had something she wanted—her book bag of papers.

He rubbed the stumps of his fingers. Truthfully, he hoped she did come. He wanted to see her, smell her, kiss her again. His body didn't seem to care that she was a lying, sneaky she-devil. He wanted her.

He rubbed the stumps of his fingers harder, willing his body to relax. Damn hand. It was strange how the fingers were still there when they weren't. Today, his phantom pinky was curled up tight, cramped. It often did that when he was tense. But he knew that nothing would help him relax until he had that woman's body underneath him. She was Odysseus's siren calling to him and no matter how underhanded she was, he wanted to make long, slow love and drown himself inside her.

Across the table, Hanger On pushed away his empty bowl and broke the silence with the one question he hated to answer. "Ugly Man, who cut off your fingers?"

He slammed his hand down on the table. "I did." He stared at the boy. "Homework done?" Hanger nodded, not looking at him. "Then let's get out there and find that girl." He looked at the empty bowls and rolled his eyes. Where did these two skinny kids put all that food? "And buy more groceries."

****

Melissa stepped off the Metropolitan Avenue bus

119

and walked down the street to the old foundry building that housed Ari's studio. It was a rough-looking place of crumbling cement and steel-barred windows, one of the last of the old factories nestled between the new condos lining the river bank. A ragged, weather-stained plywood barrier surrounded the building on the river side and halfway up the street.

Once, Williamsburg had been a depressed, low-rent haven for artists and young urbanites. It was what had drawn the white millennials and started the gentrification. Now Aristides Stavros was probably paying a fortune to stay in this rundown building. She glanced up at the new high rises towering over her. The rich executives in their penthouses must curse having to look at this wreck of a building, its walls covered with riotous pink and blue and orange graffiti.

A metal door slammed, and she drew back. Starvos and two baggy-pants youths appeared around the corner of the fence and headed up North 3rd. She waited until they turned down Wythe, then slipped inside the fence. There was some other artist's name on the mailbox, a maker of ironworks, but it was the right place. Stavros had taped his business card above it. She took a deep breath and inserted the key in the lock.

The latch clicked, and she pushed the heavy steel door open. Inside was not what she expected. The metal worker's studio occupied the entire ground floor. Light streamed through the high windows and cast the interior into sharp bands of light and dark. Welding apparatus, pipes, and heavy I-beams lay strewn across the cement. A half-finished sculpture rose twenty feet into the air. The acrid scent of sun-warmed metal mixed with the sharper tang of oil paint. Toward the back, a metal staircase suspended from chains led up to the second floor.

At the foot of the steps, Melissa hesitated. There was no way out of the second floor except by the stairs. She'd be trapped if the artist came back unexpectedly. But this was her only chance. She sucked in a breath and then clattered up the stairs, the metal rungs shaking and ringing beneath her feet.

The living area on the second floor was a large, open space with minimal furnishings. Melissa took in the kitchen alcove with high-end stainless steel cabinets and appliances, the Carrara marble walls and gigantic Jacuzzi visible through the open bathroom door and, at the opposite end, a half-wall delineated an expansive sleeping area with a breathtaking view of the New York skyline silhouetted against the setting sun. This was no low-rent housing. The outside might be disreputable, but inside Aristides Stavros lived with as much elegance as any of his penthouse dwelling neighbors.

The only incongruous area was the battered work table occupying the center of the living room, littered with half-finished sketches and greasy pizza boxes, and in the far corner of the workspace, a tousled heap of bedding topped with plastic bags from several clothing stores and someone's school books tossed every which way.

She wandered into the bedroom. The only furniture in the room was a huge neatly made-up king-sized bed and a nightstand covered with brushes and tubes of oil paint. But it was the painting stretching across the wall that caught her eye. She swept around the bed and stared. Under a pearly blue sky lay white hills and golden sand touched by an azure sea, the colors so soft and precise they stole her breath. Tipping her head slightly, she searched for the nude she knew must be there.

The painting blurred, reformed, floated before her. Then it came clear. The nude, faintly lined in, rose like a diaphanous spirit from the sea. She moved closer and with an outstretched finger traced the outline of the figure. It was magnificent. There was no denying that Aristides Stavros worshiped women's bodies. She touched her lips where he had kissed her so gently in the dark. Would she kiss him again in the light of day? Kiss a monster? She scrubbed at her mouth.

Heavens. The man was a murderer. What was she thinking?

She turned away and dove into her search. Ten minutes later, she wanted to scream. There was no sign of her knapsack or notes. Besides the kitchen cupboards and the bathroom vanity, there were no places he could have stashed them. No closets or chests in which to lock things away. Keeping her eye on the clock, she searched in his suitcase, underneath the mattress, beneath the bed, and with a paper towel wrapped around her hand, picked through a ragged duffle bag full of too familiar spray paint cans. She found nothing.

She sat down and rested her head on the work table. All that subterfuge and groveling to Tuccio wasted. Her bag was not here. She scanned the room one last time, looking for some hidden storage she might have missed. Her stomach tensed. Maybe she'd misjudged, and he had not taken it at all.

Down below, the metal door opened with a bang. Melissa froze, her heart rate soaring. Footsteps clanged up the steps, the sound echoing off the walls, pounding in her ears. She spun around for a place to hide and dashed into the only totally enclosed space, the bathroom. She cracked the door slightly and watched as the artist crossed the room and dumped two overfull plastic grocery bags on the counter. She huddled down lower, grasping the edge of the door to keep from falling.

Heart thumping in her ears, she rubbed her neck with a sweaty hand and risked another peek. The artist moved about the kitchen. His long black hair was gathered back in a sleek ponytail, and his white T-shirt clung to a body of honed rock-hard muscle that rippled as he put away food in the cabinets.

In the daylight and without the fake beard, he looked much younger than she'd imagined him to be. He whistled a tune as he tossed meat, milk, vegetables, and Greek yogurt into the fridge, placed two loaves of French bread on the counter, and stacked cans of soup, jars of tomato sauce, and boxes of pasta in the cupboard. It looked like he was planning to feed an army.

There was a rush of noise down below and then the army appeared. A passel of scruffy street kids tramped up the stairs equally loaded down. They dropped the bags at his feet and looked up expectantly. "I know. I know." He pulled out his wallet and gave them each a five. "Now off with you. Until later." The troop scrambled back down the stairs and dashed out with a bang.

A lanky, thin boy in a faded blue Mets cap worn backward held back. "Sure you don't want me to stay?"

Ari stopped in the act of rolling up his shirt sleeves. He narrowed his eyes. "Just do what I told you."

The boy saluted. "Aye, aye, *El Capitán*." He patted his pants pocket. "Text me if you need any help. And don't forget, Bedford Station at midnight."

"I'll be there," Ari said.

With a tight little nod, the boy turned and then whizzed down the stairs and out the door, slamming it behind him. Silence fell.

Melissa breathed a sigh of relief. Now all she had to deal with was the monster. She pulled away from the door and listened to him finish putting away the food. It grew quiet. She peered through the crack. He was nowhere to be seen. He must have gone into the bedroom. Now was her chance to escape.

Holding her breath, she slipped off her sandals, slowly opened the door, and tip-toed the eight feet to the stairs. So far so good. Clinging to the railing, she stepped down, the metal cold on her bare soles. Beneath her foot, the staircase shook. She looked down at the open metal steps chain-suspended above the huge metal working shop. She was small and light. She could do this. Knees trembling, she gathered herself together and stepped down to the next step. But this time, her sweaty bare foot slipped on the metal and fell through the open back of the stairs. She tipped forward, hands flailing, sandals flying. At the last moment, her fingertips clasped onto the railing, and she held on for dear life. The stairs swayed and then stilled. But her sandals continued down, striking each step in turn. The thump, thump, thump thundered in her ears.

"You're late. Take off your clothes," Ari called. "Throw them anywhere and get over here so I can see you. I don't have all day."

Drat, he thought she was a model applying for the

modeling job. She tried to untangle herself, but the stairs swayed beneath her, and her feet could find no purchase. His footsteps came nearer. She glanced down at the exit door. No way she'd reach the bottom on her shaking legs before he discovered her. Better to play along. Try out as a model and weasel out of him where he'd put her notes.

She turned and confronted the battered face peering down at her. "Uh. Hello."

"Ah—*Melissa*—from the gallery. Now this is a lovely surprise." He reached out one of his huge hands. She hesitated a moment and then seized it like a life ring. He pulled her back up onto the steps and steadied her. "You are interested in the modeling job?"

She nodded and stepped back into the loft. In the sharp light of late afternoon, she could see the damage that had been done to what must have once been a very handsome face. The puckered line of the scar slashing his cheek stretched from the bottom of his upper lip to the corner of his eye. Any further and he would have lost his sight. His nose curved to the left and flattened out on the tip, a hard lump marking the break. Her eyes drifted to his lips. He was licking them, his eyes riveted on her.

Heat shot through her and set her knees to shaking. She glanced down. Heavens, she was still holding onto him. She extracted her hand and cleared her throat. "Yes, I need the money."

"*Sígoura,* of course, the money." He put his hands on his hips and looked her up and down. "Have you modeled before?"

"Yes." Fully clothed in high school art class. But he didn't need to know that.

"So let's see if you'll do. Take off your clothes and put them over there on the chair." He leaned back against the wall.

She hesitated, her heart beating wildly like the wings of a trapped bird.

He shifted closer. "Now. I haven't got all day."

He was going to watch? But of course, that was the whole point. He painted nude women. He needed to see her naked. Her fingers trembled as she unbuttoned her blouse and slipped her arms out of the sleeves. She pulled her tank top over her head and let it fall. Cold air raised goose bumps along her arms. Eyes closed, she pushed down her jeans, praying every prayer she knew.

"The bra." She glanced up at him. His face was expressionless, but his gaze, potent with male interest, flickered over her. She reached back to unclasp her bra and let it fall. "Good girl." He straightened and got a sketchbook and stick of charcoal from the work table. He tucked the book under his arm and pointed with the charcoal. "The panties too."

Her stomach tightened as she slid the thin nylon down one leg, stood on one foot and slipped off the other. She'd been naked before in front of a man when she'd shacked up with Colin, but she had never felt so totally exposed. She turned away and wrapped her arms across her breasts.

"No. Don't do that." He walked over and pushed her arms down. He lifted her chin. "Never hide who you are. Stand up straight."

He was inches away. She could feel his breath hot on her cheek, smell his delicious scent. Heavens, she was face to face with a murderer—maybe Bella's murderer. He could kill her at any minute. Say she slipped down the stairs and broke her neck.

She almost had.

She ran her gaze over him and tried to imagine those big strong hands with the missing fingers closing around Bella's neck, squeezing out her life. But all she could think was those same hands on her breasts, rippling down her skin, flowing over her thighs. She shivered. What was wrong with her, attracted to a murderous beast?

He stepped back. "Better." Hand on his chin, he circled around her. "I think you might do. Move into the next room."

She followed him into the bedroom area. He spread a large fur of white rabbit skins on the bed, then stood to the side, and waved his hand. "Lay down."

Trembling she climbed up on the huge bed and curled up, the fur soft against her skin.

The artist pulled a white cloth out of his pocket. "On your back, Melissa." She flipped over. "Yes, exactly like that." He stood over her, his eyes squinted. "I will be working on a study for the painting behind me. The session is twenty minutes during which you are not to move or even twitch. Do you understand?"

"Yes."

"Then let us begin." He pulled a white cloth from his pocket and shook it out. "I find models are often distracted by my appearance so if you don't mind—"

The white square of cloth floated down, light as organza, heavy as a coffin lid. It settled over her face and draped across the ridges and valleys of her facial bones. She inhaled, drawing the fabric against her nostrils and into her mouth, the linen dry against her tongue, its scent his. It was too much. She spit it out, twisted, and flailed her arms. "Please—I—I have to—"

He lifted the cloth slightly. "Perhaps, you wish to reconsider?"

She choked in a breath. "No—I'm sorry. Go ahead." She clamped her fingers into the fur and concentrated on breathing in and out. The cloth settled. She could do this—lie naked for twenty minutes, her face covered by a piece of cloth no bigger than one of the old-fashioned men's handkerchiefs Jana favored for her nights on the town, and in return, she'd uncover this man's secrets.

"Ready?"

"Yes." She gulped in air heavy with the scent of oil paint and turpentine, and then the cloth came down again. Her breath heated the small space under the linen. She wrinkled her nose and took tight little breaths.

"Now. Bend your right knee and slide your foot back—yes, like that. More. All the way until your heel touches your derriere."

Cool air swept across her. Her nipples tightened. Something shuffled. Cloth rubbed. He must have moved to the other side. She opened her eyes and stared up through the cloth, but could see nothing except a million tiny stars where light pierced through the weave.

"Now without bending it, slide your left leg out to the edge of the fur. Hold. Perfect."

A timer began ticking. A click. Music began to play—something New Age, soothing like the rise and fall of the sea. Cool currents brushed against her skin as the artist flipped a page in his pad. Charcoal gritted against paper, long strokes, then short, then long again—a faint scratching that made her want to twitch. She sank her fingers deeper into the fur and tried to picture what he could see, what he was drawing. Never had she bared herself in such totality. She curled her fingers into her palms and squeezed until her nails bit into the skin. Heavens, he could do anything to her. She should leap up and run as fast as she could. She took a deep breath and forced her hands to relax. No, retrieving her notes was too important. Finishing her dissertation meant the difference between having a successful career and whipping up cappuccinos for the rest of her life. Besides, Tuccio knew she was here. He'd said he'd keep watch. A shiver ran down her spine. What could happen in twenty minutes?

The clock ticked. Minutes passed. Above her, his breath came in short bursts. His spicy scent rose from the bedding and surrounded her. Her nipples peaked. Moisture gathered between her legs. Her body remembered the strength of his biceps. Her lips quivered at the memory of his lips sucking and caressing hers, so different from Tuccio's icy plundering. She wanted to throw off the cloth and fall into his arms, and it didn't matter he was a murderer or ugly as sin.

But she couldn't. She swallowed down her unwanted urges and concentrated on the ticking of the clock. She was here to get her field notes and leave. That's all. Surely, the time was almost up?

But the clock continued to tick.

Twenty minutes. It hadn't sounded like much when Stavros said it. She wondered why he'd pay so much. Now she knew. Fighting her wanton thoughts, every second stretched into torment. Blood pooled in her limbs. Her back prickled, then her stomach. Her leg muscles quivered and burned. Sweat collected where her skin touched the fur. Heat built between her thighs. Every part of her wanted to turn and twist and fly into his arms. She puffed out a breath of air, and the cloth slipped sideways. Without thinking, she lifted her hand to put it back.

"*Sto diávolo.* I'm paying you to lay still, woman." Something fell and landed with a thud. The music stopped, and the cloth whipped away from her face. He loomed over her, his eyes narrowed. "Get up."

She rolled over to the edge of the bed and lifted herself up, right into his arms. He pulled her against him and spoke into her hair. "I don't know who you are or what you want from me. I don't even know your last name. But I want you, and I think"—he brushed a finger over her lips—"you want me."

She opened her mouth to protest, but he claimed it with his. His lips were warm and gentle as butterfly wings. His hands moved up and cupped her head, drawing her closer. He licked her lips until she opened beneath him, and his tongue slid inside, filling her, binding her to him. She moaned into his mouth, and his hand slid lower, skimming along her shoulder and down over her breasts.

She was in the hands of an artist. He painted her skin with the pads of his fingers—slow, deliberate, gentle strokes, every sweep, every glide, a moment of worship. Beneath his touch, her whole body throbbed with need.

Heat suffused her, and she leaned in, sliding her hands up under his T-shirt, pushing it past his face, over his head. He tore it off and tossed it to the side. Thick, dark hair covered his muscular chest. She pressed against him, reveling in the strength and maleness of him. She had never wanted a man the way she wanted this one.

His hands fell away, and he lifted his lips from hers.

She tugged on his hair. "No. More. Please."

"You're sure? You want this?"

She peered into his deep-set eyes, warm brown in the late afternoon light. She should be afraid. She didn't know what he'd done in his past, but a man who painted women's bodies the way he did, who touched her as if she were made of spun glass, would not kill her. Besides, her body had already made the decision for her. She could refuse him nothing. Her answer was little more than an exhalation. "Yes."

He moaned as she tangled her fingers in the dark hair that covered his chest, found his nipples and settled her mouth on the left one, sucking and licking as she unbuttoned his jeans and slid the zipper down, touched the hardness of his erection. She was powerful too.

Chapter 20

Ari closed his eyes. She'd said yes, looking at him full in the face in the daylight. He didn't care if she'd been sent by Vernon or worked for Tuccio. He'd had enough whores to know that this girl was not faking it. She truly wanted him. He would not question this gift, not now. That would come later.

He shucked off his jeans and wrapping his arms around her, pulled her down onto the fur. He kneeled above her and studied his prize. She lay beneath him, her lips swollen from his kisses, her nipples erect on perfect breasts, her hips writhing in invitation. He ran a finger between her cleft, found her bud, and circled it with his finger. Slowly, he inserted a finger into her warm passageway. She was dripping wet for him. His throbbing cock wanted to thrust inside, but he held back. He would show her he was not a beast who used women for his own pleasure. He removed his hand and sat back.

She snatched at it. "Please. Don't—stop."

"Hush, little bee. I am not planning on stopping." He leaned over the side of the bed and swooped up a paint brush. He leaned in and whispered in her ear. "I'm going to paint you. And this time, you have my permission to move."

He rolled to one side and gathered her body against him, her neat little skull tucked perfectly in the crook of his arm. Then he picked up the soft sable-hair brush and ran it down the side of her neck. "Your skin. It is the most marvelous color." He brought the brush around and down between her breasts. "It is like dawn over the sea. Not pink or peach. Not pale, but golden. It glows like the rising sun." Beneath him, her head fell back and her arms spread out over the fur. "I could look at it forever."

He trailed the tip of the brush around each breast, avoiding Tuccio's trademark bite that set his stomach burning for revenge. But that was for later. Now was for her, and the gift she was offering him. He leaned down and licked her nipples until they tightened, while his hand welded the brush with all the consummate skill he had.

Lower and lower, he swirled the brush, her breath growing more rushed, her hips arching up, begging for more. Gently, he spread her thighs. He ran the brush up and down the inside of each long leg, drawing invisible lines and patterns, ancient symbols passed down six millennia from his Neolithic ancestors: a stippled wave cresting along the inside of her thigh, a sun with shooting flames on the slight convexity of her stomach, dancing plants with curling leaves on the inside of her arms, and the sacred spirals of the mother goddess on her breasts. He could feel her trembling beneath him, sucking air, struggling toward release.

He moved down, drawn by her scent. Discarding the brush, he painted her tender nub with his tongue, light flickering strokes that swirled round and round like the rays of the morning sun glancing over the waves. She tasted like some exotic honey made specially just for him. He wanted to devour her, make

133

her his forever.

Beneath him, her breath came in ragged gasps. He licked again and again spiraling around and around. Her cries grew softer, breathier. She was close. He reached up, pinched her nipples and took her over the edge.

"That's my girl, my beautiful Nereida, my golden skinned siren of the sea." He laid his head on her stomach as waves of convulsions rippled through her.

She sucked in a deep breath. "I've never—that's never happened before." A wave of angry pride swept over him. This woman was a treasure, she deserved to be cherished, cared for. Not used. He would find out whatever hold Vernon and Tuccio had over her and free her. But first, he had to claim her.

He tossed the brush on the nightstand, snagged a condom, and pulled it on. Then he rose over her, poised at her entrance, and froze. Her eyes were wide-open, peering up at his face—his horrible beastly face. Her mouth opened, and he waited for the scream sure to come. Instead, she grasped him by his upper arms and invited him in with a breathless *yes*.

She tilted her hips to meet him, and he sank into her slowly, knowing in doing so he would never have another woman like this one. They fit perfectly. Despite the raging need for release, he fought for control as he thrust deep and fast. At the last minute, he lowered his mouth over hers and, breathing in rhythm, sucking and pushing the air from each other's lungs, they climaxed together.

****

Melissa feathered her fingers through the long dark hair of the man lying with his head pressed against her thundering heart. She wasn't like this—one of those women who fell into bed with strangers. Sex had never played a major role in her life. She didn't pick up men in bars. It took Colin months to weasel his way between her legs. It had been pleasant with Colin, curling up next to him afterward. But she had never felt passion and release like this.

Melissa studied the muscular arm wrapped around her, the deep olive skin against her pale gold. It had taken this monster with the touch of an angel to awaken her. Ripples of pleasure still coursed through her. And he had done it all with those huge mutilated hands. She placed her palm over his and fingered the rounded stumps where the fingers had been neatly cut off at the knuckles. She peered up at the painting on the opposite wall.

So deep and sensual, painted with the same loving strokes he had used on her. Another ripple coursed through her as her skin remembered the swirling brush and imagined the designs. What had happened to this man, this artist, to disfigure him so?

He withdrew his hand and rolled over on his back. "That's you in the painting."

"But how—?"

"I've been obsessed with you since I saw you at the police station." He ran a finger over her breast. "I have never seen skin like yours."

She pushed his hand away and sat up, pulling her knees against her body. In the slanting light coming through the high windows, every contour of his body was revealed. His flaccid penis rested in a nest of black curls that trailed up to his navel and covered the bulging muscles of his chest. He was a mass of muscles and tendons, broad-shouldered, narrow-waisted, a glorious example of the male body—one you might see on the cover of *ESPN* or *Sports Illustrated*. Except for his face, he was perfect. She shifted slightly and stared at his scar. Her hands tightened around her knees. "Why were you at the police station?"

He ran a finger down her spine. "I had hoped the afterglow would last longer."

Melissa curved her back away from that tantalizing finger. She could quickly become addicted to his touch. "I'm not like this. I don't jump into men's beds." She shifted further away. "Especially—ones I don't know."

"I'd never hurt you, Melissa." He folded his arms under his head. "So to answer your question. I went to report my sister missing."

"Your sister?"

He gave a low laugh. "Even monsters have sisters, little bee."

A knot loosened in her stomach. He hadn't been following her. "Who is your sister?"

He glanced at her. "Sirena Patras. You call her Bella."

"You can't be. Bella would have mentioned having a brother. I recorded her life history as part of my research."

"A fairy tale, I'm sure. As far as my sister is concerned, she has no brother. We have been estranged for seven years. She's been living in New York, and I have been living on an island in Greece."

"So she went into hiding to avoid you?"

"No. She didn't know I was coming."

"Then why are you here?"

He rubbed a hand over his face and sat up. "I'm here to sell paintings. Make money."

"And bed strangers."

He leaned over and kissed her. "Oh, little bee, that was an unexpected pleasure."

She turned all wobbly inside and pushed his hands away. "No, I need to understand. Bella's my friend. I'm worried about her."

"There's no need."

Melissa narrowed her eyes. Was he truly Bella's brother? Could she trust this man?

From down below came a knocking on the door. Melissa jumped up. "Tuccio. I forgot."

Suddenly, the hands that had touched her so gently were clasped around her arms like iron bands.

Ari glared at her. "Tuccio?"

"Let me go. He's a—friend."

"Some *friend.*" He touched the bite on her neck. "I've been a fool. Go. Get out of here." He spun around, grabbed a tube of black paint from the paint stand and squeezed it across the canvas. Thick lines of paint zigged and zagged across the delicate figure like the cuts of a knife.

Chapter 21

Melissa dashed into the white marble bathroom heavy with the monster's scent and leaned back against the door fighting back tears. What had just happened? Stavros had gone from gentle lover to raging maniac in seconds. Her hands shook so much she could barely pull up her leggings and button her blouse. The doorknob fought her until she remembered she had locked it in self-defense. Ha. All he had to do was touch her, and she turned to putty in his hands.

She reached into her pocket and pulled out the tiny pin Tuccio had given her. She held it on her palm and studied it. It looked innocent enough. "To help the Agency find Bella," Tuccio had said. Ari would lead them to her. She looked around the bathroom and saw a tan floppy hat hanging on the back of the door. He was a monster. He deserved to be kept track of. She slid the pin into the inner band of the hat. After a quick check to be sure she hadn't forgotten anything, she released the lock and stepped into the room.

All evidence of the splashed paint had disappeared. Sunlight poured through the windows and illuminated Ari, dressed in low-slung jeans, his chest bare, sitting at the worktable drinking a strongly scented tea, huge hands wrapped delicately around a bone china cup decorated with country roses.

He set down the cup and placed the mutilated hand

with its missing pinky and ring fingers on the counter as if to make sure she saw it. She stood straighter. He'd not intimidate her.

"Good thing it was your left hand," she said, tipping her chin toward it.

"Good?" He made a spitting sound and peered at her as if he could see right through her clothes. She shivered. Of course, he could. Not even Colin had ever examined every inch of her skin the way she'd allowed this man to do. There'd always been sheets and darkness when they'd made love. He took another sip. "I'm left-handed."

She cleared her throat. "About Bella—"

He turned his hand palm up and wiggled the three fingers. "None of your business."

Tuccio banged the door again. Ari stood. "Mustn't leave without your pay. Truly you didn't earn it. You are not—*professional*." He came around the counter heading toward her. He stopped inches in front of her, sucking up space and air, and took her hand in his. "Your skin"—he trailed a finger across her palm and up her wrist—"it is liquid gold. It floats over your muscles and bones like luxurious silk. And I know every inch of it." He dropped her hand. "I dreamed of painting it, loving it. But I will not share with Tuccio."

He stuck a hand in his pocket and pulled out a wad of bills. He pulled off several and stuffed them in her hand. "Your fee. This—*job*—it is not for *amateurs*. Now run down and let your *friend* know you have survived an hour with the monster. And don't think to come back." He made a fist. "I won't lose my head again."

Melissa threw up her chin. "Well, neither will *I.*"

She hugged her jacket to her chest and didn't budge. "But my notes. You have my notes and the sketches Bella drew for me."

"So you claim." He drove her nearer the steps. "Is that why you were sneaking around my apartment? I assume Tuccio gave you a key."

He came close, but not close enough to reach her. He wasn't going to touch her. For all the anger she sensed inside him, he wouldn't hurt her. She planted her feet and threw her shoulders back. "You bastard. You knew I wasn't a model." She waved her arm at the destroyed painting. "That—that was all pretense—and you took advantage and you—"

His mouth curled up in a smile. "Did what? Gave you the best sex you ever had, little bee?"

"Damn you, I am not your little bee. I'm not *your* anything. So hand my papers over. I can't write my dissertation without them."

"But you see, I think you're lying. There's no name anywhere. Just pages of interviews and checklists. Wouldn't a smart researcher put her name on her work?"

"Don't be an idiot. Ask any of the tattoo artists in Williamsburg. Hell, ask my advisor at NYU. He'll tell you they're my notes."

He ran a finger over his scarred lip. "I think I'll have to wait and ask your Bella about them." He raised an eyebrow. "I did find them in her apartment."

"Bella is missing, maybe dead. I can't wait until the police solve the crime. They're bumbling idiots who never solve half the murders in the city." She gave it one last try. "Please, the notes are useless to anyone but me." His face turned hard as marble. Down below,

Tuccio frantically called to her, kicking the heavy steel door.

Ari lowered his voice to a soft growl. "Sirena is my concern, not yours. Now run back to Tuccio and play nice."

She grasped the railing and took a step down. "You're a weasel, Mr. Stavros. I bet you do this all time. Running that ad. Getting innocent girls to come model and then enjoying them in your bed. Well, I won't stand for it." She shook her finger at him. "Unless you hand over my notes, I will report you to that gallery of yours for abusing models."

"*Sto diávolo.* You little witch." He ran a hand across his scarred lip and then stepped back. "All right, you win. But the notes are not here. I have them in a safer place. I will deliver them to your apartment tonight. What's the address?"

Melissa hesitated. It would not do for him and Jana to meet. In no time at all, Jana would know she'd slept with him. Better somewhere public. "Not at my apartment. Meet me outside The Gristle tat shop."

He narrowed his eyes. "Fine. Now go tell your dear friend to stop banging on my door. And thank him for sending such a responsive whore."

Whore? He thought her a whore because she'd tumbled into his bed. She raced down the steps. So much for first impressions. Ari Stavros was no romantic lover. She rubbed her wrist where he had touched her and shook off the frisson of warmth that remained. No, he was a creep. A dangerous one.

At the bottom, she yelled back. "I hate you, you ugly bastard."

She stepped out into the dying light of day, straight

into Tuccio's arms. Tuccio swept her off her feet and carried her to his limo, like Superman rescuing Lois Lane. "My darling, what did the bastard do to you? I thought I would have to summon the police."

For a moment, she feared that she had run from one foul man to another. But Tuccio was all gentleness. He set her on the seat and got in next to her. He ran his long carefully trimmed fingers through her hair, so different from the thick, powerful fingers of the artist with his broken nails stained with paint. He whispered in her ear. "Did he hurt you, darling?"

Melissa struggled to sit up. "The man's a lying pig. He—he tricked me. Called me a whore."

Tuccio ran a finger along her cheek. "Did he now? And did you oblige?"

"That's none of your business."

"Oh, but it is, and I think you did." His fingers dug into her thigh and his mouth slipped down to whisper in her ear. "So did you accomplish my little task?"

He curled his body around hers and pulled her against him. She nodded. Inside she cringed. Tuccio was as unpredictable as Aristides Stavros. One minute, he was a white knight, and the next, he made her feel like she was entwined with a pit viper. She hated his touch, the possessiveness, the cold, expressionless face and the flickering eyes that bore into her and scooped out the truth.

She felt guilty—dirty. Stavros had paid homage to her body. He brought her to heights of passion and release she'd never experienced before, and she betrayed him by pinning that tracker to his hat. Why had she turned to Tuccio for help? Planted that device?

She wiggled free of Tuccio's exploring fingers and

pressed a hand against her stomach. "I feel sick. Take me home, please. I don't want to vomit all over your car."

Chapter 22

Ari climbed the staircase to the roof and stepped out into the evening cool. He watched Tuccio's limo drive off and then walked toward the shore side of the building. He leaned on the railing. Below flowed the East River, a black ribbon reflecting a city of silver lights, an image immortalized by many a tourist's camera.

He spit over the side, and then wiped his lips with the back of his hand. He was paying five thousand dollars a month rent so he could have this view. He'd been very specific with his agent. A water view so he would not lose his tie to the sea. But this East River was not the Mediterranean. Underneath that glitter, there was a cesspool of filth and pollution, the effluvia of a city of uncaring souls, laboring like ants in a sand hill to make the rich richer and the poor poorer.

He pushed away the image of the girl with her huge hungry eyes and stubborn desperation. He'd been a fool to chase her into Tuccio's arms. Who knew what hold the bastard had on her? He must not forget the power Vernon and Tuccio wielded over others.

He licked his lower lip and savored the lingering taste of her. Still, it was better this way. She was too beautiful for him, a goddess deserving of a columned temple on top of Pelion, not the rankness of hell within his clutches.

But *Zeús*, how he wanted her. So much so he'd broken his own rule about work sessions and actually touched her, made love. She'd been soft and tender-skinned like the crisp oval apples that had grown in his papa's orchard when he was a boy.

A sweetly tart, golden apple—a *Firiki*—that's what she reminded him of. He turned away and stared up at the darkening sky.

A jet lumbered overhead, its lights flashing, engines rumbling, a hovering silhouette against the lavender-speckled clouds, heading east. What he wouldn't give to be on that plane flying home—away from this business with Vernon, away from this girl who looked him in the face and didn't flinch. Who belonged to Tuccio.

He gripped the railing tighter. He could not abandon the villagers and the last of the seals they protected. They were relying on him. He would never let them down. The only way he would ever leave this city would be when Vernon was defeated or when he was dead.

He turned back and stared down at the water. If he lost, Vernon's guys would probably just toss his body into that muck they called a river. He grasped the balustrade and climbed up on the railing. He exhaled all the air in his lungs, released his grip, and balanced on the balls of his bare feet, his arms spread wide. He could jump and save them the trouble. His body wavered in space for a long moment. His heart thumped. His lungs demanded air—demanded a decision.

He sucked in a breath, heavy with the stink of eight million people and their machines, seized a vent pipe projecting from the roof and jumped down onto the deck. He couldn't do it. Not yet. Sirena and the villagers, along with the seals, depended on him.

He'd survived prison. Survived base brutality. He would survive this. First, he needed to find a way to stop Vernon and his filth from ruining his village, save Sirena—and maybe the girl.

No, he needed to forget her. The little sneak was nothing to him. Not a memory. Not a lover. Just another rat belonging to Vernon and Tuccio, wanting to gnaw away at his soul. But he'd bedded her, gotten her out of his system. He hoped.

He slid open the roof door, picked up the knapsack he stashed on the top step, and then headed down the stairs to his bedroom. He dropped the bag by his bed to examine later. The bed covers and fur were still strewn in wild disarray. Her sweet, honeyed scent infused the room. His stomach knotted.

He sank down on the floor, tugged his sketch pad out from under the bed, and flipped through the pages, studying his drawings of Eudokia—the ancient white stone houses, the wrinkled face of Thea Eleni working at her loom, the seals playing in the lagoon. The last page was folded under. He pressed it open and stared down at the beautiful face. Ritsa.

Tuccio would pay for what he'd done to her. He rubbed the tattoo marking the skin of his wrist—once he and Tuccio been sworn blood brothers, protecting each other in hell. Now, they were sworn enemies.

He looked at the canvas he'd mutilated. The special commission was due by Friday, and he needed that money to complete the trust fund that would protect Eudokia and create a sanctuary for the monk seals.

He'd have to start over.

But it would be easier this time. He didn't have to imagine Melissa. He knew her in his fingertips, knew her in his blood—the taste of her, the scent of her, the texture of her skin. He picked up the brush he'd feathered across her golden body and ran it over his palm. Yes, painting her would be easy. The hard part would be never touching that glorious body again, never feeling that silken skin beneath him. She'd never rejoin him in bed, not after what he'd said and done. It was no more than he deserved.

He pulled the canvas down. But damn it to hell, Tuccio wasn't going to have her either.

****

Melissa bit her thumbnail. She would have to tell Jana about her run-in with the artist. Tuccio and Jana were co-workers after all, and Prince Uncharming was sure to mention she'd been at Stavros' place. She glanced down at her bitten fingernails and then over at Jana's perfect ones. "I took your advice." She leaned back on the futon trying to avoid inhaling the scent of Jana's nail polish. "I auditioned for the modeling job. He—Stavros had me take my clothes off."

Jana bent over and painted her toenail ruby red. "Well, la-di-dah, babe. That was in the job description wasn't it? To be naked? He didn't touch you or anything?"

Melissa tucked her hands between her thighs and willed her face to blandness. "No. He was a perfect gentleman." Except at the end when he turned into a raging demon. "God-awful looking man. Oh"—she riffled through her pocket—"he did pay me." She laid the money on her lap, counted the bills. Dirty money.

She'd jumped into his bed without hesitation; no wonder he thought her a whore.

Jana leaned over and scooped up the bills with her free hand. "That's something. All five hundred—look at that." She took three hundred and pushed the rest back. "That covers the rent you owe." She tucked the bills into her bra. "Have you found another place to stay yet? Remember my stupid roommate will be here in little over a week." She leaned over and painted the next nail. "Though I may be getting a place of my own soon."

"I think Daniela will let me stay with her."

Jana raised her eyebrow. "Who?"

"Daniela Reyes."

Jana set the nail polish down. "Oh, Dumpy Dee. God, is she still around? All three hundred pounds of her?"

Melissa's stomach soured. This was what she hated about Jana—the snide comments and the bullying. Laura had been a different person, a meaner person, when she hung out with Jana and her gang. She stood abruptly. "Holy heavens, Jana. Grow up. High school and all its petty cruelty are over. It's what's inside people that counts."

Jana pointed her foot in the air and admired her toes. "So she's still fat. What's Humpty Dumpty doing?"

"Daniela's a social worker. A great one. She makes a difference in peoples' lives."

"Hey." Jana screwed the nail polish closed. "I make a difference too. I put roofs over people's heads." She pursed her lips. "And make a load of money doing it, not chicken shit like a goddamn social worker makes. It's you who has a problem, not me. I think you want to be poor. What the hell will writing a dissertation about tattooing and getting some professorship do to save the world?" She gave Melissa a long look. "Why don't you shack up with Tuccio? Now there's a man with money enough to treat a woman well. And he's besotted with you. All he ever talks about is you."

Melissa studied the cracks running like broken veins across the ceiling. "He's cold, Jana. And he is rough." She rubbed the bite on her neck. "Truthfully, I'm afraid of him."

"He's the bad boy type." Jana slid over and put an arm over her shoulder. "Sometimes it can be exciting to have a little rough sex with a guy like Tuccio. Imagine having your hands tied, and those perfect lips trailing over your body while those clever fingers do wicked things to you." She whispered in her ear. "Makes me hot just thinking about it."

"No." Melissa extracted herself from Jana's hold and stood. It wasn't Tuccio she pictured doing that to her. "I know he's your friend, but I don't trust him. I think he's just using me for his own purposes."

"Right. His purpose is to get you in his bed, idiot."

"But I don't feel anything for him. His kiss leaves me cold."

"Gad, you are hopeless, Mel. You sound like some romance novel heroine searching for her perfect mate. It ain't like that. It's all about lust. The world's full of men and women just waiting to be tasted and savored and explored. But not to live with forever after. That bastard Colin Burke deserves a whip for making you think you're frigid. I say open your legs for Tuccio and let him bite you and teach you how to bite him back. Discover real sex."

"Lay off, Jana." She tugged her shirt collar higher and prayed the bite didn't show. "I don't need Tuccio to teach me *anything.*"

"I think you are over-thinking Tuccio." She clapped her hands. "Oh my goodness. Wait a minute. I think that Ari character did touch you." She stood and circled around her.

Melissa shook her head.

"Oh, yes. You can't fool me. You had sex with the artist, didn't you? Woo hoo." She giggled. "And I bet he didn't find you to be a cold fish. The man radiates sexiness. Let's celebrate." She padded into the kitchen and popped open a bottle of wine. She poured two glasses and held one out to her. "Here's to poor handsome Theo. Beat out by a monster." She narrowed her eyes. "So when are you going to see Mr. Monster again?"

Chapter 23

Melissa waved goodbye to the group of tattoo artists and left the store. She'd stayed way later than normal, but she didn't want to be around Jana anymore. Ever since Volcano Mouth had found out about her fling—or whatever you called it when you jumped into bed with a stranger you detest—she'd been on her case to go back and insinuate herself further with the man.

Tuccio was pressing her too but in a different way. He wanted her to do small tasks for him in return for the great favor he'd done for her—drop off a note here, pick up a package there. Worse, he'd begun showing up at her work and at the apartment at odd times. Once his limo had pulled over and offered her a ride as she came up out of the subway. It was like he was stalking her. For a moment, she wondered if he had planted a tracking device on her too. She shook off the idea. That would be too creepy.

Aristides Stavros, the lying bastard, on the other hand, had not shown up at The Gristle with her notes. But she wasn't going near his sublet again. It was bad enough he haunted her dreams.

All she wanted was her old life back—working at the café, writing her dissertation, no monsters and evil princes chasing after her. Getting away from Jana would be the first step. Daniela had agreed to let her stay with her for a few weeks until she found something she could afford on a barista's salary. She'd move out of Jana's place next week right in time for Jana's highfaluting roommate's return home. That was to the good.

She tucked her portfolio tighter to her chest and hurried across the street. She was starting over on her research. Her advisor said he'd look into a teaching fellowship for her. But it would add another year, at least, before she could get her degree.

And Bella was still missing.

She tapped her fingers on the stiff leather of the portfolio. The Siren stayed dark. The shop door stayed closed. Her customers dissipated to other shops. It was like Bella Bell had disappeared off the face of the earth, and no one cared.

She stopped at the corner. At least, no dead body had been found.

A knot of hope remained that somehow her friend was still alive. But all her searching and sneaking around had done was stir up more questions, create a guilty conscience, anger two untrustworthy men, and leave her with a passel of cats to feed on her limited budget.

Cats. Melissa reversed direction. She'd forgotten to feed Bella's cats behind the studio. She checked her watch. Eleven—a little late. Usually, she went after work to feed them. She cast a glance around. The streets were quiet, but there were still couples walking back from dinner and groups of young people heading to and from the bars. It would be all right. Besides, it was better than twisting and turning in bed unable to sleep.

By the time, she reached The Siren, the street was

dark, the coffee shops and boutiques closed up tight, the crowds of would-be hipsters looking for tattoos and trendy clothes gone home to Mommy and Daddy in the burbs. Melissa took Bella's keys out of her pocket and opened the door.

The light from the street barely penetrated the interior. She stepped inside and stopped. After a week and a half of Bella's absence, the scent of disinfectant and ink had dissipated. In its place, a damp mildewed smell rose between the ancient floorboards and mixed with something feral and dead. The stink permeated the studio and made everything Melissa touched feel damp. She fumbled her way to the wall switch behind the counter and flicked it on. Nothing happened. Drat, the electric must have been shut off. With Bella gone, nobody was paying her bills. Melissa peered into the gloom. How long before the landlord tossed out her tools and her belongings? And the poor cats. Where would they go?

At that moment, a yowl rose from behind the shop and then another. Something banged against the back door. The poor starving things must have heard her in the shop.

Kicking herself for forgetting to come in the daylight and cursing the electric company to hell, she extended her arm and, trailing her hand along the wall, found the opening to the hallway and groped her way to the back of the shop through the dark tunnel of the corridor. Halfway there, her foot caught on something solid, and she went sprawling. She threw out her arms to catch herself, and her elbow struck the door molding. She landed on the floor, excruciating pain shooting up her arm. She sat up and rubbed the bruise, blinking at the shock of it.

As the pain subsided, she became aware of the fur-covered lump under her leg. Yikes. She scuttled back against the wall and peered at it in the dark. Too big to be a rat. For a moment, she sat there afraid to move. Then she remembered her cell phone. She pulled it from her pocket and turned on the flash app. The light illuminated the body of a large cat—the orange tom with the ragged ears who'd taken a special liking to her. She shone the light down the hall. Three other cats lay dead, two of them the kittens she'd been taming to eat out of her hand.

How had they gotten in? No windows were open. She'd made sure of that, even hammering plywood over the one she'd broken. She stuck out her foot and nudged the tom's body. The head fell back, its throat slit.

She pushed herself up from the floor, trembling. Someone had killed Bella's cats on purpose and left them here for her to find. She stepped back. Whoever it was had watched her feed them, knew which cats she favored. Her heart went cold. Who could have done such a horribly cruel thing? Only two people knew she was feeding them—Tuccio and the monster. And only one was a murderer.

Something banged against the back door—the mother cat desperate for her kittens? She took a step toward the door and stopped. Or was it the killer come to get her? Her breath caught in her throat.

She glanced down at her cell phone. Should she dial 911? No, it would be stupid to report dead cats in a place she'd broken into herself. She'd be lucky if all the cops did was laugh. If she called Tuccio, he would expect recompense. Better she get out of here now and deal with the dead cats tomorrow in the daylight.

She rushed back to the front of the shop, swept up her portfolio and the keys. She slammed the door behind her and struggled to relock it. Although why she was bothering when other people obviously could get in at will, she had no idea. Finally, the lock clicked, and she took off down the street heading to Jana's. Jana might be a bullying sex fiend, but she would keep her safe.

Never before had she been afraid to be out on the streets late in the evening. She'd been living in Williamsburg for the last five years. She knew every inch of it. But tonight, walking the five blocks to Jana's was like being in a horror movie. Every sound in the night was magnified. The rustle of a rat nosing in a garbage can sent her careening across the street. The wail of police sirens several blocks away sent shivers up and down her spine. The hoarse coughs of a homeless man curled up in a doorway made her jump. She glanced at him as she hurried by.

From beneath a crumpled fedora from some other age, hard beady eyes stared at her out a face covered in a thick black beard. She'd seen him often in the last two weeks, even brought him a sandwich. Tonight, a long-fingered hand reached out toward her and beckoned her closer. She shook her head and hurtled across the street. Three blocks to go.

She was almost there when she sensed rather than heard someone come up behind her. She sped up, stepping off the curb just as the light changed, not seeing the car whipping around the corner right at her. Someone grabbed her by the shoulder and yanked her back. She whirled around hand fisted, knee raised to strike and stopped.

It was the homeless man, but somehow he was no longer slumped and limping. The beard gone, he was tall and broad and smelled like an exotic paradise. Goddamn, it was the monstrous artist. "You." She beat him with the heels of her hands. "Let me go."

"God no." His mouth came down on hers.

Heat swirled through her. She put her hand on his chest and pushed. She would not let him befuddle her again. "Don't you dare touch me. You—you—murderer"—she spat at him—"you killed Bella's cats."

"What are you talking about?

She backed away. "Her cats. Their throats slit. At her studio."

He let out a huff of air. "Hell. Damn it, Melissa. You have to listen to me." He seized her by the arm. "I can explain." She spun around and scratched at his eyes with one hand and stamped with all her might on his instep. But the man was made of iron. He just tightened his hold as he slowly dragged her into a covered pedestrian walkway running in front of a construction site. He wedged her into the corner of a small alcove.

Her jacket caught on the plywood barrier. Gravel and sand crunched beneath her feet. "Let me go this minute or I will scream."

He lifted his hands up, palm out. "I am not going to hurt you. I would never hurt you. Just please listen. I didn't kill any cats. Or Sirena—she's my sister, and I'm looking for her just like you."

Melissa wrapped her arms around herself to control the tremors rippling through her body. "Why should I believe you? After that crazy outburst at your studio.

After stalking me for days and scaring me to death."

He reached out and ran a finger down her cheek. "Your body believes me."

She jerked back. "No. You're wrong. Tuccio says you're a cold blooded killer."

Ari spit on the ground. "He describes himself."

"Is that what this is about? Petty jealousy between the two of you?"

"No, it's about keeping you safe, little bee."

"Why do you care? You called me a whore."

"I was wrong. I—jumped to a conclusion about you."

"Tuccio warned me about you."

"*Tuccio.* We have a long history, and I assure you he's bad milk. I don't know what his hold is over you, but you have to stay away from him. He's poison in a jeweled bottle. The best thing is to stop looking for Bella."

"I thought she was your sister?"

"Look, she's alive. Bella—Sirena's alive. I've had a ransom note."

He moved closer, his expression hidden in the darkness. "I'm on your side, Melissa. I want you safe and well and far away from here. Stay out of this. Trust me. I'll take care of my sister." He pulled a wad of papers from under his coat and held them out to her. "Here are your notes. I apologize for not delivering them as promised."

Melissa reached for the stack of papers. Their hands met, hers small, city-pale, his huge, sun-dark. His scent of spicy herbs and pure male enveloped her. Heat thrummed through her and set her body afire.

He was still talking. "I read what you wrote. Every

single word. It's what took me so long to return these to you. You have a gift, a way of saying things that make them come clear." Ari's hand tightened on hers. "What you say here about the women—how they become their tattoos, how the meaning seeps inside and changes them unknowingly—it's true."

She gazed into his shadowed eyes, tried to find the monster, but found only pain. "I don't—"

He ran a hand down his face. "I've become this face, this beast. It lives inside me. Makes me bitter. I had no right to do what I did to you at the studio." He pushed the papers at her. "Take your notes and stay far away from me and all these troubles."

"You're not a beast." She ignored the notes and seized him by the shoulders. Papers fluttered down around them. Their lips met and melded together. Their tongues touched in greeting, and she deepened the kiss. She inhaled the sheer maleness of him, tasted him, and kissed him harder, the hunger for him driving out all reason. His hands slipped up under her sweatshirt and cupped her breasts.

He moaned his pleasure into her mouth, setting her whole body vibrating. His thumbs swirled around her nipples, feathering them with a touch as light as his paintbrush. Pleasure shot through her. She grew wet and hot between her thighs. The blood in her veins swirled and hummed. He moved her back against the plywood, one hand sliding lower, slipping inside her jeans. His fingers found the core of her and rubbed gently. Tension built until she was thrusting her hips against him. "Please. I need you inside me. Now."

He moved his mouth to her neck. "Melissa, I have never experienced this hunger for a woman before. I can't keep my hands off you. But it is wrong. Tell me no. I am not worthy of you. Send me away."

"Never. I want this. Take me to heaven again."

His magical fingers stilled.

"Please." She reached down and ran her hand along his length. Beneath his baggy jeans, he was hard, radiating heat. How could a man be so hot? She fumbled with the button and unzipped his fly, releasing his hard cock. It sprung into her hand like it belonged there, and she wrapped her hand around him and slid her fingers up and down the silky length. It was as massive as the rest of him. She ached to have him inside her.

He seized her hand. "You drive me insane, woman. I dream of you doing this to me. But not here on the street in this dirt and filth." His breathing was ragged, his voice strangled.

"I don't care. I need you inside me now."

"We can't. I don't have a condom."

"I do." She fumbled in her pocket for the condom Jana insisted she carry at all times—she owed her one for that—tore the package open with her teeth, and stopped. "I don't know how."

He glanced over his shoulder as a car drove by. "Maybe we should stop. I'm sure this is illegal. In a public place."

Waves of desire washed over her. "No. Finish what you started."

Intense black eyes stared into hers. His breathing roughened. He shook his head. "So be it. I cannot refuse you, little bee."

He slipped his arms out of his oversized trench coat and held it out, shielding her from view. "Take off your sandals and jeans."

She shucked them off and let them fall to the pavement.

"Hold onto the coat. With luck, anyone passing by will think me a crazy homeless man pretending to be a bat."

Melissa laughed. "No, just batty." She stretched out a hand on either side of his neck and gripped the coat by the lapels. "Like this?"

"Yes. Now don't let go." He took the condom and slipped it over his cock. Then he made a seat of his hands under her buttocks and lifted her up like she was light as gossamer. "Wrap your legs around me and don't make a sound."

She hooked her legs around his hips so that he was positioned at her entrance. He groaned. "Yes, like that. Forgive me, little bee. We must be fast."

"Fast is good."

He thrust inside her hard and stayed deep, not moving, his hands shielding her bare skin from the rough wood behind her.

Melissa curled against his chest, whispered in his ear. "Move. You're driving me crazy."

"Hush. Trust me." He adjusted the angle so he pressed against her most sensitive places and rocked back and forth, his hips circling round and round, his cock deep inside her, slow and controlled. The muscles in his arms clenched around her with the effort, his whole body taut as a tenderfoot waiting for the tattoo needle to pierce the skin. The contrast between his hard body and his gentle rocking against her inner core set her ablaze.

Her strength left her, and her head fell onto his

shoulder, leaving her a quivering mass of sensation, no longer caring they were on a city street, risking arrest. He increased the rhythm, bringing her closer and closer to the edge. Heat pooled between her legs. Tension built inside her, setting her whole body aflame. Inner muscles she hadn't known she had fluttered, contracted around his penis, matching his moves.

Their mouths found each other and joined, their tongues mirroring the subtle roll and push of his thick, iron-hard cock. Their breath synced. Her blood pulsed, bathing her in a perfect storm of pleasure.

He stilled and then thrust even deeper. Everything exploded. She came with her entire body, her limbs shaking, her only support his powerful arms.

****

He was lost. Shaking and sweating, Ari held her against him as his release swept over and over. He snugged her to him. Now he knew why he had trained as a wrestler. Not to please his unyielding father, who thought him too bookish as a boy, but so he could hold this woman in his arms forever. He clasped her tighter against him. He didn't know who she was, or what her role in Sirena's kidnapping might be. It no longer mattered. She was his to love and to protect

She was right to be worried about the dead cats. She was in danger. Whether because of him or because she was involved with Tuccio, he did not know. But someone was targeting her, trying to scare her. He clasped her tighter, still inside her, and marveled at the way they fit together. He inhaled her scent redolent of sweet vanilla and honey and sex. How could he keep her safe when he lost all control when he came within a breath of her? Her scent alone stole away all reason.

She shifted against him.

"Ari?"

"Yes." He nuzzled his nose in her hair seeking her scent.

"I don't understand. This urge to join. Be together. It's like we're one soul." She rested her head on his shoulder. "I've never felt it before. Only with you."

He burst with pride. He may not have been her first lover, but he was the first to awaken her to the heights of passion.

Melissa's lips brushed his ear. "I thought—I thought I was made wrong. They said I was cold—a frigid clam."

"I don't know who *they* are, little bee, but whoever they were they were pigs. Good sex is as much an art form as the paintings I make. It takes—" He stopped. He'd been about to say a loving man. That would have been a mistake. He had no right to love anyone. Not now, with his plan to save his sister and the island in motion. When his legal trickery might mean his death. He swallowed the desire boiling up inside him, stifled the words of love clawing to get free, and let the beast out. "It takes practice and skill. Any man could satisfy you if he knew what he was doing."

"I see. And you're very *skilled* with all those models to practice on." Melissa pushed a trembling palm against his chest. "Put me down please."

He lowered her gently to the ground. With an aching heart, he took the coat from her and stepped back, shielding her from the street. Silently, she slipped on her jeans and buckled her sandals without looking at him. His heart thumped loudly, every cell in his body shouting at him to seize the moment and profess his love even if they only had hours or days, even if she planned to betray him, sell him out to Tuccio and Vernon.

He opened his mouth and closed it. No, he would not give them another pawn, besides his sister, in this chess game they were playing. He realized his fly was still open. He closed it with a curse and kicked at the papers at his feet.

"What are you doing?" His Nereida, her face flaming, gave him a push, swooped down and gathered up the trampled papers like a fury on a rampage. "My field notes are ruined, you—you—bastard."

Well, he deserved that. He bent over and helped her gather up the papers. "Look, I'll get them retyped."

"No." She clutched the tattered notes to her breasts like a shield. "I want nothing more to do with you. I can't explain this"—she shook her head—"what just happened between us. This fire you stir in my belly with your *practiced* skill. But it is over. Never touch me again." She bit her lip. "And I will not stop looking for Bella or feeding her cats. I do not desert my friends."

The chill autumn air wrapped around him, and the hairs rose on his arms. He'd convinced her of nothing but that he was a beast with no heart. Well, it was the truth. He had deserted the few people who loved him years ago when the world had been a very dark place. There were not too many who could forgive a man with innocent blood on his hands.

"As you wish." He backed out of the walkway and stumbled up the street like a drunk man. *Zeús*, he had betrayed her again. To take her on a public street like a whore was the height of foolishness.

He should have escorted her to a Starbucks or a

cozy luncheonette like the Park or better yet, a five-star restaurant in the light of day, and over latte and brioche or a grilled beef burger and feta or steamed oysters and paté, bestowed her notes on her like a civilized man. In a suit with his cock tucked neatly away, they might have had a reasonable conversation in which he explained exactly why she was a target and told her who Tuccio really was. But no, he had to play cloak and dagger, dress as a tramp and follow her around like she was a dog in heat. He really was a monster.

It was only a matter of time before Tuccio with his suave ways had her in his bed, doing his bidding. And when he tired of her, she'd be passed on to the next of his *good* friends.

He rubbed the bloody backs of his hands where they'd scraped against the plywood in the act of protecting that glorious skin, sucked on the embedded splinters, and welcomed the pain as just punishment for what he had done to the woman he was coming to love.

Chapter 24

Melissa sat cross-legged on her bed and shook off the tingly heat that suffused her body every time she thought of the incredible sex Ari had given her. For her, it had been life-shattering. For him, the work of a skilled and practiced Lothario. Confound the man. One kiss and she'd acted the whore he thought she was.

Enough. She pushed away the memory of him buried inside her and hunched over the papers spread out on the bedcovers. Slowly but surely, she was piecing her field notes back together. A small kernel of hope was growing that she would actually be able to produce a credible dissertation in time for the January deadline.

Jana peeked around the doorframe wearing a thigh-high slinky black dress. "Hey, Mel. Still up?" She bounced into the room and sat down on the bed, crushing the papers under her.

Melissa swiped at the papers. "Get off, you're ruining them."

Jana picked one up and frowned at it. "What—these filthy things?"

"My field notes. Ari gave them back to me tonight." She gave her a push. "Now get."

"Ari? Now that sounds real friendly." Jana pulled more papers from under her and dropped them on the floor. She leaned in. "Is that all your monster gave you?"

Melissa sat back on her heels. "I'm working, damn you."

"Boring." Jana tapped her chin with her index finger. "I know. Let's call up Tuccio and ask him to take us to Output." She rolled her shoulders and gave a little shake. "I feel like dancing."

"You call him. I have no interest in the man."

"Well, he's definitely interested in you. Took me to lunch the other day and asked all kinds of questions about you."

Melissa carefully put down the paper she was holding. "What kind of questions?"

"Oh, things like your birthday and what you are researching and who your friends are and whether or not you slept with the Monster Man again."

"That's none of his business. I hope you told him to shove off."

"Come on. He's like my boss, and it doesn't hurt to make Prince Charming a little jealous. Anyway, I just told him you were besotted with the monster." Jana smiled. "But I didn't give him the nitty-gritty

Melissa pulled a paper out from under Jana's thigh. "I'm not besotted. It—it just happened."

"That's the way lust works, girl."

"It won't happen again. He's responsible for this mess." She waved her hand at pile the papers.

"Oh, so you don't care for him? That's great." Jana stood and pulled her dress over her head. She had nothing on underneath except a black lace bra and matching thong. She put her hands on her hips. "Don't you think I would be the perfect model for one of his paintings? And I've never slept with a wrestler. All that raw male strength. He must be some lover to have managed to satisfy you. "She wiggled her behind. "Yes, I think I will mosey over there and give him a little booty."

Melissa's chest tightened. The man was a beast. She shouldn't care, but she did. "He doesn't even know you exist, why would he sleep with you?"

"He'll remember me. We had—what is that old-fashioned word? Yeah, a *speaking glance* at the gallery. I think I whetted his fancy. Besides, he had no trouble bedding you on the spur of the moment, did he? With his face, he must be in high alt anytime a woman opens her legs for him." She tossed back her hair and gave a little shimmy. "I think I'll go tomorrow."

"Jana, tell me you're joking. You don't even like men."

"You have two men slathering after you. Don't I deserve to share the fun, too? Men have their uses."

"Just leave Ari alone. He's—he's a murderer."

Jana drew in her chin. "A what?"

"Tuccio didn't tell you?"

"We talked about you, not Mr. Monster."

"Tuccio's not who you think he is. He's an undercover immigration agent surveilling Ari for the government."

Jana laughed. "Tuccio's undercover all right." She stared at her. "Gad, I think you are in love with him."

"I can't stand Tuccio."

"No—with the Monster."

Melissa smoothed out a paper. "Don't be ridiculous."

Jana kneeled on the bed. More papers ended up on the floor. "You're grasping at straws, Mel. Trying to stop me from seeing him. Well, let me tell you something. I'm more curious than ever to give the man a try." She poked her in the ribs with her finger. "A wrestler and a murderer—so you say—who can make a frigid bitch like you walk around like you're high as a giraffe might just be able to turn me on, too."

Melissa gathered up her papers. "If you go near him, I will hate you forever."

Jana grinned. "Gotcha. Look at you. If you're not acting like a woman getting the good stuff, then I'll eat my thong."

Melissa sank down on the bed and covered her face with her hands. "I'm afraid to love him, Jana. He's raw. Hard. Scary. But I think I do. I ache for him. I want him so much. He makes my blood fizz."

"Oh, Mel. I'm sorry I upset you." Jana sat down and rubbed her back. "I would never have slept with him. I was just teasing to find out how you really feel. You never say. Keep all your feelings inside. Nothing shows on your face, you know." She patted her on the back. "But I sure riled you, didn't I?"

Melissa pulled away. "There's no such thing as just teasing like it's a joke or something, Jana. Words hurt as much as if you took a knife and stabbed me." She buried her head in her arms. "You and my sister were always teasing me. I was too short. Too yellow. Too stupid." She swallowed, but she couldn't stop the bitterness from spilling out. "And when Laura was killed, you continued to tear me apart every time you put on that little smirk and called me Wise Buddha— like I knew something about her murder that no one else did. It was cruel." She stared at her. "What I can't figure is why you took me in this year and been so helpful."

Jana shrugged. "Guilt, I guess. I wanted to be Laura's sister. Live in your house. Have your parents. My dad—he—wasn't kind. I was so jealous of you having a great family, having her to love you. And when we met up again, and you were in such a miserable relationship with Colin, I thought I would make amends to her memory by helping you out." She kissed her forehead. "But as usual I just made a mish-mosh of it as always. Let me make it up to you." She stood up. "Hmmm, I wonder if Mr. Monster loves you back. Now wouldn't that be a stitch. So how about I go and pretend to be a model and see if I can wheedle out of him how much he likes you. What do you think?" She put a hand on her waist and gave her hips a shake.

The image of Jana seducing Ari mushroomed in Melissa's brain. She jumped up. "Forget it. He's not in love with me."

"Afraid he's a cad? I promise all I'll do is talk. I won't touch him even if he's willing. And you know what I'll do? I'll plant a little video cam by his bed. The kind we use for surveillance on the properties we supervise. Then you can see if he's bedding other models. How's that for a plan?"

"Absolutely not, Jana. How could you even think of doing such a thing? That's an utterly horrible invasion of someone's privacy. Probably illegal, too. Besides, I really don't want to know anything more about him."

Jana slipped the dress back on. "You're such a spoilsport with your high-blown morals. Drove Laura crazy, you know. Always tattling to your parents. Gad, she could never do anything without you finding out and spilling the beans."

Melissa crushed the paper she was holding. "What are you talking about? I never told on her."

"Yeah, like you never talked to those detectives the day she disappeared. After she told you never to say anything."

"I was a kid, Jana. And I was scared. Those detectives cornered me and pestered me until I broke down...I am sorry I implicated you—but I thought you'd forgiven me."

"Yeah, yeah, it's all fizzy water over the dam—a stupid mistake and nothing came of it." She came over and wrapped her arms around her. "I'll always be your friend for Laura's sake. Just don't play Miss Morality with me, okay?"

Melissa put her arms around Jana's waist. "Thank you for everything you've done. The loans, letting me stay here, putting up with my moods. I couldn't ask for more. I know you are just trying to help, but promise me you'll stay out of my love life. Leave Ari alone. Please."

"Sure. Sure." Jana patted her on the back. "Though I don't think a fling with a deformed monster and leading poor Tuccio around by the balls counts as a love life." She flicked her on the nose. "Not fair for you to have two guys. So I'm warning you. If you don't make a move on Ari and find out where his heart lies, then I *will* consider him fair game."

Chapter 25

Ari laid down his paint brush and shook his head. Despite his misgivings, the Whole Car Paint Off had gone without a hitch. There'd been four crews. One crew stood guard at each entrance. The rest manned their weapons of choice—homemade paint marker mops, paint rollers in an array of lengths, and their cannons of spray paint. With each member assigned to one task, the green, silver, and black paint flowed down the side of the car like one of those time-lapse videos speeded up to the fastest speed.

Seventy-five seconds later the car rolled out of the station wearing its new "Art not Ads" top to bottom.

He gazed at the canvas in front of him. Now if only he could finish this painting as fast. But he couldn't. Every stroke of paint reminded him of the warmth of Melissa's skin, the silk of her hair, the way her breath sped up when she was on the edge of her climax.

He dipped his brush in a puddle of golden paint and ran a brush stroke along the edge of one delectable thigh. It wasn't real skin or real woman. It didn't reveal her gentle kindness to animals, her brilliant mind. But it was the best he would ever have of her after the fiasco last night, and someday it would hang in some rich bastard's home. Probably over the hot tub.

He threw the brush down and stepped back. It wasn't up to his usual level of perfection, but he didn't care. The buyer would never notice as long he could see tits. And he couldn't bear to put another stroke of color across the canvas. It hurt too much. He'd never paint his Nereida again. Probably, he'd never paint again. Putting brush to canvas would break him.

Ah well, Vernon would solve that problem soon enough. He gazed out over the river. It was supposedly a sunny day, but today New York City sat in a drab haze of pollution that dulled the sky to a limp yellow-gray. Overhead, jets roared. Down below, cars honked. To his left, a ferry sputtered across the river, turning up liquid green filth. Sparkling new penthouses rose all along the Brooklyn shoreline. Why would anyone pay millions of dollars to view a degraded city full of sin and crime?

On Eudokia, the sky was so intensely blue you could taste it. On hillsides heavily scented with wild oregano and sage, shepherds herded flocks of sheep and goats. Down below, families threshed wheat and barley using toothed threshing sleds, while in the courtyards women ground grain in stone hand-mills for the ancient cracked wheat cereal dish they called *trahanás*. A living history preserved through the years by his father and his grandfather.

For centuries, the sea had protected it. Even today, the island's hidden harbor could only be accessed by private boat. He squeezed the lump where his nose had broken. Only Vernon and Tuccio had found their way, the location beaten out of him in prison.

He'd caused it all to happen. All of it. He deserved to die. But not yet.

He turned away from the view and headed to the bathroom. Time to get ready to face the lawyer and sign the papers establishing the Eudokia Island trust and sealing his death warrant.

****

Fifteen minutes later, Ari stepped out of the shower and flicked the water out of his hair. He dried himself off and then did something he rarely did—he glanced at his face in the mirror. One glance was enough.

He ran his fingers over the crooked nose and across the hard ridge of the scar. He could still feel Tuccio and his gang's knuckles pounding into his face over and over until he was sure he would die. The prison doctors fixed the worst of it, the crushed eye socket, the broken jaw. His father had wanted him to get restorative plastic surgery after being released from prison, but he'd refused. He deserved to look like this. It matched the monster that lived inside him. Besides, by then, he'd had Vernon to worry about.

He slipped on his jeans, fumbling at the buttons with his mutilated hand. A beautiful girl like Melissa deserved someone whole. He imagined them walking down the street. People would say he bought her with his money. They'd think him a beast capable of hurting her. He couldn't do that to her.

He scrubbed his hair dry with a towel. T-Crew was late today. They usually showed up in time to clean out his refrigerator before a night of tagging. He couldn't come with them anymore. His lawyer had read him the riot act after the last escapade, and until he settled the deal with Vernon, he couldn't risk getting deported.

Clunk. Clunk. Clunk.

"Sto diávolo." Not rocks on the door again. The landlord wasn't going to be happy.

Ari shook the remaining water from his hair, slung

the towel over his shoulder, and stalked from the bathroom. *"Erchomai."* Oops. Ought to be speaking English. "Coming." He barefooted his way down the stairs. Annoying kids. T-Crew'd been doing fine before he'd barged into their lives with his I-know-more-than-you-do attitude. After all, they'd done better than he had. They'd survived to the ripe old age of twenty without ending up convicted of murder.

Clunk.

"Coming." He ought to let them wait. Pretend he had already left. It would be easier than saying goodbye. He unbolted the door and yanked it open. "Stop—"

A woman stood on one foot, holding a high heel shoe. "Hi, remember me? Jana Firth. Friend of Melissa Dermont—that Asian girl who modeled for you. Thought you'd never answer." She slipped her shoe back on. "Resorted to my heels.

"I was in the shower."

She gave his naked torso an appreciative nod. "So I see."

Who was this blonde-haired siren? Where had he seen her before? Ari searched his memory. That's right, she'd been at the gallery. Introducing Melissa to Tuccio. He gripped the door handle harder. Was Melissa in trouble? "How can I help you?"

"I've come to check out the studio. I have a client interested in subletting after you vacate. Here's my business card."

He pinched the embossed card between his fingers. Just what he didn't need—a nosy real estate agent. "I was on my way out."

"Oh." She licked her lips. "But Melissa seemed

quite taken with the living quarters." She pulled out a camera. "I thought I'd take some photos for my client. Won't take more than a few minutes."

"It's a mess. I'm in the middle of packing up my paints and canvases."

"No biggie. I'm an expert at making messes look good. Besides, my client is an iron worker. Does some fancy kind of twisted metal sculpture. He's not looking for ambiance, just sufficient workspace."

Ari opened the door. "Come along then."

Jana snapped some photos of the lower level. "Those your canvases over there? Any new paintings I could get a peek at?" One side of her mouth tilted up. "It would be a real coup to see something no one else has ever seen."

"Blanks. Didn't have time to paint."

"Oh, what a shame. I thought you were hiring models."

"Didn't work out."

"But Melissa modeled for you."

"She proved an amateur. Didn't last twenty minutes."

"I guess she won't be hanging on someone's wall then." The woman was like a cat in heat. She rubbed up against him as she took another photo. "I wouldn't mind one session modeling for you." She eyed his bare chest. "I think you'd find I'm not an amateur."

He moved back. "Not interested in whatever you're offering."

"You sure?" Her eyes moved down lower. "Melissa gave such rave reviews. *Impressive,* she said."

Zeús. A bitter taste filled his mouth. He thought what passed between them had been something you

175

didn't giggle about with your friends. He stood straighter. "There are no modeling jobs at the moment, madam."

"Well then, Mr. Monster." She waggled her finger at him. "Melissa calls you that, you know. Shall we go upstairs and see the apartment?"

All he wanted to do was throw her out, but she was already on her way up. She climbed the stairs, all wiggling curves on sexy high heels. He followed after her, breathing in her expensive perfume. She was the type of woman he enjoyed. Worldly, experienced, no expectations and willing to ignore his face for a good fuck and a nice bundle of dough. A few weeks ago, he would have had her under him in two minutes flat. But now, after holding Melissa in his arms, making love to such a woman seemed tawdry.

The real estate bombshell had moved into the kitchen. He trailed after her as she opened cabinets and snapped photos of the room from different angles. She wandered into the workspace and fingered a drawing on the worktable. "This your sketch?" she asked, holding up the camera.

Zeús. Those were El Toro's sketches from the Whole Car Paint Off, incriminating evidence that didn't need to be in a real estate portfolio. He grasped her by the upper arm. "No photos. My work is copyrighted."

She looked down at his fingers. "Are you sure you're not interested?"

He withdrew his hand like he'd touched fire. "How is Miss Dermont?"

She gave him a strange look. "*Miss Dermont* is angry at you for destroying her field notes." The woman fingered through the sketches and held up a study of breasts. "No face showing here but is this Melissa by any chance?"

He glared at her. "No. It's the Venus de Milo."

She put it down and picked up another. "Ooo, is this one a picture of what I think it is?"

He pulled it from her hand, gathered it up with the rest, and shoved them into his portfolio.

"No need to be testy." She snapped a picture of the ceiling. "I'm worried about Melissa. She's in deep trouble, you know."

All sorts of wild thoughts scrambled through his head. He held his breath. "Trouble?"

She headed for the bedroom alcove. "Well, she's seeing this guy Theo Tuccio. He's wining and dining her, turning her head, if you know what I mean." She stopped and took a photo of the bedroom. "So this is the bed. I didn't expect it to be so huge." She glanced over her shoulder. "Ah, but then you do seem to be generously proportioned. Does it come with the studio?"

"I purchased it. I'm particular in my sleeping habits."

"I'm sure you are." She sat down and gave it a bounce.

"It's staying."

She narrowed one eye. "My client will make better of use of it than you, I suppose."

He pressed his lips together. "About this Tuccio character. How is he troubling Miss Dermont?"

"I'm afraid she's going to, you know, shack up with him?"

"Shack up?"

"Move in, get in bed. Whatever. She's broke, you

177

know. Her debts—they're astronomical. Between her student loans and paying for her mother's expenses at the nursing home, she barely gets enough to eat. Earns peanuts at that coffee shop. And in a few days, she will have nowhere to live. My roommate arrives in from Paris in three days."

His bile rose, a sickly taste in the back of his throat. Melissa wore thrift store clothes, carried a knapsack nearly worn through. He should have known she needed money. But he hadn't, and whose fault was that? They hadn't done much conversing in their last two encounters. He fisted his hands. Hell, she was ripe to be picked off by Tuccio.

"You'll think of something," Jana said with a wave of her hand. "Meanwhile," she rolled onto her back and spread her legs. "Be a good man and give me a quick tumble. Looking at those sketches of yours has made me horny as hell."

She had no underwear on. Ari closed his eyes, whirled around, and stared out the window. "You're disgusting. What kind of friend are you? Get out of here this instant."

The Firth woman sat back up. "Pooh. A big fellow like you. I expected more." She played with the buttons of her blouse. "I just need to freshen up a bit. May I use the bathroom?"

He slapped the side of his head. *What next?* He'd left clothes and towels and what else strewn everywhere. "Other side of the kitchen. But I'm warning you, it's wet and stinky. I wasn't expecting guests."

She disappeared into the bathroom. He glanced down at his bare chest. He'd been entertaining the woman half-naked. All sorts of warning blinkers went off in his head.

She'd been taking photos. Had she taken one of him? The last thing he needed was for his patrons to see the prison tat on his arm. He ran a hand through his hair and looked around for a shirt. He'd better get Hanlin to find out the name of her boss and get those photos impounded.

Shirt buttoned, he waited outside the bathroom door. Had she said quick? No woman was quick in the john. He wandered over to the kitchen and pulled out the containers of chili he'd ordered delivered for his goodbye dinner with the T-Crew boys. He dumped the spicy mixture into a pot to reheat and glanced at the clock. Six-thirty. Where were they?

The bathroom door opened. And he let out the breath he'd been holding Thank goodness Miss Firth would be gone before his guardian demons arrived. He glanced over. The bitch. She blinked up at him wearing a snake-ate-the-mouse expression on her face and nothing else.

"Like what you see?"

She was one of those women who looked like she'd stepped out a Victorian pornography card. Heavy breasts, narrow waist, generous buttocks. Just weeks ago he would have been happy to take what she was offering. Not now, this was Melissa's friend.

His cock disagreed. She stared hard at his crotch and walked toward him. "I think you do."

He backed up. "Go get dressed, Miss Firth. This is just not going to happen."

"Of course it is, you beastly man. Unless what is running through your veins is thin paint instead of hot male lust." She ran her hands up her sides and cupped her breasts. "I've heard you paint your models. Paint these." She put her fingers on her nipples and pinched.

He was full of hot male blood all right. She was a beauty with perfect features. But it wasn't her face he'd paint. His heartbeat thundered in his ears. His skin burned. The blood pounded through his veins. He wanted to turn her around and bend her over the drawing table and give her the fuck she was begging for.

She moved closer and ran a finger through the hair on his chest slowly edging lower and lower. She looked up at him smiling as if she'd won. His brain freefell as all the blood ran to his cock. Maybe she had. Maybe being inside her would wipe away Melissa's memory, the threatening love growing inside him. Let him prove he was truly the cruel beast who broke hearts like Sirena thought he did.

His hands slowly slid around and grasped her generous buttocks and pulled her against him, watching her eyes. Not many women could look him in the face for long. They had to really lust for his body to ignore what he looked like. Miss Firth's eyes were heavily made up, thick black eyeliner, fake lashes, a yellow eye shadow that brought out the warm green of her catlike eyes. He held her gaze, making sure she saw his face.

She gave it a good try, but she couldn't hold his stare. The quick glance to the right was a dead giveaway. It was all pretense, her lust as fake as her eyelashes, her performance that of a hardened whore. He slowly dropped his hands.

"I appreciate the offer, Miss Firth. But I think not."

"I swear I'll not tell a soul." She rubbed up against

him.

Entrapment. The word blasted through the last of the sexual heat numbing his brain. Of course, she would tell. That was the whole point, idiot. Tell Melissa. Tell the world.

From down below, the door opened and a gabble of voices echoed through the building. T-Crew had arrived.

Ari pushed past her. "Get dressed. Now."

But the woman had other ideas. She latched on to his arm. "But I want to meet your friends."

"In hell, madam." He extracted himself from her grasp, snatched up his jacket from the sofa, and raced for the stairs. "Gentlemen, hold up. We're going out to dinner." He took the steps two at a time. Spreading his arms, he herded the group back toward the door. "How about we get pizza at Fornino's?"

"She coming?" Fur Tree asked. Ari looked up. Miss Firth in all her naked glory leaned over the railing. She waved. "I'll keep the bed warm."

"*Zeús.*" He shook his head and took out his phone and jabbed in Delaney's number. "You'd better be gone in five minutes, madam. My security man is on his way." With that he spun around, picked up his duffle of paint cans, and headed out to do just what he'd been told not to. Leave his mark on this city that bred women from hell.

Zara West

Chapter 26

Melissa slammed the bag of cat food on the kitchen counter and tore off her windbreaker. She glanced around at the sun-dappled walls of the apartment she'd called home for the last three months and rubbed her aching head. She had to be out when Nancie returned, and she had nowhere to go.

With a groan, she thumped down on the kitchen stool and kicked off her sneakers. Twelve hours on her feet doing double overtime at the coffee shop and waitressing part-time at Lenny's, then running back and forth between Bella's place and the Siren to feed the cats was destroying her feet. At this rate, by the time she earned enough money to rent a place of her own, she'd not be able to walk to it.

Ha. As if she could earn enough. The cheapest room share she'd found online was five hundred and sixty a month plus a month's deposit down. An impossible sum to accumulate in five days.

She rubbed her feet and considered her options. She'd hoped to crash at Daniela's until she'd saved enough. But over coffee this morning, Daniela had tearfully rescinded her offer to put her up. The poor woman was nervous. She would pick up the two girls hiding at Lenny's and get them into the safe house as a last gesture of friendship. But when that was done, she never wanted to see her again.

With a groan, she shoved the cat food bag to the side. Pussyballs would have to wait till tomorrow. She lowered her head onto her arms. She could ask Tuccio for help. Though what she'd have to do in return she didn't dare imagine. Still anything was better than a shelter. She remembered his cold lips on hers, his groping hands and tongue. Maybe.

Jana peeked out of her bedroom, a glass of red wine in her hand. "He's delightful."

Melissa half-lifted her head. "Who's delightful?"

"Your monster."

She pushed herself upright. "Did you go and bother the man?"

Jana took a sip of her wine. "I wouldn't say *bother*." She fluttered her fake eyelashes. "He has the biggest bed. Nice and bouncy. Well, you already know that. And such stamina. A real man if you know what I mean. Commanding"

Melissa's heart did a flip. She shouldn't feel jealous, but she did. "You're despicable." She crossed the room, seized Jana's wine glass and threw it in her face. "I hate you."

She dashed into her bedroom and slammed the door. Tears streamed down her face. She had to get away from Volcano Mouth before she exploded. Wildly, she yanked her few clothes from their hangers, emptied the bureau drawers, and tossed the wrinkled mess into her suitcase. She gathered up her field notes along with her laptop, stuffed them on top, and zipped the suitcase closed.

Images of Jana and Ari together in bed raced through her mind, his practiced hands caressing Jana's body the way he'd touched her. Would he paint Jana too—tell *her* how beautiful her skin was?

She glanced down at her thin body with the small breasts Tuccio wanted "improved." A connoisseur of women, like Ari, would surely prefer Jana's voluptuous figure over hers.

She shut her eyes as if that would stop the thoughts poisoning her brain and snatched the apartment keys out of her pocket. Bella's keychain fell to the floor.

She bent down and picked it up, fingered the gold mermaid. Of course, she could stay at Bella's place. Who'd know? Zeya no longer peeked out her door when she showed up at odd hours to feed the cat. And it was quiet there. She'd be able to get her writing done in time to get the first draft out to her committee. She grasped the handle of her suitcase, slung her knapsack on her shoulder, and stomped back into the kitchen. Jana stopped scrubbing the wine stain and glared up at her.

She threw the apartment keys on the counter. "I'm leaving. I don't know what my sister ever saw in you. You wouldn't recognize loyalty if you tripped over it."

Jana jumped up. "Melissa. Don't go crazy on me now. I was teasing. He didn't touch me. I promise. I made it all up—well, not all, I did go there but just as a real estate agent looking over the apartment."

"You promised not to."

Jana threw her arms around her. "Please forgive me, sweetie pie, for Laura's sake. I don't know what gets into me sometimes. It's like a devil takes over my mouth."

"I can't take it anymore, Jana. One minute you're clawing out my insides and the next you're all syrup-sweet."

"You have a place to stay?

Melissa squeezed Bella's keys in her palm. "I'll find somewhere—a shelter—if I must."

"You can't go to a shelter They're full of filthy vagrants." Jana picked up the apartment key and pressed it into her hand. "Just in case."

"Fine." Melissa stuffed Jana's key in her pocket. "Look, it's been great you taking me in and all. Let's part as friends." She gave her a hug. "I'll stay in touch."

Jana refilled her wine glass and sat back down. "You could give Mr. Stavros a call. Take advantage of that great big bed."

"You've got to be kidding." Melissa wrapped her hand around the handle of her suitcase. "I wouldn't let that monster touch me again if he crawled on his hands and knees the entire length of the Williamsburg Bridge."

Jana took a sip of her wine and smiled. "He'd do it, that monster. He loves you, you know."

****

Ari peered through the car window at Melissa's apartment. He should go up and tell her what he'd done for her. Apologize for his rudeness. Give her cash so she could get free of Tuccio. But he wasn't sure he could keep his hands off her. He'd taken her on the street and trampled her field notes while rutting like an animal. She was probably so disgusted by him she'd not even open the door. And that Firth woman would be there, spouting lies.

Delaney pushed back his chauffer's hat and looked over his shoulder. "Sir, are you getting out? We can't park here. This is a bus stop, and I can see the bus coming up behind us."

185

"Drive on, then."

"Where, sir?"

"To the studio." He opened the briefcase on his lap and took out the papers. He'd done it. Created a perpetual trust to preserve Eudokia from development. It had taken almost all his millions, but what did that matter? Money hadn't brought him happiness. Better it buy justice for the people of the island.

Now all that was left was to deliver the deed for the villa to Vernon and somehow extract his sister from the bastard before Vernon discovered the legal fences he had built. He hadn't quite figured out how that would work. He would have to rely on his sister doing the right thing—he rubbed the spot on his inner wrist with the incriminating tattoo—and Sirena had never been reliable as far as he was concerned.

The car moved slowly up the street and stopped at a traffic light. Up ahead, a girl in a hooded jacket pulling a huge fire-engine-red wheeled suitcase with one hand and clasping a white grocery bag in the other, jostled past the slower-paced window shoppers. Something about the way she swung her shoulders seemed familiar. She turned her head, and he caught a glimpse of the small straight nose, sturdy elfin chin, and up-tipped eyes. It was Melissa, and it appeared she was moving out of Jana's early. Good. That blonde seductress was toxic. But where could she be heading with her luggage? The airport? His stomach tightened. Leaving New York and getting far away from him would be the wisest choice for her, but it would be like losing part of his heart.

Wait. Not the airport. That Jana creature said his Nereida had no money. She had to be going somewhere nearby.

Out of the corner of his eye, he spotted a snake of a man dressed in a fancy leather jacket and a ball cap following close after her. The hair rose on the back of his neck. The minion had to be one of Vernon's or Tuccio's, and they wouldn't be following Melissa unless they had a use for her.

He leaned over the seat. "Delaney, see the girl with that awful red suitcase? Let me off somewhere behind her."

"I'll do my best, sir. But she's moving fast, and we've a stop light ahead."

"All right. Let me out here."

The car came to a shuddering halt. The legal papers flew off his lap. He couldn't leave them in the car. Ari folded them into a small rectangular wad and tucked them into his jeans pocket. Then he shucked his suit jacket and dress shirt, grabbed his paint satchel, floppy hat, and old coat, and yanked the car door open, zooming in on the suitcase wheels rumbling on the pavement ahead of him.

Chapter 27

He should have figured that was where she was headed. Ari found a shadowy doorway and ducked inside. Across the street, Melissa unlocked the door to Sirena's apartment house, jerked her ugly suitcase over the threshold, and disappeared inside. On the opposite corner, the leather-clad snake following her leaned back against a parked car and lit a cigarette.

Ari glanced up and down the street. He needed to warn her she was being surveilled and convince her to go into hiding. But he couldn't be seen doing it. He wanted no ties between Melissa and himself that his enemies could knot together.

He headed around to the side of the building away from the entrance and stood below the old fire escape where he'd first met El Toro. Good. His sister's apartment was on this side. With a quick peek to make sure the watcher was focused on the other side of the building, he hopped up on a trash can, hooked his hands around the bottom rung of the fire escape and swung up. Placing each foot down lightly to avoid making the rusty steps rattle, he headed up.

He stopped at the fourth floor landing and peeked in. The window opening off the fire escape gave a good view of the living and kitchen areas. After checking to make sure he was well hidden in the shadow of the building behind him, he put his palms on the window sash, ready to throw it up and charge inside.

But the sight of Melissa standing at the sink opening a can of cat food and emptying it into the cat's dish brought back the memory of their first confrontation. He dropped his hands and rested them on the weathered window sill. He didn't want to frighten her again.

Inside, the cat curled around his sea nymph's legs and she squatted to pet it, her perfect breasts outlined under the thin cotton T-shirt she wore.

Ari swiped a hand across his forehead. All that beauty could be destroyed in a second by Vernon, or worse, turned to making a profit for Tuccio's call girl business as she was passed from one rich playboy's bed to another. Men paid a hefty fee for submissive Orientals.

He glanced back at Melissa. Nothing submissive about her. Looking for his sister had been a brave thing to do. Making love to him with her eyes open was courageous. And she was smart, highly-educated. He'd understood enough of her field notes to see that her research on tattooing was well-designed and comprehensive. She'd have a doctoral degree when she was done and a bright future in academia, something denied him by his own foolishness.

He rubbed the stumps of his fingers and returned to the Melissa show. Back at the sink she washed out the cat food tin while bouncing from one foot to the other as if listening to an internal song. Finished, she turned off the tap and ran her wet hands through her hair. Then with a little wiggle that sent currents of desire coursing through him, she strode over to her bulging suitcase standing inside the doorway and opened it.

He stared at the fire-engine red monstrosity. It looked like it contained everything she owned. Was that what she was about? Moving out of Firth's? Getting ready to move in with Tuccio? But why drag the thing to his sister's just to feed the cat? She could have called Theo and been chauffeured to his Park Avenue penthouse. The image of Melissa in Tuccio's bed made him clench his fists.

He peered up at the heavy yellow sky and wanted to howl his frustration. He wanted to break the glass and leap in. Make her sit down and listen until she understood the danger she was in. But she'd just run or end up under him in bed. He was hard just thinking about her, only a pane of glass between them.

He leaned on the windowsill again and forced himself to wait. Silky underthings flirted at him over the edges of the opened suitcase. She pulled out a long ultramarine blue silk robe and laid it across a chair. Then she yanked her T-shirt over her head and reached back to unfasten her bra. Ari held his breath. The bra fell away revealing the rose tan of her nipples. He pressed against the glass. He wanted to touch her, see her smooth golden skin flush again with desire. He wanted to kiss those tiny buds until she writhed beneath him asking for more.

He closed his eyes. When he opened them again, she was slipping her hands into the waistband of her bikini underwear, pushing them down, stepping out of them. *A Diós*, there was her dark triangle of hair, pointing like an arrow to the heat of her, to home. His cock twitched. He wanted to touch her sex, make her wet and ready for him. His cock swelled even more at that image of her opening to him and letting him drive into her wet sheath.

He sank down below the window and leaned back against the building wall, struggling to regain control. He cooled his ardor by imagining what Tuccio would do to that beautiful body if he thought her a turncoat. The bastard was known for his fancy knife work. He'd seen what the man was capable of up close and personal on Eudokia.

When Vernon and his crew invaded the island, Tuccio had taken up with the café owner's daughter. Ritsa had stars in her eyes, dreams of escaping the village and living high. But Tuccio had no use for her outside the island. She'd been a convenience for his sexual needs, that's all. But the girl had made a scene when he told her he was leaving. "You love me that much?" the bastard had asked her. And when she confessed her love, Vernon's brutes held her while the bastard carved his initials into her cheeks. "To remember me by."

And it had been all his fault. His fault that he'd been in jail, unable to defend anyone, not even himself. His fault that Vernon and Tuccio's gang had found the island through a slip of his tongue. He shifted against the wall. The wadded-up copy of the trust papers pressed against his hip. Well, he was no longer defenseless. Money was magic when you had enough and were willing to die in the process of giving it all away.

But not before Melissa was safely out of Tuccio's grasp. He would not be responsible for another girl's destruction. He peeked in the window again. Melissa had put on the robe. The silk flowed over her skin, hiding its glory but revealing the long, lithe shape of her. It was perfect. She was perfect.

****

Melissa dug through her suitcase. The sun hadn't quite set yet, but despite the glint of red striking the window glass, light had fled the apartment. But she didn't need light to find her most precious possession. Her fingers searched through the hurriedly packed clothing, touching and discarding until they met smooth silk satin. She drew out the garment and shivered slightly as she slipped her arms into the glorious Chinese robe her father had given her on her thirteenth birthday. She missed him so much.

He had been her only beacon of love in a long and lonely childhood. Once, when it had been just the two of them driving to a softball game, he'd told her of the woman he had left behind in Vietnam when the war ended. The woman he had truly loved. For a long time, she'd thought he meant her real mother. But when she got older, she realized that the war had ended fifteen years before she was born. She was a nobody, a waif he'd picked her out of a picture book some international adoption agency had shown him—an abandoned child with no past except that which was stamped on her skin.

It explained her adoptive mother's hatred of her. The heavy-set Italian girl with the bad teeth, who had waited for her soldier, prayed for his survival and stayed true, would always be second best to some slant-eyed foreign whore. And the foreign orphan with her coarse black hair and muddy yellow skin was a constant affront.

Melissa ran her hands over the embroidered peacock design on the sleeve. She'd seen the robe in the window of a department store at the mall and begged him for it. To her, it had seemed magical. With childish imagination, she'd dreamed it would complete the missing piece of herself.

The night he brought it home, she'd overheard her mother snapping at her father like a rabid terrier. "Sentimental fool. We should be Americanizing the girl, not encouraging *this*. She still has that sing-song accent after all these years. Why, Laura told me she doesn't even tell her friends they're sisters."

She'd been sure she'd never see the robe again. But the next morning, the wrapped package sat on her bed. Her father strong-armed his wife like he did the buyers of the cars he sold. It'd only made her mother hate her more.

Melissa loosened the sash and lifted the silk away from her skin, the air too close, her father's ghostly breath raising the hairs on her scalp. She crossed the room and slipped the window open a few inches. He'd died the summer after Laura's murder, his already broken heart torn further apart by a massive heart attack.

He'd abandoned her like everyone else. Leaving her to be the scapegoat for her sister's death.

Enough. She retied the sash, gathered up her belongings, and dragged her suitcase into the guest bedroom. She'd done no more than peek inside the second bedroom in her hunt for clues and thought it plain and utilitarian. She flicked the light switch on. The décor was stark, completely at odds with Bella's outlandish personality and the flamboyant red-orange color scheme and wild array of patterns and textures in the living room and in her bedroom.

The small guest room had been designed for a different woman—not for someone named Bella. Melissa stepped inside and took a deep breath. The air held the faint scent of eucalyptus. The furniture was minimal—a black platform bed covered in white linens, the walls softly painted a rich slate gray. She opened the closet door and peeked inside. Elegant suits and dresses hung grouped by color—clothes of a wealthy, sophisticated business woman. A yoga mat stood rolled up in a corner. It was an oasis of peace and quiet, an inner space where someone could curl up with a book of poetry, meditate, or listen to music.

She rolled her shoulders, uneasy in the silence, and turned. Breathtaking poster-size photographs of sea, sand, and gentle hills hung in a perfectly aligned row on the wall opposite the bed. Something vaguely familiar about them tugged at her memory. She moved closer and examined each one.

One showed a lagoon, the water that sapphire blue found only in the Mediterranean. In another, she could make out small fishing boats moored in a harbor encircled by white houses. The largest photo showed sheer cliffs rising from the sea and what appeared to be seals playing in the water below. She stepped back and surveyed the pictures again. Recognition sent a shiver through her. Of course, these photos were the same place where Ari painted his reclining nudes. In fact, she recognized the undulating hills that formed the background of the painting he'd been doing of her. She slapped her hand over her mouth. It was true then what he said.

Aristides Stavros was Bella's brother.

She glanced around. There'd been a photo of a

boy—that's right, in the living room. She padded through the doorway, trailed by the cat, and picked up the picture. She ran a finger down the straight nose, studied the strong cheek bones, and the arch of the unscarred lips. Black eyes, sparkling with joy instead of bitterness, peeked out from under a mass of black curls. He'd been beautiful once.

She wandered back into the guest room, set the picture on the nightstand, and sat down on the bed. Pussyballs jumped up and curled beside her. "It has to be him," she whispered, praying she was right. And if he told her the truth about that, what other truths had he told her? Was her life truly in danger? She scanned the shadowy room and shivered.

She gathered the robe more closely around her shoulders, the satin gliding along her skin, with a lightness that recalled Ari's fine tipped brush trailing over her. Her whole body tingled at the memory of the way he'd worshiped her with such gentleness. Even in their mad frenzy on the street, he'd been gentle. She shut her eyes and pushed the image away. He was well-practiced. He didn't need her. He could have any woman. He could have Jana.

A well-thumbed copy of the *Collected Poems of George Seferis* lay on the nightstand. She tried to imagine the outlandish woman she knew as Bella reading poetry. Orange Man and the other tattoo artists would never believe it if she told them. She looked again around the bedroom. Red-haired Bella with her tattoos and gypsy outfits, who'd sat cleaning her tools, and answering her questions, was a complete lie. Sirena Patras was a sophisticated, well-educated woman with impeccable taste, money to spend, and a brother who loved her. The only truth left was that she was missing.

The book drew her. She skimmed the back cover note surprised to find Seferis was a Noble Laureate, picked it up, and fingered the mosaic on the cover. She let the book fall open in her lap like a paper fortune. She looked down. The poet's words rose like a Delphic prophecy.

And a soul
if it is to know itself
must look
into its own soul
The stranger and the enemy: we have seen him in
the mirror

She shut the book with a bang and rolled over. She would search the apartment again tomorrow.

Chapter 28

It was too tempting. Melissa had opened the window just enough to allow him to get inside without forcing the sash or breaking the glass. Silently, he raised the window, stepped over the windowsill, and slipped into the guest room.

A faint glow cast by the lights of the city bounced off the cloud cover overhead and filled the edges of the room. His Nereida lay bathed in the soft light, Bella's cat curled protectively against her back. She'd fallen asleep reading Seferis. He slipped alongside and carefully removed the book from her hands.

The cat rose and stretched in welcome. He stroked its head for a moment, and then lifted the purring creature to the floor and claimed its place on the edge of the bed. "Sorry, Puss," he whispered. "She belongs to me."

He sat still, content to listen to her breathe, afraid to wake her. She was a skittish thing, his little bee. Ready to flee. Not that he blamed her.

Melissa gave a faint lady-like snort and then flailed out an arm. Her eyelids flickered, and he wondered if she was dreaming of him. He could not resist. He ran the pad of his finger lightly over her jaw, up her chin, and across her lips.

Her eyes half-opened. "I dreamed you would come." Her voice soft, sibilant, full of longing, swept over him.

All thought of talk fled as his cock rose, demanding this woman. He had to be inside her. Now. He bent over and lowered his mouth to hers. She inhaled against his lips and then pressed back. She tasted like heaven. He prodded with his tongue until her lips opened, and he could slide his tongue inside. Her arms came up around him, pulling him down. Without removing his mouth, he unbuttoned his shirt and slipped it off, divested himself of his jeans and lifting the covers, climbed in beside her. The silk of the robe pressed against him. Her warmth evaporated the evening chill from his skin.

She moved against him, the length of satin tangling between them, separating them. He untied the sash, opened the robe wide, and rucked up the silk until it was spread out around her like wings. One hand found her delectable breasts. The other searched lower. He slipped a finger between her thighs and found her tender little nub. Slowly, he swirled his finger round and round, over and over, in rhythm with the beating of her heart.

She gasped and pulled him closer, her body heating until he felt like he'd ignited a furnace. Her legs opened, allowing his fingers to find her opening. He inserted one finger and pushed it in and out, deeper and deeper. He wanted her begging, begging for him—her dream lover.

He brushed his lips down her neck, over her breast, nipping at her nipple. Then he slid lower, spread her legs and kissed her deeply, worshipped her body with his mouth, listening to her intake of breath, feeling her back arch up from the bed as he ran his tongue between her legs over her inner core again and again. He thought of his paint brush and imagined he was painting her glorious little cunt with his softest brush as he licked and sucked the salty, rich taste of her, running his hands up and down her thighs and calves. Feeling her become wet and ready for him.

He edged closer and angled for a deeper taste. He worshiped her as a goddess risen from the sea. He inserted a finger into her vagina, then another, and felt the ripples beginning. She was on the edge of her climax. With his other hand, he gently squeezed the tender nub, and she came in waves, her back arching off the bed, her release a long sigh. It made him feel like the most powerful man on earth.

Her hands came down and grasped his shoulders, pulled at him until he slid up, his cock hard and insistent against the inner flesh of her thighs, needing to feel all of her. To be inside. But she had to want him, rough, hard, and ugly, not some dream man. He gritted his teeth and waited as her small fingers ran over his face, rested on the bridge of his nose, traced the scar across his lip. There was a slight slackening of tension in the hand grasping his shoulder. She'd tell him to leave now. "Ari?"

"Yes." It came out as a growl.

"Bella—Sirena—really is your sister."

"Yes." His heart pounded, his cock throbbed. It took all his strength to hold still and not drive into her, to not profess the love that was blossoming inside his chest for this brave woman who had woken up to a sexual orgy with a monster and had not screamed. "I have my secrets to keep, but I would never lie to you, Melissa." He ran his hand through her hair. He'd always thought he'd loved women with long hair. But her short crop felt like velvet under his fingers, the bones of her skull fine and elegant. She reminded him of one of the monk seals he was trying so hard to save.

There was a startled moment. Her mouth closed and then opened. "We all have secrets." She ran her hand between them and found his hard cock, took it in her hand and ran her thumb over the tip. "You like that?" She ran her hand up and down.

He groaned.

One side of her mouth winked up. "I think you do."

"Please."

"Come inside me. I want you."

It was all he needed to hear. All blood drained from his brain and pooled in his groin. Later. They would talk later. Right now he wanted to be ridden to heaven.

"Oh, little bee. Fly for me." He flipped her over so she sat atop him. Somehow he retained enough sense to reach down and fumble in his jeans pocket for a condom. He handed it to her and nearly came as she tentatively slipped it over his hot rod.

"Come. Take me." He positioned himself beneath her entrance, sliding back and forth against her clitoris. He watched the tension in her face slacken as her head fell back and her lithe body arched over him. Her hips moved rhythmically up and down, driving him deeper and deeper inside her with each long smooth stroke.

He wasn't having sex. He was giving her everything he was—his whole being. His entire world reduced to this moment inside this woman who fit him so right. Filling the emptiness he had thought a permanent part of him. She wrapped her legs around his hips and tipped forward and back. With each suck and pull, the words he'd never said to any woman pounded louder and louder. As his heart beat faster. As his blood rose. The words echoed inside his head like waves against the shoreline. *"S'agapo. S'agapo.* I love you, *melissaki mou."* He drove in again and again, harder and harder, delaying his own release until she convulsed above him. Then he drove in one more time, and they came together in one blinding explosion.

****

Melissa's body rippled with pleasure. Behind her eyelids, stars fell. The unmistakable scent of her lover filled her nostrils. She opened her eyes. Ari lay half atop her, skin to skin. His head rested on her shoulder, his hand cupped her breast. It was like she had summoned a Greek god from Olympus and captured him. She smoothed back the long black hair covering his battered face and trailed a finger down the scar. Her imperfect god.

From the side, she could see the lost beauty hinted in the photo. The strong chin, dark with stubble, the elegant nostrils, the generous mouth with the slightly bowed upper lip, the heavy lashed, deep-set eyes with the tiny wrinkles at the corners from squinting in the Aegean sun. She wanted to look at him forever.

She had once wandered through the Ancient Greece section of the Metropolitan Museum. This man would blend right in with those classical sculptures. Her hand swept down over the hard biceps and massive shoulders, over the muscles and tendons corded with thick veins and covered with curly black hair, cradling her so gently. Even his fingers had hair across the knuckles. He was truly a beast. Her hairy beast.

Ari shifted slightly, capturing her roving hand. His

long, powerful fingers wrapped around hers. She did not doubt they were capable of breaking bones, but they were also capable of the lightest of touches. She turned her head and looked at him. Ari's eyes were open, a faint smile curving his lips. A well-satisfied man. A good time to root out his secrets, learn who he really was before she totally lost her heart.

She tipped her head at the photos. "The pictures. On the wall. You and your sister are from there—that paradise?"

"Paradise? A city girl like you would hate it." He turned her hand over and kissed her palm, ran his tongue across her wrist. "Mmm."

He was trying to distract her. She wiggled her hand free and looked into his dark eyes. "Why would I hate it?"

He rolled onto his back and stared up at the ceiling. "Sirena and I grew up there. Eudokia. It's an island in the Northern Sporades, one of the many small islands off the coast of mainland Greece. Our family has lived there for generations. There's only our villa and one small village. No electric. No running water. No ferry. Just a handful of fishing boats. We raise all our own food the way it's been done for centuries. There's a small monastery with one monk. Very isolated. A place of contentment and contemplation and for you, boredom." He sucked her index finger. "It's not even on Google maps."

She leaned up on her elbow and played with the hair on his chest. "Obviously you and your sister love the place. This room is a shrine to it. Your paintings immortalize it."

He trailed his hand down her back. "I paint to

protect it. The shore is craggy with unscalable cliffs and sea caves half under water. Monk seals live there, some of the few left in the Mediterranean. There is one small inlet where you can bring in a boat if you know where the rocks are. In ancient times, my ancestors could defend the island from invasion with walls and rocks, spears and arrows. Today you need a cohort of lawyers and paid guards to keep out the yachts and the thrill seekers and to handle the tax collectors." He folded one arm under his head and rested the other on her stomach. "For that you need money. My father ran a quarry on a neighboring island to pay the upkeep until he died. I sell paintings."

"You're lucky your paintings sell for so much money, then."

He shifted slightly. "Not luck. Strategic planning. My father expected me to run the quarry. But I was an artistic child, a dreamer. I hated the dirt and dust of the quarry. At sixteen I was all rebellion and raging hormones. I would have left and never looked back if he had enforced his will. Instead, he challenged me. Said if I could earn as much from a single painting as he did in a week from the quarry, he would sell the quarry and set me up as an artist.

"But no one, no matter how grand, would buy my pretty landscapes. I roamed all over Europe looking for buyers. It was Sirena who suggested adding the women. With a nude, the price quadruples." He closed his eyes. "Rich men like to hang them in their bedrooms or bathrooms—for the decor."

Melissa let out a slow hiss. "That sounds so mercenary. I thought—well, I am no expert on art—but I think your paintings are far more than room decorations. These photos are lovely, but your paintings capture the soul of the island. The nudes are the goddesses protecting it."

"Sometimes."

She picked up his mutilated left hand and ran a finger over the stumps. "And you do it all with only three fingers. How did you lose the others?"

He jerked his hand out of hers.

"Is that one of your secrets?"

He held his hands up above him and stared at them. "No. Merely humiliating." He dropped his hands. "It is not a pleasant story, not one I want shared—I was a Greco-Roman wrestler. Do you know how we fight?"

Melissa could feel the pain radiating off him. She snuggled closer, twisted her fingers in the thick hair on his chest. "No. I have no interest in sports."

He laughed. "Except bed sports." He cupped her head and drew her lips toward him, licked them, kissed her gently. He slid his hands down and cupped her waist. "In Greco-Roman wrestling you clasp your opponent by the waist or shoulders and try to lift him up and toss him to the mat. I'd worked in a quarry from the time I was fourteen. I had developed tremendous upper body strength and strong legs hefting marble slabs, and a practical knowledge of physics from dodging my miscalculations."

He threw his head back on the pillow. He'd been so full of himself back then. Finally, he had found a way to please his father. The day he'd made the Olympics was the only time Papa ever smiled at him. "You know how when everything seems golden and suddenly it is ripped open, revealing the muck inside? That's what happened. I thought I was top banana. My painting career was taking off. I'd made Greece's national wrestling team, performed at the 2004 Olympics, did decently, came in fifteenth in the world. But I was wild. On my own in Athens and out from under Papa's thumb for the first time. I ran into a bunch of former schoolmates and decided to show them a good time. We're in a bar and some bruiser of a kid a head taller challenges me. My so-called buddies are urging me on. 'Give him a throw, Olympian,' they shouted, pushing me forward into him. So I did. I wrapped my hands around his waist, picked him up and threw him. In the ring, on the mat, he would have sat up, scowling at me, but alive. In the bar, he hit his head on a marble table top as he came down. Broke his neck. I can still see him lying there, his face frozen in surprise. He was sixteen."

He sat up, drew up his legs, and wrapped his hands around his knees. "I wanted to kill myself afterward. I went back to my room, got a fish knife, and intended to cut my wrists. But then I thought that was too cowardly. So I drank myself into a stupor and started cutting off my fingers so I could never paint or wrestle again. I couldn't even accomplish that. Passed out after the second one. My landlady found me and got me to a hospital."

"Tuccio said you went to prison."

"That's no secret. The boy's parents took me to court. Judge said someone with my level of skill and training—an Olympic star—should have known better. I'd embarrassed the nation. Despite my father's expensive lawyers, he convicted me of manslaughter. I was sentenced to ten years in prison." His head fell forward. "I'm a killer, little bee. I killed a man—a boy."

She pushed his hair out of his face. "But 2004—

that was over twelve years ago. You must have been just a boy, too."

"Eighteen. Old enough." He closed his eyes. "And stupid. I thought prison would be like staying in a hotel. A place where I could continue to paint, read, contemplate. Instead, I was placed in Korydallos with the hardcore murderers, drug dealers, white slavers. Six brutes in cells meant for four. I figured out how to survive. I'm not proud of what I did there. Joined a gang for protection, and in return, they owned me. I did their dirty work for six years until I was paroled. Horrible things—" He broke off, sat up and ran his hands through his hair. "So now you know who you've been sleeping with, little bee. A murdering monster."

Melissa picked up his mutilated hand and held it against her cheek. She lowered her mouth to his hand. "It was a terrible tragedy, and you've survived. This is not the hand of a remorseless killer. It is the hand of an artist, a lover." She kissed each stump. "The past is the past. I love you, Ari Stavros. The man you are now." She flicked his hand over and nuzzled his palm, licked along the lifeline, over his pulse and stopped.

"What's the matter?"

"That tattoo. I've seen it before."

Ari looked down at the little blue mark staining his inner wrist like a splatter of paint gone wrong, suddenly chilled.

She snatched her robe from the bed and held it up in front her like a shield, her face white as a ghost's. "Who are you?"

The pure hate in her eyes cut into him. It had been all words then, her profession of love, just the ebbing endorphins of the love making. He spat the raw fact at her. "The man who just had sex with you." He slid across the bed toward her. "Fucking good sex."

She backed up against the nightstand and worked her way around it. "My sister—Laura—what happened to her? What did you do to her?"

She was going to bolt. He slid a little further over toward her, confident he could block her if she tried to run. "I have no idea who or what you are talking about."

"You must. *That tattoo.*" She pointed at it, the blue circle with the intricate design inside. "My sister—I saw it the day she went missing."

His muscles tensed. Not another girl lost. He'd buried himself in his art. Hidden away on his island. Abandoned his sister. Pretended the evil he knew existed didn't matter because he would never do violence to another again. "Missing?"

She was backing away, a look of horror on her face. "Murderer. You made all that sad story up just to get me to—to think I loved you."

He shot out his hand and seized her by the wrist. "I didn't murder anyone but Yannis." She tugged hard like a seal caught in a net. The delicate bones twisted beneath his fingers—so easily broken.

He let go and fell back on the bed, ran his hand over the empty sheets still warm from her body. She was right to be afraid of him.

It was only later, after the bed had grown cold, the cat had disappeared out the open window, and the police cars drew up in front the building, sirens wailing, that he remembered what he'd come to tell her.

Chapter 29

Melissa sat huddled on Zeya's sofa, a porcelain teacup balanced in one shaking hand, the other holding her robe closed.

The old lady came in and shut the door behind her. "The police left. No one in the apartment."

Maybe she dreamed the whole thing. She didn't remember how she'd gotten out of Bella's place and down three flights of stairs with her suitcase. All she remembered was the panic and the fear—the blue tattoo mocking her. Her skin still tingled from Ari's touches. His scent lingered on her skin. She'd let him seduce her. She'd excused his brutal murder of a stranger. She'd told him she loved him. Laura's murderer.

Zeya was looking at her through narrowed eyes. "I don't like disturbances in my building." She pinched the sleeve of the robe. "Caused by a lying freeloader." She settled down on the sofa next to her and took the rattling tea cup from her hands. She set it gently on the glass coffee table. "I enjoy your visits. You seem a sensible girl to me. Good to the cat. So I do as you asked. I didn't let the police know you were here. Now I want to know the truth. There was no prowler, was there?"

Melissa twisted the silk tie of the robe around her wrist. Her father had always said lies never solved anything. But she couldn't seem to help herself. Ever since her sister was murdered, her whole life had been a lie. She looked into Zeya's kind old face. The best lies held a kernel of truth. "No. It was Bella's brother."

"Ari"—the old woman sat back—"that young man so nice—he comes to find his sister. He helped me remove the graffiti from the front of the building—he attacked you? I don't understand."

"He's—not what you think—he's a murderer."

Zeya clicked her tongue. "I think you make much out of little."

"He has this tattoo on his wrist. I saw it. It—it has a bad meaning. It's a gang symbol."

The woman touched the dotted swirls on her cheek. "Tattoos stay forever. Meanings change. Maybe he's changed?"

Changed? Nothing could change the fact that Laura was dead. Her beautiful sister. Dead. The whole world should have stopped and cried on the day of Laura's funeral. At the very least, it should have rained. Instead, the sun shone, and children played in the park. Inside the airless chapel, her eyes had refused to adjust to the dark, refused to see the cold still doll that had been her sister lying in the silky white festoons of the elaborate coffin her parents had chosen for her—death's virgin bride. She twisted the sash tighter around her wrist. All she had to do was tell the truth, and her sister would still be alive. She'd betrayed Laura once. She would not do it again.

She gave herself a shake. Tuccio had warned her to not trust Ari. She'd been as entranced by Bella's brother as Zeya. Ari Stavros had weaseled his way beneath her skin, brought her body alive with his trickster fingers, made her trust him with his sad story.

He would not do it again.

She touched Zeya's aged hand. "You must stay away from him and his associates. Don't let any strangers into the apartment building. I'm afraid he'll come back."

Zeya straightened and patted her baseball bat. "No worries. Zeya Aung knows how to deal with bad men." She rose and picked up the tea cup. "But you are not welcome here anymore. The landlord will be very angry at me for this trouble." Her face softened. "I will feed the cat for Bella. Where you go, Melissa?"

Melissa leaned her head against the sofa back. It was time to accept Tuccio's offer. "I have a friend I can call. He'll pick me up."***

****

The limo was as airless as the last time, the air heavy with Tuccio's over-expensive cologne. Melissa tucked her arms in tighter against her body. She hadn't expected Tuccio to come himself. His hand rested familiarly on her thigh. "So what did you learn that sent you scurrying to me?"

"Stavros has a tattoo."

His fingernails pressed into her thigh. "You called me because the man has a tattoo. I thought, perhaps, you'd found out where he's stashed Bella."

She pulled her leg away. "It was—familiar. The man who killed my sister had the same one." Her heart thumped so loudly she was sure Tuccio could hear it. She glanced over at him. "It connects Stavros to my sister's murder. Don't you see? You can have him brought in for questioning. Prevent him from killing another woman."

Tuccio's mouth twisted. "It is not enough. What

about Bella? He tell you anything about her whereabouts? What he plans."

"She's his sister."

"Is she?"

"He said so, and I—I—believe him. There was a photo."

"So gullible, darling. It's what I love about you." He signaled the car to stop. The chauffeur got out. "We need to know what he is planning. Where he thinks his 'sister' is. You will have to go back to him and find out." He pulled her closer and whispered in her ear. "Do what you must to get back into his good graces." His nostrils flared. "That shouldn't prove too hard. You must have gotten very close tonight. You reek of him."

"But I thought you wanted—" There was a thud as the chauffeur hefted her suitcase from the trunk. Tuccio seized her nipples, still tender from Ari ministrations, and squeezed hard. She winced and put a hand on his chest to push him away. "Stop it. This is sexual harassment. I'll report you to your superiors."

"My superiors?" He threw back his head and laughed. "A girl who knowingly beds a murderer? Look." He whipped out his cell phone and showed her a picture of her and Ari in bed at Bella's, taken not twenty minutes earlier.

She slapped her hands over her gaping mouth. "How?"

"Just doing my job." A grin spread across his face. "For now, *I* am your superior, my darling Melissa." He snapped the phone closed. "Only I can prevent you being charged as accessory to murder. As long as you do what I say, you are safe." He pressed his Adonis lips against hers. "Welcome to *my* world. Soon Aristides

Stavros will be gone, and you'll be mine. Now go. Find out what he plans to do about Bella. Any way you can."

The chauffeur opened the door, and she edged out onto the pavement. Behind her, the car door slammed shut with a resounding click, and the limo zoomed off. She had done it again, let herself be fooled by a badge and the authority of government. Tuccio, despite his elegant appearance and gentlemanly bearing, was as dangerous as Ari. She was trapped. She had no one left to trust.

She stood for a moment staring blindly down the street. Cars whizzed by in a steady stream of lights, carrying people home to their families, home to their lovers. She squeezed the handle of the beat-up suitcase containing all her worldly belongings—thrift shop clothes, notes for a dissertation she'd likely never finish, a dead sister's angora sweater slightly pulled, and sketches of a tattoo that tore her heart open. She couldn't face the suffering anonymity of a shelter tonight. She looked up at the building in front of her. Heaven help her, Tuccio'd dropped her back at Jana's. Shifting the weight of her knapsack to her other shoulder, she crossed the street, inserted the key Jana gifted her into the lock, and trudged up the stairs, words of apology thick as cement on her tongue.

Chapter 30

Ari stood in the shadow of Sirena's building, clutching her cat. On the corner, Tuccio's chauffer loaded Melissa's red suitcase into the trunk of the limo. The little sea witch. From his bed to that slime's. She hadn't believed a word he'd said. How could she think he'd killed her sister? Not that he blamed her. No woman believed a man with a face like his—an admitted murderer.

He dropped the cat to the ground. It crouched for a moment, its green eyes boring into him, and then jumped up onto Zeya's windowsill. The old woman opened the window, crooned to it in her lilting tongue, and the cat scurried in. Zeya shook a finger at him and slammed the window down. Another woman angry at him.

He pulled out the papers wadded up in his pocket and searched for the one in Melissa's name—the one that gifted her the unsold paintings at the gallery. He'd meant to share it with her tonight, hoped she'd laugh, be a bit shocked at his generosity, and pleased. She admired his work, she'd said. And the money she'd get from selling them would support her for years.

He clenched it tighter in his hand. He could still rescind it. But that would mean another trip to the lawyer. He folded it back up and stuffed it in with the rest. There was no one else to give them to. Let her have them. It didn't matter who benefitted from his work. Not once he was dead.

A police car cruised by, going slow, looking for Melissa's prowler. He flipped up the collar of his jacket, pulled his floppy hat lower, and hunched his shoulders like a homeless man searching for a place to bed down for the night. He headed toward the corner. T-Crew would be waiting for him. He'd promised them a surprise.

Tonight he would lay out the plans for a graffiti tour business and studio, show them the store front he'd bought for them with the fully outfitted art studio, and the furnished apartments above for them to live in. All he needed was their signatures. It was a grand scheme that had Walter Hanlin shaking his head as he signed the papers. "From homeless to businessmen overnight?" he'd laughed. "You're one crazy Greek, Mr. Stavros. One crazy Greek."

He spotted a penny and picked up it up, fingered the coin sticky with the sooty dirt that clung to everything in this god awful city and then tossed it down. It rolled along the pavement and disappeared down the drain. Was that what he wanted? To throw away the love he'd found in Melissa's arms? Let Tuccio have her without a fight?

Tuccio.

He pushed up his sleeve and stared at the tattoo. Her sister had been murdered by someone wearing this tattoo?

"*Sto diávolo,*" he whispered under his breath. He needed to know more about Melissa's sister. But first, he would deliver his surprise to T-Crew.

****

Four hours and fifty tags later, Ari opened the first apartment door in the building he'd bought. The chemical reek of fresh paint and varnish told him the work he'd ordered done had been completed.

"Welcome to T-Crew's new home base," he said, smiling. He waited for the cheers. Five blank faces frowned back at him. He glanced from face to face. They didn't believe him either. "Look. It's yours. The whole building. Free."

"Nothing's free," Fur Tree said, crossing his arms over his chest.

El Toro moved forward and ran his hand along the glistening kitchen countertop, opened a freshly painted cupboard door. "Explain free."

"The whole building belongs to T-Crew." Ari pulled out the papers. "Taxes and maintenance paid by the T-Crew Foundation I've created for as long as any of you are living in it. There are three two-bedroom apartments like this one and three one-bedrooms, more than enough for each of you to have your own if you wish. The empty ones can be given to people you know who need a place to stay or you can rent them out. That's up to you to decide."

El Toro's eyes widened. "You trust us—to manage a whole building?"

"And the tour business. You can run it out of the commercial space on the first floor. The foundation will pay for it to be spruced up, and for advertising."

"Tours." Fur Tree tapped his foot. "We don't know nothing about running a business."

Ari glanced at each one. "But you do. T-Crew is a business. You purchase supplies, advertise, work incredibly hard, and give tours to strange Greek guys."

He winked at Hanger. "You just aren't getting paid for it."

Neto slouched near the door, a sour look about his mouth. "Just another do-gooder. Think to buy us." He turned to El Toro and waved his arm at the room. "We do this. Take this. Start a legit business. We have our names in the paper. Big man there will get all the credit, and what we gonna do when the police show up—and the social workers"—he glanced at Hanger—"wanting to know what a bunch of losers is doing with a fine building on the main drag in Williamsburg?"

Ari put up a staying hand. "I will be gone in a day or two. There will be no publicity except what you decide on. Your names are not attached to the foundation in any way. All legalities will go through the law office of Walter Hanlin, the man who pulled Fur Tree out of the Tombs. The owner is officially registered as a foreign corporation. As far as I am concerned you can abandon the place—let the building turn into a neighborhood eyesore." He shrugged. "Or rent out the apartments for thousands a month and go live in the Bahamas. It's up to you."

Hanger tipped back his hat. "You're leaving?"

Ari avoided the kid's eyes. "That's the plan."

The boy's mouth twisted. "When?"

"I'm waiting for an answer to a message. Then *pah*! I'm out of here. Meanwhile"—he shoved his hands into his pockets and half-turned to the door—"that girl Melissa, the tattoo junkie. I need your help to find out everything about her."

El Toro closed the cupboard door with a bang. "Why, Ugly Man?"

"She needs some convincing."

El Toro shrugged. "Waste of time."

"It's all right," Hanger said with a quick look at his brother. "We'll help find her for you."

El Toro sketched an imaginary tag on the counter top. "So where do we start, Ugly Man?"

Ari looked at the ragged members of T-Crew and grinned. "First you sign these papers for my lawyer—your names will be kept absolutely confidential—so he can represent you legally. Next stop—the library."

Fur Tree wrapped his arms around his head, elbows askew. "No way you getting me inside a library with all those stinky books."

"Not going to be looking at books. We're going to search the newspaper archives. I want to know exactly what happened to a girl named Laura Dermont."

Chapter 31

Melissa inserted the key in the lock and pushed the door open as quietly as she could. Jana lay sprawled on the sofa, her head thrown back, her long bare legs hanging over the end. Light from the street filtered in through the shades, highlighting the generous curves of her body. Half-naked, in thong and bandeau, she looked like one of Ari's paintings.

Melissa swallowed the bile rising in her throat. She'd been a fool to turn on Jana. Their ties were tenuous. A dead sister. A false police report. Yet, Jana had taken her in and cared for her in her own unique way after Colin did his dirty. She turned and headed for her bedroom. They'd talk in the morning.

She glanced at the clock on the wall. Drat, it *was* morning. But she'd forgotten Jana's careless housekeeping, and in the dark, stumbled over a stack of dirty dishes sitting in the doorway. China crashed. Silverware clattered.

Jana jerked up. She rubbed her eyes. "Melissa?" She swung her feet to the floor. "Woo hoo. You're back."

Melissa let go of her suitcase and dropped her portfolio. "Please forgive me. I—I need you."

Jana stepped over the dirty dishes and cups on the floor and gathered her into her arms. "I've been waiting for you to say that for ages, Little Miss Independent."

She put her hand on the small of her back. "Now come. Let me make you some breakfast." She pushed her toward the kitchen. "Then you can tell Auntie Jana all about what happened."

"What's to tell?" Melissa slumped down on the kitchen stool and rested her head in her arms on the counter. "My life's a mess."

"That's nothing new." Jana rifled a can of cola from the fridge, zipped off the tab, and slapped it on the counter. "Here, get some caffeine and sugar in you fast, you look half-dead."

"I wish I were dead." Melissa took a sip. The carbonated liquid fizzed against her tongue, sickly sweet. She swallowed. It burned all the way down her throat.

Jana ripped open a package of instant oatmeal, searched for a clean bowl, and shook in the flakes. She splashed water on top, shoved it into the microwave, and set the timer going. "That bad, huh?"

Melissa coughed to clear her throat. "I'm in love."

"Well, we knew that. The question was with whom—Mr. Monster or Mr. Prince Charming. They're both wealthy as sin." She glanced at Melissa's outfit of black leggings and faded sweatshirt and pursed her lips. "Able to keep you in a style you are unaccustomed to." She dug in the dirty dishes in the sink and came up with a spoon caked with dried yogurt. She turned on the tap and rinsed it, picking at the dried-on goop with a fingernail. The microwave dinged. She put the spoon on the counter and turned to get the hot oatmeal. "After your outburst, I'm pretty sure it's the monster. So spill it."

"He's a murderer, Jana. He murdered Laura."

"Laura?" The bowl of oatmeal slipped from Jana's hands and splashed to the floor. Hot cereal splattered across her left foot. She hopped up and down, cursing.

"Heavens!" Melissa leaped from her seat and rushed to help. She ran cold water on a dish towel and pressed it against the burns. Already the skin of Jana's instep was turning red.

"Aww." Jana pounded a fist on the countertop as Melissa reapplied the towel. "Stupid. Stupid. Stupid. I tell you"—she caught her breath—"I can't cook or clean worth bananas."

"You need a live-in maid."

"No, I need you. Miss Neatnik."

Melissa re-wet the towel under the faucet. "To tease."

"That's me, the Big Tease. Damn that hurts." She rested a hand on Melissa's head. "Look, I've truly missed you, sweetheart. It's been dead lonely here."

"Don't be silly. I haven't been gone"—she glanced at the clock again—"for more than eight hours." She bent down over Jana's foot, fighting back tears. Eight hours in which to lose her soul to one bastard and become the slave of another.

The reality of it all struck her. Tuccio had a photo of her with Ari. Prince Charming set her up. He must have a webcam planted in Bella's place. What had Ari called him? Poison. The Greek might be a murderer, but he was a better judge of men than she was. She might as well have "Idiot" tattooed across her forehead.

Jana sniffed. "The place was so empty when I got home. Just some big old spider crawling on your pillow."

"Ha. Would you have preferred I'd left a gigolo or

two in my bed instead? "

Jana blinked. "Now who's the tease? Anyway, you weren't here to splat the spider—don't give me that inscrutable stare—you were pretty angry—said you would go to a shelter rather than stay with me. Mel—I almost went back to visit your artist—make you pay for not believing me. I might have got him into bed this time."

"No. Don't even think of going near him. He's Laura's murderer."

Jana jerked the wet cloth from Melissa's hand and sat there holding it. Water dripped onto the floor. "Laura? I don't understand. I thought—how do you figure that?"

"He has a tattoo like the one on that guy who picked up Laura. Has to be the same man."

"But you told those detectives you didn't see the driver."

Melissa shook her head. "I didn't. I just glimpsed the bastard's arm hanging out of the car window."

"I don't remember you mentioning a tattoo at the time."

"I was a twelve-year-old with her head in a book. What'd I know about tattoos? The only tattoo I'd seen was on Johnny Depp in *Pirates of the Caribbean*. This one was really small—like a round circle and on the inside of his wrist. Thought it was a stain or something. I didn't know what it meant until later." Much later. After she'd buried herself in researching tattooing practices in preparation for her dissertation.

"Well, you sure mentioned plenty of other things. Like my being there when I wasn't." Jana put a hand on Melissa's. "You shouldn't have done that."

"There's lots of things I shouldn't have done." Melissa dropped her eyes and concentrated on examining Jana's foot. "I don't think the burn is too bad. You'll have trouble wearing shoes for a while. But if we keep cold water on it, I think you can skip the hospital."

Jana held her foot out and turned it left and right. She winced. "Yeah. Oh, speaking of the hospital. Your friend—Dumpy Daniela. She was hit by a car."

"Daniela?" Melissa jumped up. "How is she?"

"No idea. It was on the six o'clock news."

"On the news? It must have been bad. What hospital?"

"Didn't say. Happened near the bridge."

Melissa dug her cell phone out of her sweatshirt pouch pocket and rang Daniela's number. With each ring, her heart beat faster. Iza and Gracine, the two women she'd been hiding—Daniela had promised to pick up them up and move them to the safe house yesterday. They'd be in a panic by now. Running out of food. And if Daniela were incapacitated for days or months—or died? Her poor children. It didn't bear thinking. When the call went to voice mail, she stood. "She's not answering. I have to go."

Jana's eyebrows went up so high they disappeared behind her bangs. "Go? Now? At six-thirty in the morning? You don't even know what hospital she's in."

Melissa shoved her cell back into her pocket. "There's something I have to do. I'll be back."

Jana's voice rose a pitch. "For Dumpy Daniela? What about my foot?"

"I said I'd be back." Melissa slammed the door closed behind her and took the stairs two at a time, mentally calculating how much food she could afford to buy with the cash left in her wallet.

She hit the street running and had to swerve to avoid bumping into a bag lady pulling a shopping cart. A group of young men with duffle bags hoisted over their shoulders and ball caps worn at varying angles surrounded her for a moment, and then swept past, in a parade of color and noise. She looked over her shoulder at their retreating backs. She knew them. The last two hadn't been dressed the same, but they had to be the same identical twins that had been hanging outside Ari's studio when she'd fled that day. Was it only four days ago? The day she let him paint her into ecstasy.

Heat shot through her, and she bit her lip hard. What was wrong with her? How could she have these feelings for the man who murdered her sister? She never wanted to see him again. She faced forward and ran right into a hard male body. She looked up.

"Twelve years ago I was in prison."

"What?" She put her hand on his sternum and pushed. It was like trying to move a very warm cement wall. He didn't budge. Beneath her palm, his heart thumped.

"Do the math, Melissa. Twelve years ago on the day your sister was murdered, November 8, 2004, I was in prison *in Greece*."

She glanced down at his wrist and stepped back. "But the tattoo. The man who took my sister—I saw it on him."

"I'm sure you did. But it wasn't me."

Melissa halted. It hadn't been him? He'd been in Greece. Something fluttered inside her, something that had been dormant for too long—it felt like hope. God, she wanted this man. She thought of Tuccio, and what he wanted her to do. She fought the urge to throw herself into his arms and cling to him. She forced herself to step back. She would not do Tuccio's dirty work for him. Better she stayed away from him.

He narrowed his eyes. "There are monsters in the world worse than me, little bee."

Yes, there were. She stared at the lopsided face with its crooked nose and puckered scar. The beloved face that belonged to the man she loved. She tucked her bag tighter under her arm. "I have to go."

He put a hand on her arm. "But we need to talk—about my sister and a man named Vernon Newell."

She backed away. "I really have to go." She looked down at his hand. "Now."

"I thought—" His hand fell away.

She whirled away and dodged blindly across the street, fighting back the tears, ignoring the gaping emptiness inside her. The aroma of hot dogs and popcorn wafted around her. Everyday smells on a day that was far from ordinary. She turned the corner and headed toward Lenny's—forced herself to concentrate. Food. She needed to buy food. The women she sheltered depended on her. She gave a quick glance over her shoulder. If Ari wasn't the man who murdered her sister, then who had?

****

By the time she burst into Lenny's Fast Eats, it was past seven and the place was crowded with commuters. Lenny made a little huff when he saw her and continued ranting to the customers waiting in line about the latest plan to upscale the street by tearing down his old storefront and erecting another high rise to house the

Wall Street brokers taking over the Brooklyn waterfront. Melissa grinned. Half the people waiting in line were exactly those high financiers living in thousands-of-dollars-a-month apartments. But that was Lenny, and they loved him for it. He wiped his hands on his aproned beer belly and turned to fill a line of plates with his famous cheese and bacon home fries.

Melissa swung the plastic bag of groceries behind her and inched carefully around the crowd waiting for service. Lenny didn't appreciate her bringing in food. It wasn't enough to pay top rate for his one-room apartment and put up with his wolfish leers when she waitressed. He thought she should get all the girls' food from him. But nobody could subsist forever on the greaseball's fat-soaked cooking.

She pushed open the door to the hallway and stepped back to let an over-endowed lady and her toddler pass out from the rest room. The woman waved her hand in warning. "Phew. Filthy in there. And the smell. Wouldn't have used it, except for this one. When they gotta go, they gotta go." She shoved the child ahead of her. Melissa nodded and waited for the woman to leave.

Lenny was no shakes at cleaning the johns, but it did stink worse than usual, like someone had a major case of gas or worse. Holding her breath, Melissa pushed open the door labeled Employees Only and fumbled her way in the dark to the rear door that led to the stairs. The reek in the stairwell was enough to make her eyes sting. It smelled foul with a hint of sweetness that reminded her of a dead dog she'd once come upon in the gutter on a hot day. Were the girls sick?

She dashed up the stairs and banged on the door.

"Gracine, Iza. Please open." She waited breathing through her mouth. Listening for the familiar sounds—the blaring TV that ran night and day, the girls squabbling. The dead quiet set her nerves on edge. She shifted the shopping bag to her other hand and banged again. The sounds echoed in the stairwell like the rumble of thunder. She hesitated and then reached out and turned the doorknob. It was unlocked—a very bad sign. She opened the door part way. "Iza? Gracine?" The smell if anything was stronger.

The blinds were drawn and the room dark except where bits of daylight found its way around the edges. She flicked the light switch on and then wished she hadn't. Iza and Gracine lay sprawled on the floor, nude, their stomachs split open, a slimy trail of guts spread across the carpet as if they'd been pulled out by the handful. Blood splattered across the TV screen and down the wall behind it.

They'd been dead a while. Flies buzzed, settling on the open eyes and crawling in and out of their red-lipsticked mouths. It was nothing like a horror scene in a movie. It was worse. Butchery—the girls tortured like Bella's poor cats.

She backed away, tripped, fell. Clasping her stomach, she retched and retched until it felt like her insides were torn out. Vomit spilled onto the carpet and mixed with the gore as she scrambled back toward the door. She crawled out on the landing and sat on the top step fumbling with her phone, trying to dial 911 between choking retches.

But before she could do so, the phone rang. Shocked, she dropped it and had to lean down to keep it from tumbling down the steps. She wiped her hand on her sweatshirt and thumbed it on.

Tuccio's suave voice murmured in her ear. "Now you don't have to worry about them or your friend Daniela anymore, little doll. You can focus on your work for me. Go talk to your lover boy and find out where Bella is before it's too late for you, too." Sirens sounded from the street outside. "Right on time. The police have arrived. And I know you don't want to talk to them about your private little enterprise running hookers. I suggest you leave by the back door. Now." The phone went dark.

She stared at the screen. Running hookers? Melissa glanced back at the apartment. More like ruining lives. Death followed her like a shadow. There was nothing she could do for those poor girls. But she refused to be Tuccio's puppet. He was the real monster in her life.

She stood and grasping the railing with shaking hands, stumbled down the stairs and pushed out the back emergency exit, Ari's warning sounding in her ears. A quick glance around showed the way clear, and she took off running. Running to the man she loved.

Chapter 32

Ari folded the last of his shirts and laid it inside the suitcase. He looked around the empty studio. Nothing of his was left. He'd given his art materials and climbing gear to El Toro, his sketches to his lawyer and tossed the spray-paint-stained T-shirts and jeans in the trash. The only thing he hadn't done was straighten things out with Melissa. But it was too late now. She didn't trust him. He'd seen the panic in her eyes when she'd fled from him. At least she had gone back to the Firth woman's place and not off with Tuccio.

Better she was far away from him anyway when Vernon came for him. He'd sent her a letter informing her where to collect her paintings—and told T-Crew to keep a close eye on her.

He checked the text message on his phone. He had an hour to go before Vernon's men would pick him up. He shut the suitcase and stood it on the floor at the top of the stairs. In all likelihood, he'd not be coming back for it. Not that it mattered. Shirts and underwear, jeans and socks—the superficial skin he wore to cover his true nakedness. He locked the bag. Useless clues for the police if he disappeared.

He shook out his suit jacket and slipped his arms in the confining sleeves, adjusted the fit over his shoulders where the fabric stretched tight, and wrapped and knotted the blue-green Kobo silk tie that shimmered like the water in the seal caves. He scooped the papers off the kitchen counter and made sure the deed and plane tickets were tucked in the interior breast pocket.

He was ready—a wealthy businessman off to make a simple financial exchange—one Greek island for one recalcitrant sister.

The knock on the door surprised him. They were half an hour early. He trotted down the steel stairway, relieved. The sooner he saw Bella released, the better. But when he opened the door, it was Melissa, head down, shoulders slumped, her sweatshirt covered in rusty red stains that could only be blood. His heart skipped a beat, and he put out a hand and drew her inside. "Are you hurt?"

She looked up at him, her face pale as unpolished marble. She glanced down at her sweatshirt. "Not mine."

He wanted to wrap his arms around her and never let go. He held back. She was in shock. He feared she would break if he touched her. "Whose?"

"Some friends. There isn't time to explain. I came to warn you. You're in danger. Tuccio, he's not what he appears. He told me he was an Immigration Agent trying to deport you, but I think he's something— worse."

He leaned on the door and shut it behind her. "Of course he's worse. He's a criminal involved in all kinds of nasty business. He's a partner with Vernon, the man holding my sister."

"He's not working for Immigration?"

Ari punched the door. "That what he told you? No."

She stared up into his face. "He wants to know

where Bella is."

It was all he could do to not take her in his arms and give her the comfort they both needed. He stifled his desire. "How do I know you are not still working for him?"

"I'm not." She bit her lip, shifted her weight from foot to foot, hunched even more. She looked like a lost sparrow blown in on the Sirocco winds. "Not anymore. When you found me here that first time—when you painted me—made love to me—Tuccio had given me the key to get in—in return for me putting a surveillance device on you." She put a shaking hand on his arm. "And there must be other devices planted." She glanced around the studio. "Tuccio has pictures of us in bed at Bella's. He called me about the dead girls, called the police. He's framing me. But it doesn't matter what happens to me. I don't want to know your plans. I just wanted you to know not to trust him."

Ari spit on the floor. "I know the man—well. We were in prison together." He gave her an icy look. "We wear the same tattoo. Did you ask him about it when you warmed his bed?"

"Same tattoo?" She stepped back until she stood flush against the door. "Bed? I've never—seen him in anything but a suit."

"Since when did that ever stop anyone from shagging?" He put his hands on either side of her and leaned in. "You lie for him. Spy for him. Surely you warm his bed?"

"No. I'm terrified of him."

He raised his eyebrows. "Tuccio would like that. He enjoys dominating his partners."

"Believe me, I would never. I—I love you."

He shifted closer until they were eye to eye. "How do I know you haven't just come from his bed to do exactly what he wants? I've seen you kissing him, your arms around his neck—all dreamy-eyed over that plastic-faced Adonis."

"At first—I was fooled by him." She touched Ari's scarred lip, warm and soft beneath her fingertip. "But not for long. All he wants is Bella for some reason. I was to seduce you—ferret out where she is."

He brushed his lips against her forehead, pressed his erection against her stomach. "Well, then you've done a fine job of it, little bee. My mind doesn't trust you, but my body doesn't care."

"No, don't. We don't have time—" She tried to wiggle away.

He pressed her more tightly to the door and kissed her. "There's always time. But first let's get rid of this." He pulled the sweatshirt over her head and dropped it to the floor. He wrapped his arms around her and unsnapped her bra. He ran his thumbs over her nipples. "Whose blood, Melissa? Tell me."

"Stop it. I can't think when you do that." She wrapped her hands around his. "Two girls—Iza and Gracine. They'd run away from their pimps. My friend and I were hiding them. It's something we do to help the girls afraid to come to the shelter. We call it Waystation. We help them cover up the brands and tattoos those men put on them, and then we get them to safe houses outside the city. But somehow, Tuccio found them." She craned her neck. "He may be watching us now with a hidden camera."

"If he is, then he's seeing you do exactly what he wants. Being a good little girl for your spymaster." She opened her mouth to protest, and he kissed her, sucking away her words, hushing her with his tongue. His left hand crept down lower until he cupped her mound. He pressed and rolled his hand through the thin fabric, reveling in her wetness, her readiness for him. He felt the moment she surrendered all thought. He pressed her to him. "But I don't care if you've come to uncover my secrets. You've already stolen my heart."

She held her fingers to his lips. "Stop talking. Show me."

"Have you heard a word I've said?"

"Mmm." She undid the top button of his shirt. "You love me. I love you. All's right in the world."

He leaned his forehead against the wall. "Little Bee, nothing's right."

She pushed the next button through the buttonhole. "A vestibule is better than the street."

He clasped her hands in his. "I want you too, but first I need to tell you about my sister and Vernon. What I have to do to save my sister."

"Later." Her hands fumbled with his fly. "I need you."

"As I need you." With those words he surrendered. He slipped his fingers into the waistband of her leggings and trailed them down over her perfect rear end, removing the man-made skin off one leg and then the other, laying bare the dawn-colored perfection he couldn't get enough of. He knelt in front of her, kissing the inside of her thighs, the tiny bud between her legs, slowly working his way back up to one luscious pear-shaped breast, then the other.

She wove her fingers through his hair. "In. Me. Now."

"Yes, little bee, yes." He rose and skimmed the long column of her neck, soaking in the vibration in her throat, the hum of his little bee. He picked her up, carried her to the metal worker's steel worktable, and set her down on the edge. He cupped her head with one hand and pushed her legs wide open with his thigh.

He positioned himself at her entrance, drove inside amazed at how perfectly they fit, and held himself there, wishing he could hold back time, hold back death. That he'd been born someone different, someone worthy of this brave woman who loved him. Ripples of pleasure built around him as her tight sheath pulled him in deeper and deeper. Her body trembled in his arms.

She trembled against him. Time to bring her over. He drew back and slammed into her again and again, losing himself inside her until they merged into one.

She sobbed against him afterward, soaking his suit jacket with snot and tears, her hand wrapped tightly in his tie, creasing it into a wrinkled mess. He didn't care. It had been the right thing to do. He carried her upstairs and laid her on the sofa. Her eyes fluttered and closed as she sank into sex-sated sleep. He fought the urge to lie beside her. He'd lost track of time. Vernon would come for him anytime now. At most, they had fifteen minutes.

They hadn't used a condom either, he realized. He laid his hand on her stomach and imagined her carrying his child. Pictured that child running along the beach, picking up shells, swimming with the seals. He shook the image away. There would be no beach, no shells, no seals, and no children for him. Children had no place in a future only hours long.

He felt her intake of breath before he heard it. She

opened her eyes and rolled onto her side, pulling his hand into hers. "Let me see it again."

"What? The tattoo?"

She answered with a nod.

He released her, slid up the cuff of his shirt, and held it out in front of her.

She leaned up on one elbow and touched the blue mark. Her cold fingertip burned his heated skin. "It's the same. So intricate. What does it mean? Why did the guy who drove off with my sister have it?"

He pressed his lips together and settled on a gloss. "It's a Balkan gang symbol, little bee. Very common in Greek prisons." Where Vernon and Tuccio's thugs held sway. "I have no idea who murdered your sister." *Zeús,* he hoped that was true and not the awful feeling he had in the pit of his stomach that her sister had had a run-in with Tuccio. That would be too much of a coincidence.

Melissa looked back at the tattoo, avoiding his eyes. "It's just—I never told the police about the tattoo. Laura made me swear not to tell anything—said it was a secret that could kill her if I told. She didn't trust me, you see. I always tattled on her. I was a jealous little brat who thought it was my role in life to get her in trouble. But this time, there was real fear in her eyes when she said the word *kill.* I believed her. So when the police first questioned me about her disappearance, I said nothing. Told them I hadn't seen her leaving school or where she'd told me she was going."

"You kept your word."

"No, I *didn't*—I *did* tell where she said she was going. But too late. After three days, two detectives put me in this tiny room." She wrapped her arms across her chest. "This big burly guy with bloodshot eyes and a

234

voice that sounded like he'd swallowed coffee grounds. And a woman with great big front teeth and hair slicked back in a bun so tight you could see where the skin pulled. They went at me like banshees. Moving in and out. Yelling and screaming inches from my face. Calling me names. Saying if Laura were dead it would be all my fault."

Ari felt sick. He knew what interrogations could be like. He still carried his own internal wounds inflicted by the guards he'd thought in his naiveté would protect him from his vicious cellmates. But to subject an innocent child to such a brutal onslaught was unconscionable. No wonder Melissa didn't trust the police or him. He wondered if she trusted anyone. "You were just a little kid—"

"No—thirteen."

"A kid. Didn't your parents—"

"My parents thought I'd not told out of spite. And when the police found Laura's body—I knew I had killed her, and they were right to hate me."

"It wasn't your fault." He gathered her into his arms.

She leaned the side of her head against his chest. "My father—I'd thought he loved me." She pressed against him, straining as if to crawl inside him. "He wouldn't look at me or talk to me for weeks after. I might as well have been a ghost in the house. And then he had a heart attack and died, and I knew forgiveness would never come."

There were no words that could ever heal that wound. She'd lost too much. Carried too much guilt. So Ari did the only thing he could think of, he kissed her, and in that moment, as her warm lips melted against his, as their tongues met and he tasted the familiar honey sweetness of her, he knew he had made a grave error. He couldn't just abandon her, bequeath her some paintings to remember him by. There was more than lust between them.

There was love, and love was not what her father had shown her. It was a commitment to care for and trust each other for all time—through all. He could not walk blindly to his death at Vernon's hand, and abandon her the way those who should have loved her had. *She* deserved a future. *They* deserved a future. His head throbbed. He only had to figure out a way to survive his meeting with Vernon.

A car horn honked outside his door. She froze in his arms and then held on tighter. "Is that who you were waiting for?"

"Yes." He pulled back and looked down at her. She had made herself strong on the outside, but inside was a little girl desperate to be trusted, desperate for unconditional love, open for everything he wanted to gift her. But it was too late. They were here. In minutes, he might disappear without a trace. And she would think his love a lie, just like everyone else's in her life.

He should have told her the truth. About Sirena, Vernon, and him. He drew her into his arms, kissed her, ran his fingers along her cheek, around the whorl of her ear. He breathed in her scent, studied her perfect lips, memorizing her. The car horn blared again. "I have to leave, my love."

"But I don't understand. Where are you going? Who are those people?"

He let go, stepped back. "Come, I have to get dressed. Now." He scooped up his suitcase and dragged her to the bathroom.

"Are you going back to Greece?" She made no attempt to dress but sat naked on the sink top, her legs slightly apart.

He struggled to keep his hands off her as he tugged on his pants and stuffed his arms into a clean shirt. "No. I have something to do first."

She reached across and slowly buttoned up his shirt. "Take me with you."

"Hush." He had to leave now, or he would never leave. He kissed her again, savoring his last taste of her. "This is for your own safety. Someone will come—one of the graffiti artists—and let you out. Go with him. T-Crew will hide you from Tuccio." With a quick twist, he slipped out the door and locked it behind him. The image of her perfect face and whispered words seared his heart.

The apartment was dead silent for a long moment. Then the pounding started, small fists smacking the bathroom door. "Ari, let me out! Let me go with you."

He pressed his palm against the rattling door and whispered at the crack. "I'm sorry, Melissa. It is better this way. Remember, I love you."

"Don't leave me," she yelled. The banging came louder and harder. Each smash another nail in his soul. He spun around, seized his suit jacket, and dashed down the stairs. A man running from himself.

****

Melissa listened to Ari's footsteps clanging down the stairs, the metal door below clicking open and banging shut. He had left her. She slid down the wall onto the cold tiles. She rubbed the sides of her hands swollen from pounding on the door. Fool. She finally falls in love, and the man abandons her. She banged her head against the door, the sound echoing in the emptiness. Aristides Stavros truly was a monster.

She pushed herself up from the floor and set out hunting through the sink cabinet drawers for something rigid and narrow to wedge between the latch and the strike plate. It was time to take control of her own life.

Chapter 33

Ari stopped on the curb and glanced back at The Foundry. He shouldn't have left Melissa locked in, trapped, especially when she was in shock. Her friends murdered. But at the moment, it was the only way he could think of to keep her from following him. He didn't understand everything going on, but he knew Tuccio was at the root of it. He patted the papers in his suit jacket. Vernon would get nothing from him until he called his dog off his little bee. He took out his cell and messaged El Toro to come get Melissa.

A limo pulled up to the curb and the door snapped opened. "Get in, Olympian."

Vernon Newell had put on maybe twenty pounds since the last time he'd seen him, but he was still a good-looking man. Ari stared at the face he'd hoped to never see again and cursed the power the man held over him. Since he was eighteen, this man and his minions had controlled his life. Now they controlled his death.

Ari rested his hand on the door frame. He had to make sure Vernon would leave Melissa alone. "I need your promise—"

Vernon Newell leaned over. "Not if you want to see your sister, old friend. Get in now."

"I left—"

The stone-hard smile hadn't changed. "Get in and we'll talk. Just like old times. Then we do business."

Ari looked back once more, his stomach twisted in a knot, and then slid into the seat beside the man he hated. "A girl, Melissa Dermont, she's back at the Foundry. Anything happens to her—"

"Not to worry." Vern slapped his back. "Don't look so glum. Makes you look even uglier than normal, and it's hard enough looking at you. Tell me about my island."

He pushed Melissa out of his head. He didn't trust Vernon, but for now he needed to focus on saving his sister. "No, let's talk about Sirena."

"Your charming sister is fine. As you will see shortly." Vernon clasped his hands together. "She doesn't know you're coming, by the way. I thought to surprise her. She likes surprises."

Ari straightened up. "If you've hurt her in any way—"

"I would never *hurt* my Bella." Vernon's lips twisted to one side. "Besides, what would you do if I did? Other than requiring you to complete the legal arrangements for the transfer of the island to me, you have no leverage." He laughed. "You really are naïve, my dear boy. And quite entertaining. It's been fun watching your career soar these last ten years. You do paint like an angel. Bought quite a few myself. Of course, all those paintings will be worth a lot more when you are—how do they put it in those auction catalogs? Ah, yes—recently deceased. "

Ari clenched his fists. He'd known he was walking into a death trap, but hearing his fate roll off Vernon's sloppy lips like he was some captured pawn in a chess game infuriated him. He glanced out the window and was surprised to see they were still in Williamsburg.

The girders of the bridge peeked over the top of the buildings, the graceful arcs of the cables at odds with the gray rectangles of the city. Had they been driving in circles? For a moment, he considered jumping out of the car. He could hide away somewhere, masquerade as a homeless man. T-Crew would help—until he found a way to bring Vernon and his cronies down. He glanced over at Vernon, whose mouth was moving as if he were arguing with himself. But he would have to abandon his sister to this man, and he couldn't do that. He sat back and let silence fill the car.

The limo pulled up at the entrance to a new condo sitting at the edge of the East River. Ari got out and peered up. The building was one of those new swanky places catering to the uber-rich. Flanked by Vernon and the bruiser who'd been driving, Ari entered the expansive white marble lobby accented with huge green and blue circles that made it look like some outsized fast food restaurant. Their footsteps echoed as they guided him across to one of the elevators. Vernon entered a code on the keypad and the door slid open. The elevator had only one destination button, The Penthouse. There would no easy escape from where Vernon was taking him.

The door slid shut, and the bruiser crushed him against the back wall, pinning him there, one hand on the back of his neck, his cheek smashed against the steel. The other hand brutally whipped a leather thong around his wrists.

"Apologies, Olympian," Vernon said. "Not that I don't trust your fine manners, but I can't take any chances in such a small space with a World Class wrestler. By the way, meet my friend Gavril. I particularly chose him for this adventure." The elevator stopped. "Gav, tell our guest who you are."

Gav pulled Ari's head back. "You defeated me at the Olympics, rich little Greek boy. Me, the Romanian star wrestler. I had to go home in disgrace. I was finished in the sport after that. The money support dried up, and my family reduced to starvation." He jerked his head again. "But this very nice man, Mr. Newell, came and gave me a fine job working for him. And soon he is going to give you to me, and we will fight again. But this time—*I win*." He jabbed his knee hard into Ari's back, and Ari whipped back his head, catching the bruiser in the nose. The man snorted and slammed Ari's head back into the wall with enough force to make him see stars.

"Play nice, boys." Vernon stepped out of the elevator and signaled for them to follow. The bruiser hustled Ari into a small steel-shrouded entry area. Two guards with guns stood at attention. Vernon walked past them and stopped at a steel door that blended with the walls. He glanced over his shoulder. "I didn't think you'd mind, Olympian. I've scheduled a little private bout for a few friends. Won't be quite up to professional standards. Didn't think we'd need a referee. You might have to show off those moves of yours that kept you alive in the Kordallos. You *have* kept in practice? You were once very, very good." Vernon eyed him up and down. "But I'm thinking you won't be a sure bet anymore."

Ari struggled against the thong around his wrists. It was cutting off his circulation—intentionally, he was sure. Too much longer, and his hands would be numb, and he'd have no grip to fight with. Gav would be able to destroy him in minutes—several painful minutes. A fitting way to go, his father would have said. "We deal with my sister first."

Vernon smiled and then put his hand in the blinking red fingerprint scanner. The door slowly slid open revealing an elegantly appointed living room with a view of the New York skyline. A small alcove near the entrance hosted a well-supplied wet bar. An enormous thin-screen TV covered one wall. Across from it was a sitting area with a coffee table made from a slice of an authentic-looking Greek column and an arrangement of sofas and chairs. A thick Greek *flokati* rug in pure white wool covered a floor of highly polished cream marble swirled with gold he'd know anywhere. He'd lifted tons of it slaving in his father's quarry. Everything new and expensive and exactly how Sirena would furnish a room. Except for one thing. Above a deep brown leather Chesterfield sofa hung one of Ari's largest canvases, the one he'd done of the thieving Swedish girl lying asleep in the sand, her back turned toward the viewer, her long blond hair trailing into the sea. The one he'd thought the Guilders had bought at the gallery opening.

Vernon followed his gaze. "Lovisa. I think you called her Poppy. One of your best works. So much emotion invested. Worth every thousand I paid. She's Gav's now, you know, the little slut." He tipped his head. "He was thrilled to have her when I told him she'd been yours, weren't you, Gav?" He glanced at the Romanian, whose mouth twisted against his teeth. "But I'm afraid Gav doesn't have your sensitivities. Not the artistic type at all. But then there are all types of monsters in the world, as you know." He walked across the room and took down two glasses. "But enough reminiscing. Be seated, my old friend."

Gav jerked him over to the sofa and pushed him down. His hands twisted as he fell, and he stifled a groan. "My sister."

"Yes, time for business. I assume you have the deeds." He poured a finger of fine scotch in each glass. "One for the villa and one for the island."

Ari nodded. He didn't trust his voice. He was too angry. Better Vernon think he was a beaten man.

"In your suit pocket?" He took a sip of his drink and signaled to Gav. "Get it."

Gav took the opportunity to spit in his face as he drew the well-traveled lawyer's envelope from Ari's pocket. He handed it to Vernon who shook his head. "Sloppy. Sloppy, Olympian. My lawyer is not going to like filing something that looks and smells like something a homeless man would pad his winter coat with." He pulled out the paperwork and glanced over it. "Looks in order. Hanlin? He your lawyer? I'll have to check on him."

"Gone—out of town." Ari had made sure of it. As of three days ago, Walter Hanlin and his wife of twenty-five years were on an all-inclusive sixteen-day voyage to the heart of the Amazon. A second honeymoon. The man had earned it.

"Convenient for you."

"You can call his office. His assistant will validate that the paperwork is all in order and is ready to be filed in Greece pending your signature and mine."

"Then let's sign. I have a bunch of contractors ready to build a world class resort while I lie on that pristine beach you love to paint." Vernon dropped the papers on the coffee table. "After the wrestling match, of course. Untie his hands, Gav."

From his boot the Romanian withdrew a long thin knife, the kind an assassin carried, and sliced the thong. Ari brought his trembling hands forward and flexed his numbed fingers. Blood rushed back in. The pain was excruciating.

"Fingers a little stiff? Well, just do your best."

"Not until my sister is released."

"Oh, I almost forgot in the excitement of having my dream come true. You have this misplaced affection for the sister you abandoned. Tell Bella I need to see her, Gav."

Gav disappeared through a side door. Ari stared after him. The next moment was crucial. He'd only have a second to communicate his plan to Sirena. He rubbed the grooves in his wrists and prayed his sister still remembered the good guy, bad guy routine they'd devised in childhood to escape their father's strap.

He heard her before he saw her, spike heels tapping against the marble. She came through the door, leaner and more elegant than he remembered, a Grecian goddess, but with a touch of sadness around the eyes that hadn't been there seven years ago. He stood and held out his mutilated hand, spinning his index finger in a tiny circle. *"Xarieté, Sirena. Anápoda—"*

"Oh no. No Greek." Vernon said quickly stepping between them. He glared at Ari. "You sit."

He sat and prayed that Sirena had understood she needed to act in the reverse, pretend she hated him.

His sister whipped her head around toward Vernon. "What the hell is he doing here, Vernie?"

Ari let out the breath he'd been holding. She had

gotten the message. At least he hoped she had. Or maybe she really did hate him enough to see him dead.

"I invited him. Thought you would be delighted to see your brother after all these years."

"He's a worthless sheep turd."

"Come, sweet. He's come all this way to rescue you." He handed her the glass of whiskey. She took a sip and put it down.

"Rescue me?" She whirled on Ari. "Idiot. I told you I never wanted to have anything to do with you. Ever. You've done enough damage to me to last a lifetime. I don't need rescuing." She spoke in the wheedling voice she'd perfected on their father. "Vernon's been ever so nice. We've been renewing our acquaintance these last few weeks." She waved her arm expansively. "Gave me *carte blanche* to redecorate his penthouse. Like it?"

Had she truly gone back to Vernon of her own free will? She'd loved him once. Ari looked down at his hands. "Vernon wrote me he was holding you hostage. Wants the island and villa in return for your release." He tipped his chin toward the papers. "I'm ready to give it to him as soon as I see you safe."

Vernon draped an arm over Bella's shoulder and slowly massaged her neck. "See, I have gotten the island for you, my sweet. It wasn't right for this murdering bastard to keep you away from your home. I told you I could give you anything your heart desired."

Her lips turned up, and she cuddled closer, but Ari could see the flicker of tension under her eye. Now was the time to show anger. He stood and looked her up and down with as much disdain as he could manage. "I should have known this was your idea. The Sirena I

246

knew is gone. Dead." He snapped his fingers. "Bella is a much more suitable name for a *whore*." He took a step toward her, but Gav knocked him back down and gave him a fist in the face.

"You speak nice to the lady, bastard."

Ari rubbed his mouth and came away with blood from a split lip. He bent over, drooling bloody saliva. So much for the new décor.

"Damn. He's bleeding on the rug." Bella grabbed a napkin off the bar and surged forward before the men could react. She pressed it against his lip and dropped a small capsule into his mouth.

Ari stared into her eyes, the beautiful deep brown eyes that matched his own. Was she poisoning him or saving him? She wouldn't know about the trust. Did she think to save the island by killing him before he could sign? Or did she know Vernon was going to have him beaten to death and hoped to give him a peaceful end?

He thought of Melissa unprotected, at the mercy of these men, and prayed she was safe with T-Crew. He curled his lip and licked away the blood. There was still a chance he could weasel his way out of here, a small chance, but he wasn't ready to give up quite yet. He tucked the capsule into his gum and glared at his sister. "So I'm to believe you're here of your own free will, and this deeding over the island is your idea," he said. He noted how she refused to look him in his eyes. "So let's prove it."

She stared at him and took a sip of her drink.

"Vernon, let Bella walk out the door without a goon on her tail and go shopping or back to her studio or to her apartment. Meanwhile, you keep me here." He nodded at Gav. "We have our little wrestling match.

247

When I see that she can come and go, live her life as she feels fit, date you if she wishes. Marry you even—without coercion." He nudged the deeds. "Then I will happily sign these papers in front of my lawyer." He leaned back, crossed his legs, and despite the pain, folded his hands behind his head. "You will note that only he can be the witness and as I said—he's unavailable for a few days."

Vernon set down his glass and glanced at Bella. For the first time, he looked unsure. Then he laughed. "Well, well. You are a clever bastard." He took Bella's hand in his. "You will not like this, but Bella *is* special to me. The only woman I've ever loved. I've been trying for months to convince her to marry me. I thought that finally if I rid her of the brother who ruined her life and sent her into hiding and I had the island back, she might say yes."

Ari nudged the capsule with his tongue and glared at his sister. "Vernon Newell's criminal operation murdered more people than I can count and sent thousands of young girls to brothels. He wants to transform our island into a rich man's playground. And you can love him, Sirena?"

His sister looked away. "People aren't always who you think they are."

Vernon huffed. "Sure, I wasn't born like you with a gold spoon in my mouth. Did things I'm not proud of. But I worked my way up out of the pit. I've changed." He grasped Sirena's hand. "For *her*. I'm a financier now. I invest in new technologies. Totally legit."

"What about Tuccio and his cronies?"

Vernon shook his head. "Got my eye on them. But not working for me."

Ari sat up, his heart racing. If Tuccio wasn't working with Vernon, he had no leverage to stop him from hurting Melissa. "You've split with Tuccio?"

"All of them. I've gone straight. But Tuccio's not happy about it. Guy's a crazy murdering bastard, cold as ice under that suave façade. You spent five years in prison with him, you should know." Vernon shrugged. "When I gave up the bad stuff, he thought I should have turned it all over to him. He's been trying to bring me down ever since."

"And you haven't taken him out?"

Vernon put up a hand. "Don't do that anymore."

"I don't believe you. You plan to kill me, right?"

"Well, I do hope you survive the wrestling match, but I don't particularly want you to win. After all, it's your fault Bella left me in the first place." He gazed out at the skyline. "Everything might have been very different if a good woman had married me years ago."

Ari glanced at his sister and looked away. He remembered the first time he saw Vernon, standing on the deck of the million dollar yacht moored in Eudokia harbor. The animal he'd become in prison hated the man on sight. The international crime boss had brought a crew of thugs and a perfect face.

But Sirena had been enchanted by the man's European manners and magazine model looks. And when he found his little sister in Vernon's bed, he'd gone berserk. Ari opened and closed his hands. He could still feel Vernon's neck in his grip, the blood pulsing beneath his fingers as he squeezed, the dying gasps. Sirena trying to hit him in the head with his father's marble bust of Archimedes and hitting Vernon instead.

If Sirena hadn't stopped him, the man standing in front of him would be dead, and he would be in prison for life. He touched the capsule again with his tongue, considered swallowing it. His sister had every right to wish him dead. He bent his head. "I know you can never forgive me for what happened. Prison ate up all that was good in me. It's taken years to quiet the beast inside."

His sister gave him a hard look and turned away. "Vernon should never have brought you here."

****

Melissa woke with a jerk. She lifted her head and blinked, blinded by the overhead bathroom light. She struggled to stand, her naked body chilled from lying on the tile floor. Every muscle in her body screamed with the effort. She must have been asleep for hours. She stamped her feet and rubbed her arms, trying to restore the circulation while cursing with every nasty word she knew. Aristides Stavros was a pig. Her calf cramped, and she bent over to massage it. Worse than a pig. She comes to warn him, bares her heart to him. They have mind-bending sex, and then he locks her naked in a freezing bathroom while he goes off to who knows where.

She must be thick-headed to let the man keep touching her. He insisted he loved her. So what's new? He could join the list of people who had said they loved her. She didn't need his love. Anyone's love.

She grasped the edge of the tub to steady herself and searched for her clothes. That's right, Ari'd torn them off her. They'd been covered with blood and vomit. She dropped to the floor, her stomach heaving. The memory of the mutilated bodies of Iza and Gracine flooded over her. Those women had died because of her, just like her sister. If she hadn't convinced them she could keep them safe, they'd still be alive. Her mother said she had the *malocchio,* the Evil Eye. She hadn't known the meaning at the time. She shivered. Now she did.

She fought down nausea and looked around for something to wear. Ari's suitcase sat open on the floor. She hesitated, then pawed through the neatly folded garments, discarding freshly laundered dress shirts and well-pressed trousers, designer ties and a tailored suit jacket—the one he'd worn that night at the gallery—the night they'd first kissed.

She blinked back tears and slipped her arms into the sleeves. His unmistakable scent tickled her nose as the collar brushed the back of her neck and the silk lining settled over her shoulders. It was as if some gentle remnant of him embraced her. Was this all she would ever have of him? She shook her head and drew the outsized jacket closed, trying not to remember the warmth of his arms around her and the touch of his hands on her skin.

She rolled up the sleeves and leaned over the suitcase. She needed socks. Her feet were freezing. Surely he had packed a pair of socks. She dug deeper. Her hand struck a notebook. She drew it out and opened it. Sketches of Ari's paradise spread out before her. She flipped through the pages—rolling hills, twisted trees, sleek seals, a beautiful girl's face, and herself lying naked in a nest of fur, her body faintly lined with the symbols he'd brushed over her that first time they'd made love. She traced them with her finger, remembering.

251

She shut the book and stood. She was going do what she should have done from the start. Go far away, write her dissertation, and let the police find Bella. She picked up the nail file, slipped it between the door and the frame and fiddled again with the latch.

Something clicked. She tried to turn the doorknob, but it was still locked. Another click. She put her ear to the door and listened harder. Thank goodness. Someone had opened the downstairs door and was coming up the stairs. She dropped the nail file and hammered on the door. She didn't care who it was as long as they unlocked the door. But she hoped it was the monster. She couldn't wait to tell him what she thought of his cowardice.

The door opened. A kid. One of Ari's graffiti crew—the tall one. And he didn't look happy to see her.

Chapter 34

Ari stumbled across the street, reeling like a drunk. He'd survived Vernon's wrestling match, but just barely. From the way it hurt to breathe, he had at least several broken ribs to go with two broken fingers. His left wrist was numb and throbbing, something seriously wrong. He ran his tongue over his teeth. A broken tooth, too. Gav had been all smiles and pleasantries after the bout.

Then Vernon slapped him on the back and had him literally dumped on the street. Told him to get in touch when Hanlin got back, and they'd sign the papers. And he'd do it for his sister. Gift her the island trust he'd set up. But Melissa—they wouldn't tell him anything about Melissa.

He leaned back against a light post and tried to block out the pain, not from the broken body—that he had earned—but from the hole in his heart. He had hoped for reconciliation, some peace between him and Sirena. But his sister didn't need him. She never had. And now she had Vernon.

He patted his breast pocket. Yep, it was still there—the capsule, the rounded lump the size of a pebble from his favorite beach, Bella's questionable gift. Later, once he made sure Melissa was okay, and he had nothing else to live for, it would come in handy. He pushed away from the pole with a grunt and headed toward The Foundry.

Overhead, wispy cirrus clouds scudded across the full moon. It was the kind of night when T-crew stayed in. They'd be too visible in the moonlight. He'd head over to the crew's new place as soon as he found Melissa. Say a second goodbye. If he had enough strength.

He limped through the gate and stumbled. Fur Tree loomed up inches in front of him like a ghost rising from the cracked pavement and gripped him by the shoulder. He winced and threw the hand off.

The youth stared, his face hard as slate. "She's gone."

"Is she safe?"

Fur Tree shrugged.

His heart skipped, and he tried to bulldoze his way around the boy, but his legs turned to melted rubber and his head filled with broken feathers. The last thing he heard was someone crying out his name.

****

Ari woke up to a constant buzzing and the pervasive stink of disinfectant and alcohol. He sniffed. It was coming from him. His throat burned like he'd swallowed fire, and his mouth tasted like rubber.

"We almost lost you."

He swiveled his head to the right and a sharp pain zinged across his chest. A long-faced man in green scrubs stared down at him, clipboard in his hand.

He strained to lift his head and found it too heavy. He let it roll back. "Where...am... I?" The words wheezed out between lips he could barely move. He was surprised he could talk at all.

"Langone Medical Center. I'm Dr. Giacometti.

You were admitted two nights ago with some broken ribs, a concussion. But those are the least of your problems. The life-threatening injury was internal bleeding and a punctured lung. We did a thoracotomy." The doctor tapped his fingers on the back of the clipboard. "Splinted your wrist plus two fingers on the left hand. Not sure you'll get full movement back. You'll need intensive therapy. Live a rough life, Mr. Stavros?"

He would have laughed if he didn't hurt so much. He lifted his uninjured hand slightly.

"Well, you'll be staying with us awhile. Our main concern is your lung and blood clots. No plane flights for at least six weeks. I see you are here on a tourist visa. Is there someone we should contact in Greece?"

Ari shook his head as gently as he could. It still hurt.

"Then I will leave you to the nursing staff and send a social worker to get you an extension on the visa." Dr. Giacometti slipped the clipboard into the holder at the foot of the bed. A nurse entered and passed behind him. "This is Gwen. She'll give you something for the pain."

In the doorway, he stopped. "Aristides Stavros. You're that artist whose paintings are over at Gallery Four." He shuffled his feet and blew out a breath. "My wife's seen your work. When she heard you were my patient...well, she wondered—if in exchange for my fee—you could paint her—as an anniversary gift for me?"

Ari struggled to concentrate. The doctor's voice faded in and out. Wife? He didn't paint wives, he painted whores. Naked ones. Women paid to close their eyes and let him look with his monster face. All except one—Melissa. He saw her again, lying in the mussed sheets, all golden dawn skin and smooth curves, her eyes wide open peering into his. But he'd never paint her again. He glanced at his splinted hand. "I'm…left-handed."

The doctor pressed his lips together. "Should have taken better care—"

Ari didn't hear the rest, lost in a nightmare haunted by the pain on Melissa's face as he slammed the bathroom door.

****

He must have slept. Ari opened his eyes. Sunlight poured through the blinds, creating a bronze halo around a head of riotous black curls. Only his sister had hair like that. He shaded his eyes with his right hand. It hurt a little less this time to move, but every breath slicing through him reminded him of all the mistakes he had made. "Sirena?"

The blinds snapped shut. "Name's Bella." Her heels clicked as she crossed the room, each tap jarring his brain. She stared down at him and shook her head. "You should have swallowed that pill." She sat in the chair next to the bed and crossed one leg over the other. In the red crepe suit she wore, she looked like a demoness come to send him to hell. She waved a hand over him. "Would have saved you all this."

"I wasn't ready—" He coughed, and his throat burned.

"Hush. You need to whisper, idiot." Bella turned away, fussed with a cup, and then held an ice cube to his lips. The cold trickled down his throat.

He swallowed and continued in a throaty whisper. "To die. I have unfinished business."

Bella sat back and stared at him. "You were willing to give away our home, the island, to save me, but you didn't trust me enough to let me save you."

"Save?"

"The pill would have made you too sick to fight that stupid revenge match Vernon planned. I'd tried to talk him out of it, but he really doesn't like you too much." She shrugged. "Vernon's okay. I love him, I think. But men—and I definitely include you in that category—lose half their brain cells when they're angry. And you did make Vernon angry back on Eudokia. At least he had enough sense not to go head to head with you like he wanted." She ran her finger through his hair. "You would have hurt him." She bent over and spooned up another ice cube. Ari blinked. At that moment, she was the very image of their mother. "Lovisa is married to Gav, by the way. Very happily. I guess Vernon hooked them up way back when he was Vicious Vernon riding roughshod across the Balkans. Anyway, Vernon hung that painting up on purpose to goad you. I know your work makes money, but it's not my cup of tea. I had chosen a Greek weaving to display there. Anyway, Vernon told you those lies just to get you angrier so you'd fight harder."

"That's not vicious?" he whispered.

"He's a shark with teeth, Ari. Always will be, but he has a soft underbelly." She sat back. "Seven years ago, I was a foolish young girl. Papa wouldn't let me go to college or get a job. No villager boy would touch me, the daughter of the man they relied on for their livelihood. The only reason for my existence was to serve Papa as his glorified housekeeper. Vernon was like a flame that drew me in, promising me the world.

You were right; I should never have gotten involved with a crook. But I was desperate for attention, and you were so broken after prison."

He slid his hand over and touched hers. "I'm sorry."

"In the end, it did me good. Ran away and found myself. I've made a good life here. I'm a wicked fine tattoo artist." She flicked her arm over and pulled up her sleeve, revealing a diving monk seal. "I will never let anything happen to them, Ari."

"But Vernon said—"

"Pulling your chain. My cover as Bella was very deep. He only found me two months ago. We've been getting to know each other again."

"So he says."

Bella shrugged. "He's asked me to marry him—but I'm not ready to commit to anything permanent. Yet. Need to see if the flame still flickers enough to last a lifetime." She bent over and gave him a kiss on the forehead. "People do change, Ari. Even you." She tucked her red Prada ostrich purse under her arm and headed for the door.

At the threshold, she slowed. "Oh, by the way. There're some scruffy-looking street thugs waiting to see you. Should I let them send them up?"

Ari nodded. Bella threw him a smile and disappeared out the door. He frowned. His baby sister had become a strong, self-assured woman, but he worried she was too trusting of Vernon. He glanced down at his injured hand and remembered Vernon's comment about how the value of his work would increase if he were deceased. Not being able to use his hand ever again would serve the same purpose. Vernon stood to make a fortune on that alone. He'd been buying his paintings for years. By now, he must own half his work.

"Ugly Man." Hanger On bounced into the room and plunked down on the edge of the bed. Ari winced as the mattress tipped. The kid had put on some pounds gorging on the contents of his refrigerator.

"Down, idiot. Man's beat to pieces," El Toro said, pulling his brother off the bed. Neto and Solo came around the other side of the bed. Fur Tree came in behind them and stood off to the side, staring at the IV drip.

"Sorry." Hanger On tilted his head and stared at the wreck that was his body. The kid's face scrunched up. "You gonna live?"

"Yeah—think so." Ari tipped his head toward his left hand. "But no more tagging." He glanced up at the ring of solemn faces. The kids were taking it hard. They'd thought him invincible. "How's the new place?"

El Toro's mouth twitched up. "Awesome. We fixing things up. Got us some furniture at the flea market."

"And school? Going, Hanger?"

Hanger's face brightened. "Yeah. Got a great social studies teacher. I'm doing a project on bridges and how they're built. Been going to the library to look stuff up like we did to find out about that murdered girl. You know, the Billy Bridge is over a hundred years old and was once the longest suspension bridge in the world. And it's really weird how—"

Neto chucked him on the shoulder. "The man's hurting. He don't want to know that stuff."

Ari shook his head. "Being curious is the path to

wisdom."

Fur Tree scowled. "Wrong saying. Way I hear it, curiosity gets stupid artists hurt bad." He shuffled his feet. "We should go. Let the man sleep."

Something chill ran through Ari. "Where's Melissa?"

Fur Tree shrugged. "Don't know. The *chica* was just like gone when I got there."

"Gone?" Fur Tree was hiding something. It was there in his hunched shoulders and cast down eyes. "How?" I've got to—" Ari struggled to sit up. A wave of pain rippled through him, and he flopped back down with a grunt.

"See. I told you to keep your trap shut." El Toro snagged Fur Tree by the arm and pushed him toward the door.

"Not—his—fault," Ari puffed out. No, it was his. He'd abandoned the woman he loved when she was in danger. Worse, he had believed the rat Vernon would protect her.

Hanger On clasped his uninjured hand. "Don't you worry, Ugly Man. We'll find her for you."

A shudder crawled down his spine. Tuccio was out there somewhere, and he didn't want T-crew near him. They might think they were street tough, but compared to Tuccio and his goons, they were as vulnerable as Bella's cats. Better they think he'd lost interest. "Don't bother. She's made her choice. Now get." He lifted his right hand and waved the crew out.

He lay back on the pillow and closed his eyes. Fool. She'd come to him panicked by the bastard, covered in blood, and what had he done? Had sex with her on a workbench. He cursed. He should have done more to stop Tuccio at the start, but all along he'd thought the danger was from Vernon.

Now he had a whole new battle to wage. He might be a broken man, but he was alive. He struggled to sit up in bed. Tuccio would not destroy the woman he loved.

Chapter 35

Thump. Something hit the rear door of The Siren. Melissa froze. Had Tuccio found her and come to murder her like he had Iza and Gracine?

Thump. It banged again. Adrenaline shot through her, sending her heart rate soaring. She clutched the bag of cat food tighter and stared at the thin boards she'd nailed over the broken window, the bolt she'd neglected to slide closed. Goosebumps trailed up her arms and across her back. Any minute, the murdering bastard would burst through the door and get her.

She spun around, looking for a place to hide. But the empty storeroom lacked a door, the windowless bathroom lacked a lock, and if he were coming in the back, he'd be a fool not to have men out front too. And Tuccio was no fool.

Nowhere to hide. Nowhere to run. She didn't even have a weapon, just a stupid twenty-five-pound bag of dry cat food. She hefted the bag and imagined smashing it into that perfect face. At least she'd get some satisfaction out of that.

Trembling with the effort, she lifted the bag higher, pressed back against the wall, prepared to go down fighting.

A skittering scratch. Then another, capped by a familiar yowl. Her heart rate fell. Her death grip on the bag loosened, and she exhaled.

Just hungry cats.

One hand gripping the bag, the other on the bolt latch, she pushed the back door open with her hip and peered out into the yard. No perfidious Tuccio. No goons. Only cats.

She tiptoed down the steps, dumped the kibbles into the feed bowls as quickly as she could, then dashed back inside. She tossed the empty cat food bag on the floor and threw back the bolt. Hiding out in Bella's tattoo parlor wasn't the most brilliant idea she'd ever had, but it was the only place she could think of after escaping from Ari's. At least here, she had enough privacy to change her appearance so she could lose herself on the streets. Hide from Tuccio. She wouldn't stay long.

She released a trembling breath and slipped into the Siren's dimly lit bathroom. Drips of the Manic Panic hair coloring she'd used splattered the sink. She peered into the small mirror and smiled at the bizarre image in the glass, satisfied. It hadn't been easy to turn her thick black hair to pink. The room stank of hair stripper.

But now it was done. She dipped her fingers in a jar of gel and slicked her fingers through her hair. Spikey and fuchsia. She inserted a neon blue feathered hair clip. Step one to the new Melissa—the one with no heart to break.

Step two next. Out of the Northside Pharmacy bag sitting on the top of the toilet, she pulled the cosmetics she'd bought and laid them on the sink edge: ivory face powder, blue-black eye shadow, inky eyeliner, and NYX lip cream in *She-Devil*. She hated the muddy plum color but loved the name. With a shaking hand, she brushed the shadow over her eyelids, encircled her eyes with thick eyeliner, and lightened her skin with a dusting of powder. For the final touch, she smeared the lipstick on thickly.

She preened her head back fashion model style and studied the effect. Yep. Made her look like she was half-dead. Fitting.

With a satisfied nod, she flicked off the light, picked up her portfolio, and set off for the grand finale.

****

Twenty minutes later, Melissa lay on Orange Man's tattoo table and gazed up at the ceiling. She gripped the foam covered edge. She was doing the right thing. After this, her research would be complete, and she could hole up in Manhattan in the tiny room she'd found on the NYU graduate bulletin board. She'd spend the next four weeks completing her dissertation and be ready to defend it in time to graduate in January. Then she was leaving New York City and never coming back.

"Ready?" Orange Man picked up the tattoo machine and stepped on the foot pedal. The buzz of the machine zinged through her and set her nerves on edge. The sound reminded her of being dragged to the dentist as a child and gripping the slimy leather armrests as the bone-shaking drill ground into a decayed tooth. She'd feared the dentist. Somehow the idea of that tat needle pricking the tender skin of her breast and belly frightened her even more.

She pressed her lips together and firmed her resolve. This was a perfectly rational step. Getting tattooed would give her intimate knowledge of what women went through for the men they loved. Her dissertation would be the better for it. After all, ethnographers were expected to immerse themselves in the cultures they were studying. Hadn't Lars Krutak at the Smithsonian covered his body in tattoos as part of his research? Watching his *Tattoo Hunter* series on Discovery Channel several years back had given her the confidence to select tattooing as a dissertation topic despite every attempt by her advisor to dissuade her.

Orange Man dabbed her skin with something cool and slimy. She flinched. He glanced up at her. "Relax, sweetheart. Petroleum jelly. Makes the needle glide more smoothly."

"I know. I've watched hundreds of people get tattoos." She glanced down at the blue lines of the design staining her skin. "But this—this is completely different."

"I told you." Orange Man laughed, revealing the star tattoo on the inner surface of his lower lip. "You can observe all you like. But you don't really know what a tat is until you're under the needle." He tilted his head and studied the design she had chosen. "I hadn't expected you to want something so ambitious though. It will take several hours to complete, and you will never be able to remove something so large. Are you sure you don't want something small for your first—a rose on your ankle or a butterfly on the shoulder?"

"No. If there is one thing I've learned in my studies, it's that you can't choose a design because it's what everybody else has or because someone else tells you what you should get. The tattoo must have a special meaning to you alone. You're the one who will live with it the rest of your life. In most cultures, tattoos are done for spiritual or magical reasons. Here people get tattoos for the most trivial reasons, like their friend got one or their parents said they couldn't or someone dares them to do it."

"Or they're drunk." Orange Man shook his head. "Long history of that. Still, I'd be out of business if the idiots didn't keep coming." He turned away and dipped the needle into the black ink, then swiveled back and curled over her neck. She could feel his breath on her skin, his shirt sleeve rubbing against her arm.

His gloved fingers pressed and pulled the skin flat. The needle touched her. As the tip bit in she knew she was just fooling herself. There was nothing magical or spiritual in what she was doing. She wanted to destroy what the monster who'd broken her heart had loved—her skin. For a moment, she considered leaping off the table. But only for a moment. She fisted her hands and held still as the needle pricks scratched at her skin like hundreds of angry cat claws. She stared at the ceiling and welcomed the pain.

****

Three hours later, her credit card carried more debt, her newly tatted skin burned, and she was back at The Siren to pack up her belongings and feed the cats one last time. Then, goodbye Williamsburg. Goodbye monsters. Goodbye love.

Chapter 36

Ari rested his left hand on the white gauze-covered examining table and waited for the doctor to stop talking into his digital voice recorder. Give him athletic trainers with a roll of tape over lawsuit-worried surgeons any day. Back during Olympic training, he would have been taped up by now and hustled back to the mats with the admonition to suck it up. Not that he could do much sucking in or out at this point. Every breath hurt.

He glared at the surgeon and willed him to hurry up. He had to check on his paintings, then get back to Williamsburg to corner that Firth woman and find out where his Nereida might go. Melissa couldn't have just disappeared into thin air.

"Try bending the fingers," the doctor directed.

Ari flexed the fingers of his left hand. They barely moved, yet pain ripped up his arm like someone had driven a burning poker into it.

The hand surgeon sat back. "It's not just that the finger bones are broken, but the flexor tendon has detached. You will have to keep the splint and wrist cast on for at least two more weeks. Then we will reevaluate and do surgery, if necessary, to restore some movement, but some stiffness will remain." The physician settled in to re-splint the fingers. "You might consider becoming proficient with your right hand. It

267

can be done."

"Enough to retain my status as a world-class artist?"

"I've heard it said that artists paint with their heads, not their hands. I've seen paintings done by people using their mouth or their toes. I'd say it's up to you." He tucked in the end of the wrap and inserted the metal clip. "See you in a week."

Hand immobilized in yards of bandaging, Ari pushed up from the table and wended his way out of the doctor's office. His car was waiting for him at the entrance. He crawled inside, nodded to Delaney, and flopped back on the seat. "Next stop the gallery."

****

Miss Pinch Nose Keeler was waiting for him, tapping her toe, clipboard in hand, her eyes firmly focused on his feet. "Where did you disappear to? You need to sign off on my commission."

"Hos-ital." He was getting better at speaking without taking deep breaths, but he still sounded like he had very large marbles rolling around inside his lungs. He tried again. "Hos-ital." He stood and waited. Slowly, she ceased tapping and actually looked at him. She stepped back. "Oh, my goodness."

He forced a smile despite the pain; his mirror told him that with his swollen cheeks and black eyes he looked like the Joker come straight out of a *Batman* movie.

She straightened. "You should have let us know you were injured, we would have—"

"Thrown them out?" Sweat gathered on his forehead, and he swayed slightly. It was really too soon to be doing this, but he had to take care of Melissa's paintings until he found out where she had gone. He'd store them at T-Crew's place for now. That much he could accomplish.

"Heavens, no. Your work is fantastic. But here—" She fluttered around him and took hold of his good arm. "Sit down. I'll get you a cup of tea."

He plopped down on the leather chair because he'd keel over if he didn't, and watched Hard-Nosed Business Lady revert to little Miss Housewife as she plugged in the hot pot, arranged tea things on a tray, and fussed with the paper napkins. He stifled a snort. It seemed that wounded monsters invoked pity even from lime green witches. If he had the strength, he would carry the paintings out himself, but he could no longer lift anything requiring two hands.

He picked up the teacup with an unsteady right hand and pretended to take a sip of tea to be polite. He put the cup back down in the saucer, relieved not to have spilled it. "The paintings." He reached into his pocket with his good hand and drew out the address. "Hire a packer. Send them here."

"But they're gone."

"*Gone?*" He struggled to draw in a breath. Gone like Melissa? "Who picked them up?"

"I wasn't here. My assistant handled it." She rolled her desk chair around and pulled out a packet from the file cabinet. She flipped to the last page. All blood drained from her face. "Apparently, you did." She turned the paper so he could see the signature.

He shoved the tea tray to the side. The spoons rattled in the saucers. "I think not." He pulled a marker from his breast pocket and with his right hand scrawled his signature across her white marble desktop the way he'd practiced in therapy. It looked like it belonged to some school boy who'd been writing "I shall not fight" five hundred times.

Keeler's mouth sagged. "But—but who?"

"I aim to find out."

Keeler's gaze settled on his splint. "That's your painting hand. Will it affect your career?" Hard-Nosed Business Lady was back.

"Yes."

"Oh." Her mouth dropped open and then snapped shut. "If you have other works, we could arrange a small private showing."

"No."

Ari forced himself to get up without holding onto the back of the chair to steady himself. Everything tipped and then righted. "Better re-read my contract and forget about your commission. You'll be hearing from my lawyer."

Chin up, shoulders back, teeth clamped against the pain, he made his way out of the gallery, then crept into the car. He leaned back gasping for air.

Delaney gave him a needling glare that told him he looked as wrung out as he felt. If he had a choice, he'd crawl into a hole and lick his wounds. But he didn't. Melissa was missing, and someone had stolen his paintings. And he couldn't help but think the two were related.

He put up his hand. "Don't. Say. A. Word. North 7th and Driggs." He'd mailed the letter gifting Melissa the paintings to her apartment. Maybe Miss Fuck-Me Firth would have some answers for him.

****

The Firth woman met him at the top of the stairs

wearing a bareback teddy in some violent shade of magenta that matched her lipstick. She focused her eyes on a spot above his head and batted her false eyelashes. "I knew you couldn't resist me. When I heard your sexy accent on the intercom, I thought, 'Jana, your ship's come in.'"

If he were a ship, she'd be staring at the orlop deck, not his Gucci loafers. Ari stifled a laugh. She still couldn't look him in the face. He waited for the shooting pains in his side to die down. When he finally spoke, his voice came out a cross between a croak and a broken washing machine. "Put some clothes on, Miss Firth. We need to talk."

She wrinkled her nose and smacked her lips in a warped imitation of Marilyn Monroe. "You're no fun, Mr. Monster. Come in and make yourself at home while I change." She sashayed back into the apartment and disappeared into what he figured must be her bedroom, leaving the door open.

He hesitated on the threshold. It was a risk to have anything to do with this woman. Still, if anyone knew where Melissa might be or what happened to his paintings, she would.

Jana reappeared in an emerald green silk caftan that matched her eyes and clashed with her lipstick. She leaned against the bedroom doorframe. "Come in. I promise to behave." She led the way into the tiny living room and plopped down on the futon. With a wink, she arranged the billowing silk around her so it was half open down the front, then patted the place next to her. "Sit."

He chose the fragile-looking wicker chair instead. A stack of newspapers and a half-full Chinese take-out container occupied the seat. He gathered them up, set them on the floor, and lowered his body into the chair. It wobbled and creaked, but held. He let out the breath he'd been holding and focused on Miss Firth's half-turned face. The woman was fashion-model beautiful, but there was a hardness about her lips, a tightness along her jaw, he didn't like. He rested his injured hand in his lap and leaned forward. "I'm looking for Melissa."

"Melissa?" She gathered her legs under her, revealing more than he wanted to see of Flirty-Firth. "She's not with you?"

He pasted on a blank façade, the one he'd learned to wear in prison. "No"—he lifted his bandaged arm—"I've been in the hospital."

"Oh, dear." She leaned across and patted his knee. "You poor, poor man."

He trapped her hand under his. "When did you last see her?'

"Let's see. She flew out of here like a crazy woman at some ungodly hour. Left all her stuff." She tapped her lips with her index finger. "Hmm. That's right. Last Saturday."

The day he'd locked her in the bathroom. The day he'd abandoned her. Ari swallowed a groan. It congealed into a hard lump in the back of his throat. He swallowed again. "Your friend's been missing a week. Aren't you the least bit worried about her?"

Her French-manicured nails dug into his thigh. "Of course, but I am sure you will find her—or she'll find you." She extracted her hand and examined her nails. "As they say, it's written in your stars."

"You have a crystal ball?"

"I *have* many things." Head down, she readjusted her legs and smoothed down the caftan. "I *know* even more."

"Bad things happen to false prophets."

Her eyebrows curved up and vanished beneath her bangs. "Are you threatening me? Because I have very protective friends."

The muscles across Ari's shoulders tightened the way they used to before a wrestling bout. He shifted. Beneath him, the chair shimmied. "Do you? Do they protect your good friend Melissa, too?"

She flicked her fingers at him. "That's neither here nor there. Let's just say it would be wiser for you to stop looking for her. She doesn't want you. She doesn't want me. She doesn't want to be found. She's just— *gone.*"

He swallowed down the angry words pounding to get out and used his softest voice. The one he used with models having second thoughts. "Is she? You have no idea where she might be? With an old lover? With someone at wherever she's working on her degree? With one of your 'protective' friends?"

She gripped the edges of the caftan closed and shrugged. "I have no idea. Melissa's always been—oh, how to put it—*irresponsible.*"

Enough. He'd learn nothing from this woman. She was no friend to Melissa. He leaned on the arm of the chair and pushed himself up.

Crack. The cheap wicker snapped beneath his hand. He tipped. Lost his balance. His foot shot out, knocking over the take-out container. The reek of rancid peanut oil and soy sauce assaulted his nose. Unrecognizable vegetables, white bits of tofu, and brown sauce spread across the papers littering the floor.

"Sorry." He bent down to scoop up the mess but stopped. Beneath the goo lay the envelope he'd sent containing the information about the paintings. Torn open. Empty.

He waved it in Firth's face. Bits of sauce splattered her cheeks, spotted her caftan. "Explain this."

She rose in a cascade of green silk, tuberose, and jasmine and wiped the sauce from her cheek with a trembling finger. "Melissa must have—"

He glanced at the postmark. The letter had arrived on Monday, two days after Melissa went missing. Firth was lying through those over-bleached teeth. He glared at her. "No, you opened it." He seized her chin and forced her to look him in the face. He expected to see disgust. Instead, he saw tears. He let go.

She wiped her wet cheeks with her sleeve. "Please, believe me. I really don't know where Melissa is. The envelope—I found it lying on the floor by the mailboxes. Torn open like that. I have no idea what was inside." Still sniffling, she peeked up at him. "Was it important?"

"Nothing to worry your beautiful little head about." He lifted her hand and with all the elegance his mother had drilled into him, bestowed a kiss worthy of his aristocratic ancestors. "I will be leaving the country shortly. But if you hear from Melissa, please let her know that Bella is safe and that I asked for her."

She let her hand fall. "Melissa is so lucky to have a man like you. I hope you know—a girl can never have too many friends."

He pulled out his card and handed it to her. "Call my cell if you should need anything."

She studied the card. "You're an overly-generous man, Mr. Monster."

He stumbled out of the apartment, leaving her standing there, arms wrapped around her, mascara staining her cheeks. He thumped down the steps, his brain churning. Had he just been hoodwinked or warned?

****

Drat. Melissa slowed at the corner. The hooded man was there again, leaning against the bus stop post across the street from The Siren. She'd seen that same watcher too many times to be coincidence. His clothes changed, but always a hooded sweatshirt or baseball cap shaded his face.

At first, she'd thought it was Ari, haunting her. The man had his broad shoulder build, narrow waist, and long dark hair, but he also had all his fingers on his left hand. She could see them now grasping the newspaper he was pretending to read as if he were just another bored commuter waiting for his ride.

Besides, by now Ari was long gone, back to Greece or down a sewer. As far as she was concerned, that was for the best. The hole in her heart insisted otherwise. But broken hearts healed, maybe slightly cracked, but still functional. She should know. This wasn't the first heartbreak she'd ever had. But it sure was going to be her last.

She gave her pink locks a shake, clasped her portfolio under her arm, and aimed for the boutique just past Bella's. With a little convincing, the shop girl would let her slip out her back door, and she could enter The Siren through the rear entrance, no one the wiser.

But as she passed Bella's, she saw movement

inside. She halted and stared past the glowing neon mermaid in the window. There was no mistaking the red-headed woman bustling around The Siren.

She pushed into the shop and threw herself into her friend's arms. "Bella! I was so worried. Where have you been?"

"Who?" Bella held her at arms' length. "Melissa, the pokey anthropologist? Is this you?"

"Oh." Melissa glanced down at herself. "Yeah, my new look. What do you think?"

"You look—well—" She circled around her, touched her cheek—"like Michelle Yeoh gone Goth."

"Call it what you want." Melissa put a hand on her hip. "This is the new me."

Bella tugged on the baggy black pants and shirt. "Kinda ninja. Can't say it does much for your charms. These things add about ten pounds to your figure."

"My old karate outfit. Besides—don't need charm. I've sworn off men. Forever."

"I understand the feeling." Bella looked her up and down, touched the side of her nose. "Needs a piercing right here."

Melissa laughed. "Yep. Can you do it?"

"I'm in the process of closing up the shop for a while." She flicked the end of her nose. "But come into my lair. I can still do a piercing."

Melissa followed Bella's swinging, unnaturally red hair into the tat room and sat down in the chair. She glanced around at Bella's elegant designs. Nothing had changed. "So where did you go?"

"Needed a break. Went to visit—an old friend."

"I got scared something happened to you. Your files were all over the floor like someone rifled through them searching for something.

"Everything was in perfect order when I arrived." Bella narrowed her eyes. "How did you get in?"

"I broke the glass in the back door."

Bella sat back.

"And there were the dead cats."

"Dead cats?"

"I was feeding the strays for you. And someone slit the throats of your favorites—the yellow tom and the tabby with the kittens. They were left in the back hall."

Bella pressed her hand against her heart. "I didn't see any dead cats when I opened up."

"They disappeared a while back." When she'd return to hide out there'd been no furry bodies, not even stains on the floor. With the sun streaming through the windows, and Bella standing beside her, she felt a fool. Had she imagined everything? No, Iza and Gracine had died in a bath of blood, Daniela had really been hit by a car, and there had been dead cats here. "Maybe your brother cleaned them up. He's the only one I told."

"Brother?"

Melissa looked up. "Your brother, Ari."

Bella crooked an eyebrow. "You know my brother?"

"We kind of met at your apartment. I've been feeding your cat there, too."

Bella gave her a hard look. "At my apartment? I wondered—"

Melissa didn't want to think about how the guest bedroom must have looked. They'd both left in a hurry. "He's been looking for you too. He said you'd been kidnapped."

Bella pushed her long red hair out of her face.

"That was Vernon's doing."

"Vernon?"

"Long story. Let's just say they don't like each other and, being men, think the worst of each other." Bella sorted through her tool tray. "Have you seen my brother? He's gone AWOL himself. It's just like him. Waltzes back into my life after seven years of silence to save me and then promptly disappears immediately after. The doctors are very upset. Vernon's got people out looking for him. But my brother is a master at disappearing. Been doing it to me my whole life."

"Doctors?"

"Yeah, you don't just jump out of bed four days after lung surgery and go hoofing it off somewhere."

Melissa sank back against the counter, her heart cracking open again. That graffiti nut had lied to her. Ari hadn't left the country. "How'd he get hurt?"

"Damn wrestling match of Vernon's. Told you those two don't play nice." Bella peered out the window. "Speaking of Vernon. He's supposed to be picking me up shortly. So if you want that piercing, I'd better do it now."

Ari would hate her to mutilate her face. Melissa stood. "I think not—not yet anyway." She touched her neck. "I got a tat. Orange Man did it. I would have had you do it, but I thought you weren't coming back."

"You did right." Bella smiled. "Orange Man's the Master. He did mine, you know." She pushed down Melissa's collar. "Ooo. How far down does it go?"

"All the way."

Bella blinked. "Definitely the new Melissa."

Thump. Something shook the rear door.

Bella jerked her head around. "What?"

278

"Oh, that's just the cats," Melissa said. "They get a little wild when they're hungry. They're used to being fed at this time. I'd better put out the food."

"But I already fed them."

Melissa's body went rigid.

Crash. The rear door banged open. They both swung around. A huge bald man with protruding teeth stood there holding a taser. "Ladies, your ride awaits. Please step outside and join the gentleman in the car."

Bella tossed back her hair. "Don't be ridiculous. I'm not joining anyone."

"Don't try me."

Melissa put a hand on Bella's arm. "Maybe we better—"

Bella threw off her hand and put her hands on her hips. "Big words. Vernon will eat you for lunch if you touch me."

Pop. Taser barbs hit Bella in the shoulder, and she fell screaming and shaking to the floor.

"Bella!" Melissa bent down only to find herself lifted by the armpits and half-dragged half-carried out to a car. She opened her mouth to scream and a dirty palm pinned her mouth closed. She struggled to bite him, but the goon must have made a habit of abductions because his hand cupped away from her teeth just in time. He tossed her into the back seat of the car, where she fell into a man's lap.

"Melissa. A pleasure to see you."

She knew that voice, that cologne. Her whole body tensed and she pushed against him. "Tuccio. You bastard. Let me go." She kicked and wiggled, but he easily pulled her arms behind her and snapped on a zip tie. The big man deposited a subdued Bella on the seat next to her and slid in.

The door slammed closed. The driver took off into traffic.

"Sorry, boss, for damaging the goods. I took out both Vernon's guards smooth as peanut butter. Didn't expect there to be two she-bitches. That one bites."

Tuccio grinned. "You did fine. This one on my lap is a particularly fine specimen." He brushed his lips against her cheek. "However, the pink hair and the bruiser makeup has to go, darling."

"No, you have to go." She tried to get another kick in, but he wrapped his hands around her neck and squeezed. "You are a nice surprise, but I don't really need you anymore. Now I have Bella. Either you sit still and I promise no harm will come to you and your friend here, or I can just get rid of you now. As Bella can tell you, I do keep my promises."

"Relax, Melissa. It's me the bastard wants." Bella leaned her head against the seatback. "Theo Tuccio. What garbage can did you crawl out of?"

"Nice to see you, too. I've been having a hard time believing you've been sitting on my doorstep for the last seven years and I never knew it."

"You're in good company. Vernon couldn't find me either. How did you?"

"Been following your brother and this punk head here around for the last three weeks. Not smart, your brother. Flies in. Has a big art show. Lots of publicity. Makes millions. Even I read the newspapers once in a while. Turns out I didn't need either. You showed up at your studio like a homing pigeon. Vernon tired of you?"

Bella closed her eyes. "So what's the plan?"

Tuccio smiled. "We're off to look at some artwork I've just acquired."

Chapter 37

Ari turned the corner onto Bedford. At the end of the block, a nondescript black car sat double-parked outside the Siren, engine running. The all-too-familiar profile of the man who'd destroyed his face and made him the prison enforcer was silhouetted in the rear window. Tuccio.

The hair rose on the back of his neck. *Sto diávolo,* his sister was in danger. He broke into a stumbling run. Every step rocketed pain through his body. Every breath ended in a gasp. Every fear ripped through his brain.

Ahead of him, a bruiser of a man in a motorcycle jacket emblazoned with an all too familiar symbol shoved a flailing pink-haired Goth into the backseat, then a staggering Sirena. Ari pressed his hand against his side and ran faster. But he was too slow, too far, too broken.

Wheels spun, and the car took off, disappearing into traffic. Knife-like pain shot through him. He crumpled onto the pavement, clutching his broken ribs, wheezing in the fumes that passed for air. Too late. Tuccio'd stolen his sister. He'd failed her. Again.

He pressed his hands against his chest and waited for the pain to fade and his thundering heart to slow, for his head to stop spinning and for his vision to clear. He'd trusted Vernon to keep her safe.

Never again. It was up to him to save her and her friend. Somehow.

First, he needed to get moving. He sucked in a breath of air, resettled his hat on his head, and swayed to his feet. Pedestrians fanned around him, grumbling, making rude comments about drunks, pushing him aside.

He rubbed his head. Sirena and that girl were in trouble, and he was a physical wreck. To hell with being a hero. Time to call in the police. He halted and searched his pocket for his cell. Someone bumped into him, and he slipped off the curb and fell. The phone tumbled to the pavement out of sight, out of reach. Useless.

As useless as him.

He lay there in a gray fog. Cold from the pavement seeped under his coat and numbed his body. Footsteps shuffled past. Voices approached and receded in waves. Louder and softer. In and out. Like surf beating against the shore. The sea rolling onto the beach at Eudokia.

Eudokia. His beloved island. His home.

Lost.

Forever.

The world went gently black.

****

"Get up, Ugly Man." Someone tugged on his coat. He rolled over and blinked against the sunlight. For a moment, he thought it was Melissa. Then his vision cleared, and a familiar face came into focus.

"Fur Tree? That you?" The boy's face bore a major scrape on the cheek and a swollen lip.

Fur Tree tugged again. "Get up, Ugly Man. Phew. You been lying in dog shit."

Ari stood, wobbled a bit, and then steadied. "My sister. She's been taken."

"Man's wanting you." Fur Tree yanked off his suit jacket, dropped it in the gutter, and pushed him toward an open car door.

Ari peered up into Vernon's grim mug and tensed. Sitting next to his sister's double-dealing lover was the last place he wanted to be. But he seemed to have no choice. He fell into the seat and concentrated on breathing. Each inhalation ripped through his chest. He sucked in the pain and held onto it. It reminded him he was still alive.

Vernon leaned over him. "Thanks, Fur Tree."

Ari shook his head to clear it. "You know him?"

The car door slammed, and the car moved into traffic. "I know everyone."

"Good. So let's go bring Sirena home."

"I will. When you tell me where she is."

Ari squinted at Vernon. "I thought you had everything under control."

"I had Gav and Fur Tree shadowing Bella and your Melissa. But Gav's vanished, and Fur Tree got knocked out. When he came to, they were gone. Found you and called me."

Melissa? Ari's heart skipped a beat. He sat up and put a hand on Vernon's shoulder. "Wait a minute—the pink-haired girl was *Melissa?*"

"Must have been. She's been hiding out at Bella's last few days. Did two girls get in the car?"

Zeús. How could he not have recognized her? He glared at Vernon. "Tuccio took them both—under duress."

"Tuccio? You sure?"

Ari nodded. "Recognized him."

"Damn you to hell, Stavros." Vernon fisted the back of the seat. "Like an idiot I listened to you and all that crap about freedom and choice. So I let your sister go. Gave her time to think about my proposal. Time to get captured by that bastard." He fisted the seat again. "She was going to give me her answer today." His cell phone rang. He pulled it from his pocket, looked at the number and put the phone to his ear. "Theo. You let her go now." Pause. "No way I'm paying you fifty million." Pause. "Yeah, well we'll see about that, won't we?" He flicked the cell off. "I don't believe it. He's demanding a ransom. The rotten upstart kidnapped my Bella."

Ari couldn't help himself. "Now you know how it feels." He shifted on the seat. "And only fifty? Eudokia is worth ten times that."

"Shut up."

"And he's your protégé. Do you think he'll give her back in one piece?"

Vernon drew back his fist. "I said shut up."

Ari shook his head. "Uh-uh, Vernon. Bella would not approve. Besides, the ribs are already broken."

Vernon dropped his hand and sighed. "So—"

"You could call the police. After all, you're now an upstanding citizen, and it's a very big city with millions of rat holes in which to hide two women."

"Oh, we'll use the police when needed." Vernon smiled slowly. "But I am an expert on rats, and right now, you and I are going hunting."

****

Two hours later, Ari leaned against the side of Marv's Food Truck, sipped a shake that settled like lead in his stomach, and watched the sun set. This was a wild goose chase. Vernon had checked out five of Tuccio's supposed hideaways in Brooklyn and except for stirring up a hornet's nest of angry pimps, johns, and addicts, found nothing. It had been five hours. Tuccio might hold onto Sirena, but by now, the bastard could have stashed Melissa anywhere—flown her out of the country, sold her to one of his patrons, tumbled her into his bed.

"Pssst."

Ari peered into the shadowed doorway. "That you, Hanger?"

"Toro's in trouble. We need you."

He squinted up at the building Vernon was searching. Muffled shouts told him a verbal battle was going on inside. He was useless here. He didn't owe Vernon anything, and he didn't like his methods. The only issue was how much he could help Toro in his physical condition. "You know I can't do much with these ribs."

"Your Archimedes brain still work?"

His heart sped up. Visions of Toro trapped under a fallen wall or hanging from a rooftop flooded his mind. "Yeah, how far?"

"South Brooklyn. We'll need a cab. This way."

He stumbled after Hanger. On the corner, the kid flagged down a cab by running out in front of it. The cab screeched to a halt and the driver leaned out the window. "Get out of my way. I don't pick up the homeless."

Ari opened the door and addressed the scowling cabby. "Ignore him. He's a kid. They dress weird." Hanger elbowed Ari. "Show him your money."

Ari pulled out a fifty and waved it in the cabby's face. The driver nodded. And they slid in.

"Ferris Street, Red Hook," Hanger said through the Plexi window.

Ari spun to look at him. "Where?"

Hanger shrugged. "You'll find out soon enough."

He studied the snubbed nose face. Hanger was hiding something. He looked at his watch. "Hey, shouldn't you be in school?"

"Nah. Sort of a—holiday. I'll let the others know I found you." Hanger pulled out his cell and called. "Got him. Meet us there."

Chapter 38

The damp chill emanating from the crumbling concrete walls of the sub-basement Tuccio had dumped her in crept under Melissa's thin, cotton karate outfit and into her bones. She twisted her hands against the zip ties binding her hands behind her back. Her fingers had gone numb hours ago.

She could no longer feel her toes either. Tuccio's moronic thug had taken her sneakers and zipped a tie around her ankles after she'd kicked him in the shins. But it had been worth it to see the chipmunk-mouthed bastard who'd tasered Bella grimace. She rubbed one bare foot against the other in a fruitless attempt to warm them up.

A trickle of fear crawled up her spine and settled in her empty stomach. Tuccio'd taken Bella away a long time ago. And they would come for her next. She had to get free.

She tugged at the ties again. Her wrists chafed. Her shoulders knotted. But the thin plastic held firm. Once she'd watched a YouTube video showing how to break out of zip ties by yanking hard. But it wasn't as easy as it looked.

She leaned back against the wall and peered through the gloom. If she tilted her head to the far right, she could barely make out the location of the door. A line of light shone along the bottom edge. Every once in a while, a shadow passed by—Tuccio or one of the guards on the prowl in the hallway beyond. She bit the inside of her cheek. Even if she did break the zip ties and managed to stumble to the door, she wouldn't get far.

She closed her eyes and inhaled the stink of sewage and mold and something recently dead that permeated her prison. The situation was hopeless. She was trapped and at the mercy of the real monster—a man willing to murder to get what he wanted. Icy prickles ran up and down her spine. She could die here, and Ari would never know what happened to her.

She licked her lips and remembered another shadowy basement and the first kiss they'd shared. Heat soared through her and then fled in the dank chill, leaving only regret behind. She should have trusted Ari to come back to her.

She let her head fall. She'd been an idiot. Hoodwinked by a pretty face. If only she'd trusted Ari from the beginning.

Crash. The steel door slammed open. The metallic ring blasted her ears after the hours of silence. Overhead fluorescents flicked on, blinding her. She peeked through her eyelashes. Tuccio stood in the doorway, restraining a reluctant Bella by the wrists. They'd stripped her to her underwear and taken her red wig. Short, black hair frizzed around her face like an angry cloud. Blood trickled down her face from a cut on her forehead.

"Vernon will never pay a ransom for me, you idiot," Bella yelled, yanking and twisting against his grip.

He laughed. "I have no idea why he wants you. But

he'll pay. And in more ways than you can imagine. Now shut up, she-demon."

She swung a leg at him and caught him in the shin. "Jackass. I'm in his bad books. I refused his proposal."

Tuccio grunted at the hit and with the help of the rougher-looking of his toughs, the bald one whose lips and tongue rolled around like loose marbles, wrestled her over to the wall. "I think you protest too much, my dear Bella. He'll come. I've made sure of it." He smashed her against the cement, knocking the air out of her, then zip tied her hands and ankles.

He stepped back and glanced at Melissa. "And your beloved monster will show up, too. If not for his whore"—he waved toward the corner of the basement where a stack of wooden crates leaned against the wall—"then for his paintings." He started toward the door. "I'm afraid, however, you won't be here for his grand arrival. My buyer will arrive shortly." With that, he flicked off the lights and left them lying on the damp floor in the dark.

Bella sniffled.

Melissa whispered across to her. "Are you all right?

Bella sniffed again. "I'll survive. Got a bunch of bruises, but so do they. Listen, Tuccio is right, Vernon and Ari will come and walk right into his trap. And I don't even want to think about what he means by a buyer. We have to do something."

"But what? I tried to break the tie but—"

Suddenly the door slammed opened, and Chipmunk Man swaggered inside, a body slung over his shoulder like a sack of dirty laundry. "Company, girls." He dumped the trussed up body on the floor and stomped back out.

Melissa caught a glimpse of the face as the door shut out the light. "I know who that is," she whispered. "That's one of Ari's graffiti groupies. He must be close. We have to escape."

Bella huffed. "If you wiggle closer, maybe I could chew through the damn ties."

Trying not to think of the filth on the floor, Melissa stretched out her body and rolled toward her. "Is that close enough?"

"Good. Now sit up." Bella brushed against her. "Hold your hands up higher."

Melissa maneuvered into position and held her wrists as high as she could. Bella's breath blew warm on her numb hands. The tie tugged against her skin. Minutes passed. "Any progress?"

The tugging stopped. "Damn thick plastic," Bella said. "This will take hours"—a shadow blocked the light under the door—"and I fear we don't have hours. Here they come."

Footsteps clattered closer. Laughter rose and fell. The doorknob turned.

"They're in here," Tuccio said, stepping inside, his spicy cologne a stark contrast to the moldy damp. He flicked on the lights and turned to let his companion enter.

Melissa held back a gasp. The man accompanying Tuccio was Grease Bag Lenny. Suddenly, a whole bunch of things made sense—Lenny's willingness to let the girls stay there, how Tuccio had known about Iza and Gracine and Daniela.

The double-dealing Grease Bag had put on a suit for the occasion, but it was as oil-stained as his everyday apron. He waddled over and halted in front of them, reeking of overheated grease and burnt fries. He placed his hands on his tubby belly and narrowed his eyes at Bella. "Not that one—with the tattoos. Too identifiable." He stepped up to Melissa and ran a hand down her cheek. "This is the one I want."

"Traitor." She spit in his face, bent her legs to kick out with both her feet.

"No, you don't." For a big man, he moved fast. He lifted her up and held her against the wall. Massive rolls of fat pressed against her chest, stifling her, pinning her to the hard cement like a captured butterfly. His sausage-fingered hand flew out and wrapped around her neck. She struggled to draw breath.

"Been watching you prance by for months now, dolly. Waiting for this day." He leaned harder on her throat. Her lungs burned. Black flowers floated across her vision. There was a persistent ringing in her ears. He ran his tongue up the side of her face and whispered. "You'll soon learn to behave. Choking is a proven aphrodisiac."

He let go.

Melissa sagged against the wall, gulping air into her lungs, one thought battling to get out. She sucked in a ragged breath. "I'm—tattooed—too."

Lenny's eyes narrowed into tiny slits. He yanked open her shirt, yanked down her waistband and scowled at the images running from her clavicle to her upper thigh.

He seized Tuccio by the lapels and pulled him up against his belly in a bizarre imitation of a before-and-after body-builder poster. His jaw quivered. Spit flew out of his mouth. "She's ruined. Half. I will only pay half of what I offered."

"Then the deal's off." Tuccio brushed Lenny's hands off his suit, whipped out a long-bladed knife, and stabbed it into the heaving belly.

Lenny let out a squeal worthy of a stuck pig and fell back, eyes bulging, the knife handle protruding from his guts. Blood blossomed across his white shirt, stained his pants. He collapsed to the floor, emitting a thin high-pitched wail.

Tuccio yanked out the knife and snapped his fingers at Marble Mouth. "Dump the turd in the river."

Melissa gasped. "But he's still alive."

Tuccio whipped his head around. "Not for long." He came toward her, his eyes cold as ice. He spread open her shirt and traced the lines of the tattoo with the tip of the bloody knife. Chills ran up and down her body. "Now what are we to do with you, Miss Dermont? You've lost me thousands of dollars defacing yourself." He lifted the knife and placed it at the tip of her eye. "Perhaps I'll add a scar or two. Where you're headed now, the men won't care." He grasped her chin and pressed harder. Melissa closed her eyes to block out the face looming over her, the one she'd once thought perfect. But she couldn't block out the pseudo-velvet voice or the sting of the knife still dripping with Lenny's gore. The tip bit into her skin. Tuccio's voice whispered in her ear like a lover's. "A scar to match your Ari's." The knife stopped. "Or maybe not. Our Greek hero may be more amenable to my terms if he thinks you untouched."

Beside her, Bella hissed like a snake. "Let her go. She's useless now. You lost your buyer, and Vernon won't pay ransom for her."

He spun around and punched her in the jaw. Bella's head fell back, blood dripping from a split lip. "Your brother will. With his life."

She spit out the blood and rolled her shoulders. "I have no brother. Ari's gone—the coward. Flew the coop when the going was good."

"You underestimate the man." He tucked away the knife and glanced at his watch. "I expect your brother to arrive shortly. Without Vernon. And I have *so* many things he wants." He walked over and kicked the trussed up graffiti artist lying on the floor. The boy grunted. "Good. Still kicking. Meanwhile, you ladies and gent get nice and comfortable. The show will begin shortly."

The door banged open. "Here she is, boss." Marble Mouth held Jana by the arm. "She-devil bit me." He let her go and rubbed his arm.

Jana shook him off, then minced over to Tuccio and gave him a kiss on the cheek. She slithered against him. "What's going on, Theo? If you wanted me, all you had to do was send your comfy limo. Not that bastard. He kept touching me."

Tuccio grasped her by the chin. "You're here to join my party."

Jana glanced around. "Party? Here? In this stinking cesspit?" She wrapped her arm around him."With her?" She pointed at Melissa.

Melissa's blood froze. She strained against the zip ties. "I thought you were my friend."

"Friend? Ha." Jana walked over and slapped her. "I've hated you forever. Some gook from nowhere, lording it over me, getting me in trouble with the police with your fat trap. Had to do some rotten things to get my police record expunged. And you—Little Goody-Two-Shoes—going on and on about your dear departed angel of a sister. Near drove me crazy. Well, your sister was no angel."

Melissa's heart thudded in her ears. "What—do you mean?"

"Your darling Laura slept around. Did drugs. And I covered for her."

"What?"

"Had a drug dealer boyfriend." She whirled around and pointed to Tuccio. "*Him.*"

Melissa stared at Tuccio. He stood wide-legged, his face utterly expressionless. Was he the shadowy boy she glimpsed in the beat-up convertible that whisked away her sister that fateful day? "How—how'd she die?"

Jana pursed her lips. "Drug sale gone bad, or so I've heard. Right, Theo?"

"Enough true confessions," Tuccio said. He pushed Jana toward Chipmunk Face. "Bind her with the rest."

"Bastard." Jana tottered on her heels, found her balance, and dove at him, beat him on the chest with her fists. "But—but I did everything you asked."

"I didn't ask you to act the slut with Stavros."

"It meant nothing. I was trying to get information for you. Besides, you were messing with her." She pointed at Melissa.

Tuccio tossed Jana to Marble Mouth. "Shut her up."

"No way." Jana drove her stiletto heel into the guy's instep, pulled a knife from her pocket and ran at Tuccio. "You double-dealing crook. You promised me a manager position in the firm if I reeled in Melissa here, helped you get the paintings."

Tuccio stepped back with a laugh. His men circled closer, and he waved them away with a shake of his head. "This is my she-cat."

"Damn right." Jana swung the knife at him, caught his upper arm. A thin line of blood stained the sleeve of his white shirt.

"Enough." Tuccio grabbed her knife hand and twisted. Her fingers lost their grip, and the knife tumbled down into the murk. He yanked her against him, wrapped her hair around his hand and pulled her head back. Jana snarled and kicked, but she was no match for him. He yanked harder and nuzzled her throat. "I love your passion, darling. But you're a loose cannon with a big mouth."

He shoved her into the arms of the guard next to Bella. "Put her with the others." Holding his hand on the cut, he went to the door and invited in a younger man with pale gray eyes that matched his own. He slapped the man on his shoulder. "Kiro. Shut their traps and don't let them move an inch. If they do, I give you permission to play a bit—but no visible marks. Understood?"

"Yes, boss." The man stalked in and grinned, revealing eye teeth filed to points. "Now, ladies. Let's see who moves first."

Chapter 39

Ari stepped out of the cab behind Hanger. Abandoned two- and three-story factories lined the river side of the street. Cars whizzed by, traveling through, not stopping. Faded black paper covered barred windows. Rusty corrugated metal sheathed entrance ways. Crumbling brick walls bore faded lettering with names of companies long out of business.

Hanger looked over his shoulder. "This way, Ugly Man. Hurry."

For one moment, he hesitated. He'd been a fool to come on his own. If Toro was trapped inside one of these buildings, it would be close to impossible to get him out. He glanced around. Up ahead, a battered white van blocked the sidewalk. Pressure built inside his chest. He wanted to trust Hanger. But this felt like a trap. He fingered his phone. Should he call Vernon? Call the police?

Hanger swerved around the van and crossed the street. A long row of garbage bins, full of demolition debris, lined the sidewalk in front of a boarded up storefront. Ari trailed after him, drawing out his phone.

"No cops," Hanger whispered. He knocked the cell phone out of his hand and dropped it in a garbage bin. "Wait here. Act like a bum looking through the trash." Then he crossed over to the other side of the street and disappeared behind the van.

Minutes passed, and Hanger did not return. Ari inhaled the stink of the river and then wished he hadn't. The rotten chemical smell only added to tightness in his chest. He gave up searching for the phone and crossed over to the other side of the street.

He skirted around the van and stopped short. A little farther down the street, Hanger was standing in a dark doorway talking to Tuccio's thug, the leathery snake who'd been tailing Melissa. His heart thundered in his chest. Hanger. Innocent Hanger worked for Tuccio? No.

He pulled back trying to decide what to do. There was a familiar whistle. Ari looked up. On the roof of the factory, he saw the twins, Solo and Neto.

"Psst." Solo leaned over the cornice and signaled with his thumb. He mouthed the words: *Go round back.*

Ari nodded and headed down the narrow side street alongside the brick wall of the factory. At the back of the building, he found a padlocked metal cyclone gate.

"Here."

He peered up. Neto pointed at a rope dangling from the roof. It barely reached the top of the first-floor windows. He clenched the fingers of his injured hand. He doubted rope climbing was on the doctor's list of recommended activities. But if Tuccio was here, then so were Melissa and his sister—he clamped his teeth together—and Toro.

He seized the rope, and ignoring the fiery pain radiating up his arm, worked his way up the battered brick wall of the building, finding toeholds in the crumbling mortar and using his legs for support as much as possible. He yanked himself over the cornice and stood. The grim faces of Solo and Neto glared at him.

"Don't follow directions, do you, Ugly Man?" Solo said.

Ari cradled his throbbing hand against his chest. "How'd they capture Toro?"

"Some lady called saying she had a painting of yours to be picked up. That you had left it to us. Gave this address. Toro and I came to collect it. When we got here, a man took Toro inside to sign papers, he said. But once Toro was in the office, they threw me out. Couldn't get back in." Solo fisted his hand and shook it at him. "The man said he'd trade Toro for you. If you'd stayed where you were, Hanger would have gotten them to bring Toro to the door for the exchange. We planned to drop bricks on the thug's head before they got to you."

Ari sucked in his breath. "Bricks? These bastards have guns. You all could have been killed. We need a better plan." He reached into his pocket, then remembered the kid had tossed his cell. "Why'd Hanger ditch my phone?"

"Probably thought you'd call the police. Thugs said Toro will go to jail if the cops show up."

"Actually, I was going to call a sometime friend. Does anyone have a phone I can use?" Ari tried to move the fingers of his left hand and got no response, only excruciating pain. Useless. He dropped it to his side. "We're going to need all the help we can get."

Solo gave him a sideways look. "No, you'll put Toro in danger."

"Toro's already in danger. Trust me. Vernon Newell can deal with these thugs. He speaks the same language."

"Vernon Newell? The guy Fur Tree's been working for?" Solo glanced at Neto and then tossed Ari his cell. He typed in a call for help and pushed send, hoping Vernon checked the text message at once even though he didn't recognize the sender. He gave back the phone and then looked at the twins. He would have to give himself up and hope that Vernon arrived in time. Toro and anyone else in Tuccio's hands wouldn't last long. But meanwhile, maybe they could find where Tuccio was holding his captives and make a little mayhem along the way until help arrived.

He examined the door hatch. When they'd closed the factory, they'd used wood instead of metal, and time and weather had cracked and warped the boards. He glanced over at Neto. "Think you can widen those cracks?"

"Sure thing, Ugly Man." Neto pulled a knife from his pocket and set to work creating a gap on either side of the plank.

Someone tugged on his coat. He jerked around and stared down at Hanger's lopsided grin.

"No way you'll get that open this side of New Year's," Hanger said.

"How'd you get up here?"

Hanger scrunched his nose. "Climbed the rope like everyone else. I pulled it up too so the bad guys wouldn't climb up after me. That's what always happens in the movies."

Ari pressed a hand to his forehead and shook his head. *Zeús*, he'd forgotten all about the boy. Hanger could have fallen, and no one would have known. He wanted to hug the kid. Instead, he growled at him. "This is no movie."

Hanger stuck his hands in his pockets, walked over to study Neto's ragged digging." So how you gonna get the door off?"

"With this rope you rescued." Ari picked up the rope, tied the end to a solid cast iron vent pipe, and then looped it around the end of the board. He twisted and knotted the rope. "This is a tackle knot. It halves the force needed."

Hanger fingered the knot. "Oh, like the lever. Can I do it?"

Ari handed him the end of the rope. "Be my guest."

While Hanger and Neto demolished the hatch, Ari stared over the cornice. For the first time in his life, he would actually be glad to see Vernon Newell show up.

Chapter 40

Ari lowered himself down the hatchway. The third floor of the factory was a large open space littered with broken casings where machines had once stood. Bits of light shot through rips in the paper covering the windows and illuminated dust motes and rat turds. No one had been in this part of the building in years. Tuccio would be holding the girls down below. He studied the way the old plank floor dipped and twisted. "Not sure the floor is sound," he called back to the deco boys gathered around the hatch.

"I'm the smallest, send me," Hanger said.

Ari shook his head. No way a child was going into that place. He tried to sound upbeat. "You have the most important job—coordinator. You are in charge of Neto's cell phone. When a gang of big thugs arrive in a bunch of black cars, you text Solo. Together we will squeeze our evil friends here into a tight corner between us and my buddies."

Hanger nodded, his mouth twisted in an I'm-not-convinced scowl.

Ari signaled Solo. "Bring those loose roof tiles."

He caught the rope and swung down, waited for the twins to follow. "Now Hanger, toss the rope." He caught it and wrapped it around his shoulder. He pointed at his feet. "Step where I step." Carefully picking his way from plank to plank, he led them across the floor to the stairs and started down.

Just as they reached the landing above the second floor, the door below banged open, and two men's voices echoed up. "Woman sure can kick. Bet I got black and blue marks down my side."

"And Kiro gets all the fun with the ladies while we get to watch an empty hall."

Ari stopped short, his blood boiling. Melissa and Bella were running out of time. He signaled T-Crew to hold up. Then he leaned over the railing, located Tuccio's men, and dropped one of the shingles down the stairwell. The asphalt thudded at the bottom.

"What was that?" One of the thugs drew his gun and started down.

He dropped the second piece of asphalt so it hit the railing inches below the remaining guard. The guard turned his back and took several steps toward the sound. Good. With a sweep of his hand, he tossed the last piece so it hit farther down.

"Someone between us," the thug called down to his partner. His footsteps faded away.

"Now." Ari signaled, and they rushed down the stairs to the second floor. He glanced up and down the dim hallway. Three doors opened along the corridor. The first door was locked. The next office door stood open. "Here." They ducked into the room. It was empty except for some metal chairs and an old battle-axe of a desk. Ari half-closed the door. "Does that door over there lead into the other office?"

Solo twisted the knob and peeked in. "Yep. It's same as this."

"Perfect. Time to even the odds." Ari picked up the rope and checked the tackle knot. "First we'll set up a barrier of chairs in the other room. Then I'm going to drop more shingles. As soon as they're on the landing, Solo, you peek out the door and get their attention. Then duck back." He held up the looped end of the rope. "The door opens inward so as soon as they're tangled in the barrier, Neto, you come round, hook the rope to the door like this, yank hard, and tie the rope to the railing." He turned to Solo. "After you are through the inner door, push the oak desk against it. Once Tuccio's men are trapped, promise me you'll stay undercover while I go find Toro and the others."

Ari glanced around at the young faces and bit his lip hard. Blood welled, the taste bitter iron on his tongue. He was risking more than his own life, he was asking these youths to risk theirs. Footsteps rang on the treads. A man coughed. Tuccio's guards were coming back up. It was now or never.

Solo rested his long-fingered hand on his shoulder. "Don't worry, Ugly Man. We know what to do. You go. Save Toro and the others."

Despite the hard knot in his chest, he gave them a thumbs-up sign. "Stay low. They will shoot." Ari pressed himself against the inner wall of the stairwell and waited for the two thugs to rush by, then took off down the stairs. Behind him, doors slammed and curses slapped his ears. His body tensed, but he did not look back, did not stop. Instead, gasping for air, he sped downward, taking the stairs two at a time, every step shooting pain through his ribs, bringing him closer to disaster.

The first-floor hallway stood deserted. All the doors closed. He hesitated, listening. The faint clank of a doorknob turning came from below. The basement, of course. Blooding thrumming loudly in his ears, he continued down.

Just as he reached the bottom step, the door opened, and one of Tuccio's goons stepped out. Ari wrapped him in a head lock and banged his head against the doorframe. The man slid down, unconscious.

Ari stepped inside and blinked against the dark. He searched for a light switch, found it and flicked it on. *Sto diávolo.* Bella and Melissa lay on the floor, bound hand and foot.

Bella tossed her hair out of her face and looked him up and down. "Thought you left."

He hurried to her. "I am not the coward you think I am."

"Oh, just cut us free and get out us of here." She pursed her lips. "You did bring a knife, little brother, didn't you?"

"Of course." He pulled out his Swiss army knife, leaned down and sliced apart her zip ties.

She stood up, rubbing her wrists. "Take care of your girl."

Ari turned to Melissa and cut her free. He helped her up. He wanted to hold her, kiss her and never let her go, but the wary look about her mouth, and the coldness in her eyes stopped him. Instead, he tousled her hair. "Nice color."

She put her hand on his arm. "Your graffiti buddy is in bad shape."

He pointed to the door. "The stair above was clear a few minutes ago. Head on up. T-Crew is on the second floor. I'll get Toro and follow."

He rushed across the room and bent over Toro's

305

prone body. The boy was unconscious, a huge yellowing lump on the side of his head, his skin a sickly bluish green. Ari smoothed back the long dark hair. He'd have to carry him out. He put a hand on his ribs. Somehow.

"Monster Man."

Ari spun around. Next to the crate, Jana Firth lay on her side trussed like one of Barba Thomasi's chickens waiting for slaughter in Eudokia's butcher shop. He stared at her. "You!"

She held out her hands. "Cut me free. Those bitches would leave me here to rot. But you won't."

"They must have a reason."

She raised an eyebrow and gave him an open-mouthed smile as false as her eyelashes. "Jealousy."

"More like betrayal."

She tugged at her bonds. "Does this look like I'm in Theo Tuccio's good graces?"

"You're definitely not in mine. You're the reason my paintings are here, why my friend Toro is injured."

She gazed up at him, her make-up-smeared face a mockery of packaged beauty. "Please, I can help you get out."

As much as he detested the woman, he couldn't leave her in the hands of these brutal men. He leaned down to cut her free.

A shadow fell over them. "My dear Jana. Don't make promises you cannot keep."

Ari spun around and peered up into the icy eyes of his worst enemy. Tuccio stepped into the cellar, followed by two of his men holding his sister and Melissa, knives to their necks.

Bella struggled against her captor, elbowing him in

the chin. "Take the bastard out, Ari."

Tuccio flicked out his own knife and seized Bella by the hair. "Drop the knife, friend, and step away from Firth or your sister will lose her nose."

A shiver snaked through him. Ari put up his hands. The thug closest to him grabbed him by the shoulders and threw him onto the floor. His head rushed to meet the concrete, and everything went dark.

Chapter 41

Ari came to with a start. He was lying face down in a noxious puddle pungent with spilled blood and stagnant river water that brought back memories of Korydallos Prison. Zip ties bound his arms and legs. Every muscle and bone in his body ached. Chills shook his body. He blinked his eyes to clear his vision.

The leather-clad snake lifted him by his shoulder and flipped him over. He peered up into gray eyes cold as stone. The man smacked him in the ribs with a steel-toed boot. Pain blossomed across his chest, and he coughed.

The Snake grunted, "He's comin' round, Theo."

"Good. It's time to get the show started." Tuccio moved into his vision. "By the way, let me introduce you to my new protégé, Kiro. I've promised him first turn with your Melissa."

Snake Man Kiro gave him a grin that matched the one Tuccio once wore before the plastic surgeons had at him. Then the Snake lifted him up and deposited him against the wall.

Tuccio paced in front of him. "I knew you would come. They all said you'd left. But I know little Ari better than that. You think with your heart. I could never beat that softness out of you." He caught him under the chin with his palm and thrust his head against the wall. "Not that it wasn't fun trying. I saved you in that prison. But you double crossed me. Chased me off the island and turned Vernon, my own brother, against me." Tuccio slammed his head into the wall. "And for that you will pay."

Ari sucked in as much air as he could, and ignored the white fissures slashing across his vision. He'd taken too many blows to his head to think clearly. He struggled to get the words out. "I had nothing to do with Vernon's closing you out."

Tuccio's mouth twisted into a tight little line. "Right, nothing to do with the man who's been your patron for years, who's in love with your sister. You're two peas in a pod, you and Vernon. Because of that worthless peasant girl I knocked up. Damn, I'd been in prison for five years. I needed something soft and warm. I would have paid her well. But the high and mighty Olympian wanted to be a white knight. Bad mouthed me to Vernon. Why didn't you marry the poor thing yourself?

"Ritsa committed suicide after you carved her up."

Tuccio whirled around and punched him in the chin. "I never cut her."

Ari spat out blood. "They were your initials on her cheeks."

Tuccio shook his head and said softly, "No. Not me. Is that what this has been about? You thought—"

Ari narrowed his eyes. Had he been mistaken all these years? He remembered the girl's last words, the look on her face. No, she'd not lied. "The girl told me herself."

Tuccio threw back his head and laughed. "Almost got you, didn't I? For a moment, that softy heart of yours was full of compassion for little old me." His phone rang. He pulled it out of his pocket and glanced at the message. "Well, I have no compassion in me at all, only revenge. You're going to pay for all I have lost. Watch me destroy all you love bit by bit, and be able to do nothing about it." He glanced at Bella. "And then I will do the same to Vernon." He licked his lips. "He's on his way, you know. Coming to the rescue."

Tuccio signaled Kiro, and Ari was dragged to his feet. "Take a good look at the little ladies and your gypsy spy guy. It's going to be your last."

Ari blinked to clear his vision. Along the far wall, Toro lay prone, bound hand and foot, not moving. Melissa, incongruous pink hair framing a fear-pale face, huddled against the near wall, hands and feet bound, eyes tortured. Beside her, Bella flicked her chin in a Greek gesture of disdain and turned her head away.

He'd let her down. He'd let everyone down.

He closed his eyes and prayed that the T-Crew members hiding upstairs stayed there, that Hanger listened for once and still played lookout on the roof. He let out a steadying breath and glared at Tuccio. "It's over. You have me. Let them go."

Tuccio flexed his plasticized lips into a smile worthy of a victory salute. "Oh, I think not. They're the guests of honor at this party." He signaled his men. "Open the crate and dump out the canvases." He nudged him in the ribs with his foot. "Watch."

The men tipped the crate over and the last of his paintings—the ones intended for Melissa—spread across the floor.

Tuccio took out his knife and with savage fury slashed each one over and over, stabbing through breasts and stomachs, spines and necks, wrists and ankles until all that was left were bits of colorful canvas scattered like dying leaves across the filthy floor.

Ari tucked in his chin and tried not to look, not to think. Every swooshing blow flayed his own skin. Each rip sliced through his heart. Years of work destroyed in a moment. His last painting of Melissa, done from memory. Gone. It wasn't all his work, but it was his best.

He peered across at Melissa and his sister. He should have taken Tuccio out years ago—in prison or afterward when the bastard destroyed Ritsa. But he hadn't. He clenched his bound hands, remembered the look of surprise on the face of the boy he'd killed, the awful silence that followed, the ripping apart of who he had been.

He'd sworn never to let that murdering monster out again, never to snuff out another life. Now the two women he loved, and an innocent boy on the cusp of manhood, were trapped in this hellhole, and he knew he would kill again to save them even if it destroyed him in the process.

He rolled his shoulder muscles and tested the zip tie binding his hands behind his back. Kiro the Snake Man had learned his technique from the master. There was no flex. No room to turn his wrists and loosen the grip. He would have to break it. He glanced at Tuccio's two big toughs. But not yet—sometimes the wisest offensive was to hold back and let your opponent think he'd won.

Tuccio bent over Ari and lifted his head again. "Don't fret about the paintings. I have planned a brilliant finale to your artistic career." He leaned closer. "The art world is going to be amazed at your last tour de force. Most original artwork they've ever seen. I've titled it 'Dead Artist in a Crate.' I'm shipping you to the Biennale." He nodded to his men. "Get to it. Pack him in."

Two pairs of hands seized him roughly and carried him to the empty painting crate. Ari relaxed his muscles. It would be a tight fit. He'd built it himself, knew the dimensions to a tee. The crate was six feet by ten feet, but only fifteen inches wide.

They stuffed him in head first. His neck bent sideways. His body sagged down. His legs folded in at an awkward angle. Rough wood scraped his skin. His injured hand twisted, and he swallowed the pain.

Tuccio smiled down at him. "Look at the big man now. All tucked up nice and tight." *Bang.* He slammed the lid and picked up a hammer and a nail. "Now for the party." He hit the nail. "You get to listen to China Doll and the kid being enjoyed by my men." He whacked in another nail. "While your darling sister curses you." He drove in the last one.

Ari released the breath he'd been holding and took several shallow gulps of air. Then he flexed his shoulders and snap—the zip ties binding him broke open. Tuccio was going to pay.

****

Melissa stared at the wooden crate. Some monster. Ari hadn't struggled when they dumped him in that coffin of a box. Hadn't glanced her way. Hadn't acknowledged her. He was going to die a slow, horrible death trapped in the hold of a container ship without food and water. She blinked back tears. He hadn't even said goodbye.

There was a clattering in the hall, and Chipmunk

Man dashed out the door. He returned dragging a kid wearing baggy sweats, a battered baseball cap, and untied sneakers. "Found this peewee sneaking around, boss."

"Name's Hanger." The kid elbowed the bald guy in the gut and wiggled free. "Wasn't sneaking. Came to tell you there's folks upstairs. Got your other idiots trapped."

Melissa's stomach clenched. The kid was selling them out. She glanced over at Toro's still body. Not that she blamed him. She'd have done anything to save her sister—she tried not to look at the crate—or Ari.

Tuccio flicked his thumb at Chipmunk. "Go see."

Hanger spread his legs and glared up at Tuccio. "I helped you. Now you let my brother go. He didn't do *nothing*."

Tuccio's mouth winked up in a half-smile, and he slowly clapped his hands. "Bravo. I can use kids with chutzpah in my network. I let your brother go, you and he work for me. Got it?"

"Yeah, man. Whatever." Hanger spied Toro half-covered in torn canvas strips. "Wha'd you do to him?" He scrambled to his brother's side, leaned over him.

A shot ripped out from somewhere upstairs. Someone yelled. Kiro whirled and bolted out the door, gun drawn. Tuccio turned to follow.

In the same instant, Toro leaped up from the floor and jumped on Tuccio from behind. Spray-painted fingers dug into the thick neck. Teeth sank into the exposed skin above the bastard's collar. Tuccio gagged and spun around, trying to dislodge the gypsy demon on his back. Toro clung on, yanking and pulling and biting, but it was taking all his strength.

Melissa tugged on her bonds. If only she could get free and help.

Something cold brushed against her wrists, and she jumped.

"Don't move, tattoo groupie," Hanger whispered as he bent behind her. The zip tie sprung free. She shook her hands to get the blood flowing. He sliced open the leg tie with a penknife and moved on to Bella. Melissa stood up, wobbled, caught her balance, and blinked as the sides of the ill-fated crate fell open like the petals of a decaying flower.

****

Ari threw down the hinge pins that had held the crate together on the inside and staggered upright. Tuccio whirled past, Toro clinging to his neck.

What was the crazy gypsy doing? His heart skipped a beat as Tuccio smashed the fine-boned body against the concrete wall. Toro was tough and tenacious, but he was no match for a six-foot-two Macedonian brute. He shouted at Toro to let go, and then leaped forward with a growl and dove at Tuccio's legs.

Tuccio staggered and twisted under the new attack. With one hand, he jabbed for Ari's eyes. With the other, he bent back Toro's fingers. He swung, ducked, and sent Toro flying across the room. The youth landed hard on the cement, pushed up once, and then collapsed.

Ari's vision narrowed in on the man facing him. No more. The bastard had to be stopped. Adrenaline thrummed through him. His muscles tensed as they did before a bout. He rose up, found his footing on the rough, broken concrete, and smashed his fist into the false face leering at him.

Plastic and metal crunched. Pain spiraled through his hand, numbing it.

Tuccio laughed, reached inside his coat, and whipped out his knife.

Ari stepped back. He knew that blade and what it could do too well.

Tuccio circled around, knife flickering. "Ha. Little Rich Boy. Still afraid of my little friend here." He slashed out, aiming for Ari's good cheek. "Time to balance out that scar I gave you."

The knife whizzed toward his face. Ari flinched and jerked his head to the side. *Whoosh.* Tuccio slashed again, driving him backward across the cellar away from the door, away from the women. Ari stumbled, tripped on a board from the crate, and fell backward with a crash. Wood pieces went flying. Splinters buried themselves in his arms and legs. Above him, Tuccio kicked at his head. He latched onto Tuccio's foot and twisted, but his battered hands failed him, and he lost his grip.

Tuccio took advantage, stomped on his right hand, crushing the bones. Pain jolted through his fingers and up his arm. Ari groaned and yanked his hand free. The knife came straight toward him.

At the last second, Ari lifted his legs and rolled out from under Tuccio, then sprang up, gasping for air. But Tuccio was quicker, in better shape. He spun around and drove the knife into Ari's shoulder, gave it a twist, and pulled it out.

Ari went down on one knee, his shoulder a blaze of burning pain. His vision blurred. His whole body shook. Tuccio's destroyed face loomed over him, the lips pulled back in a grotesque smile. The knife came down again.

Melissa's scream pierced the roaring in his head. He forced his eyes open. She had the hammer aimed at Tuccio's head. Face contorted in fury, she took a step forward. Splintered wood crunched beneath her feet.

"Oh no you don't, China Doll." Tuccio jerked around, seized her by the hair and put the blade of the knife against her throat. The hammer thunked on the concrete. The glistening edge of Tuccio's knife pressed down, slitting the skin. A ribbon of blood welled.

"No." Ignoring the burning pain from his smashed hands, Ari sprang from the floor. Setting his feet, he locked his arms around Tuccio's chest like he would an opponent in a match, and squeezed with every bit of strength he had left. The first rib cracked.

Tuccio jerked. The knife slipped from his fingers. Ari kept squeezing. Another rib cracked. Tuccio's hands lost their grip on Melissa's hair. She dropped to the floor, her head thwacking against the concrete, blood dripping down her neck.

Ari gasped. Melissa. Tuccio had killed Melissa. The beast inside him leaped free. Ari squeezed harder. More ribs cracked. Tuccio's lungs strained and gasped for air. Still, Ari squeezed and squeezed.

Tuccio's eyes bulged, his body convulsed, and then went limp.

****

What happened? Melissa shook herself and pushed up on one elbow. Her head spun. Her neck burned. Voices rose and faded. Someone nearby whimpered. Footsteps stomped up and down the staircase. The acrid reek of blood hung in the fetid air.

She pushed her hair out of her eyes and glanced around. The walls still seeped green ooze. The foul aroma of the river still assaulted her nostrils. The overhead light bulb still glared. But Tuccio's broken body was gone. She wrapped her arms across her chest and shivered. The nightmare was over.

By the door, Bella leaned against a large-boned man with white-blond hair. From the way they were kissing, she guessed he must be the infamous Vernon Newell, and upstairs, the tramping must be his men rounding up the last of Tuccio's thugs.

In the distance, sirens grew louder.

Beside her, Ari moaned softly. She shifted toward him. Blood stained his shirt where Tuccio had stabbed him. Deep gashes encircled his wrists where he'd fought to free himself from the zip ties. Scraps and splinters covered his cheek and forehead. His lower lip bled where it had split open. Tucked close to his side, his crushed right hand hung swollen and limp. His breath came in widely-spaced snatches.

She wanted to kiss him, throw her arms around him, tell him she'd been wrong to think he'd abandoned her, that she understood he'd been trying to protect her—she touched the cut on her neck—from this.

But she didn't want to hurt him. Tentatively, she placed her fingers on his arm, one of the few places he seemed uninjured. He flinched away, and she dropped her hand. "Lie still," she whispered. You're badly wounded. An ambulance is coming."

"I'll live." He used his elbow and torso to twist himself up to a sitting position. He bent over and noisily sucked air in and out, his face etched with pain. "Toro?"

"Over there."

Ari followed her gaze. Toro lay in a heap against the wall, his brother holding his hand, tears running down his face. *"Sto diávolo."* He gathered his legs under him and half-crawled, half-staggered toward the broken body. He collapsed beside Hanger.

"She can't feel her legs," the boy said. There was a shattered look about his eyes.

Melissa jerked up. *She?* Toro was a girl? She studied the prone body. Swaddled in the baggy clothes, the body was a mystery, but there was a swan-like curve to the neck, and elegance to the limp hands. Ari's gypsy could be as much female as male.

A hard lump formed in her throat. She sat for a moment, the damp of the concrete seeping into her bones, emptiness enveloping her. Then she pushed herself up and on shaky legs wobbled toward them. Several feet away, she stopped, her skin chilled.

Without the tugged down hat and the wild hair, the graffiti artist's face was softly feminine, the heavily-lashed dark eyes gentle. Many young men had delicate builds. But only a woman in love wore that look.

"Sorry I lied," she was saying. The thin body shuddered. Her breathing roughened. "'Bout being a boy. It was safer on the streets that way—for Hanger and me."

Ari moved closer. "Hush. Help is on the way."

"But if I can't walk—my art—I can't live like that—a cripple."

Ari bent down and kissed her on the forehead. "They'll fix it, Toro. Fix you. You have a future as a great artist." He leaned closer. "I'll see to it. I promise."

The corners of Toro's lips twitched. "I love you,

318

Ugly Man."

Melissa stepped back, put her hand on the cold concrete wall, and steadied herself. She didn't belong there with them. Hanger grasped Ari's jacket like a lifeline. Toro lay relaxed, one hand resting on Ari's thigh. Matching curly dark hair. The same olive-toned skin. They looked like a family.

Ari had a beautiful young artist to care for, to love him. He didn't need her.

Melissa lifted the collar of her shirt and lightly touched the tattooed skin. All he'd had with her was hot sex and trouble. She buttoned her collar closed. And he would hate what she had done to herself.

The sirens stopped. The ambulances had arrived.

Melissa took one last look at the man she loved and slipped out the door.

Chapter 42

Ari peered out at the viridian water, at the line of pale gold where the water met the sea as the sun tipped the horizon. He kicked at the sand. Everywhere he looked, he saw a painting—he saw Melissa.

He closed his eyes and bent the fingers of his left hand as hard as he could. Most of the pain was gone, but the fingers barely moved. Paint. Bah. He couldn't even hold a fork to eat. And using the crushed fingers of his right hand had proved—well—awkward. The mess of paintings stuffed in the trash bin up at the villa bore witness to that.

He waded out into the water and dove in. Gentle waves ebbed around him, welcomed him and cradled his body. Little fish nibbled at his toes. He turned onto his back and kicked farther out. The villa on the cliff grew smaller. The figures of Hanger and Toro in her wheelchair eating breakfast on the veranda became fainter.

They would be here soon—Bella and Vernon. Come to take possession of their villa. He flipped over and settled into a slow sidestroke. Bella insisted he could stay, but he'd moved his stuff to the shepherd's hut above the lagoon last night. They'd all be more comfortable with him out of the way.

The sun rose higher. Golden light splashed over him, turned the water around him to emerald and chrome green. He floated for a while, watching the light climb the cliffs, strike the white walls of the villa, touch the red roofs of the village. A rooster crowed. A donkey brayed. A small fishing boat sailed out of the harbor. A yacht motored in.

He wished them happiness. He dug his arms into the water and started swimming again. So much was gone—his home, his talent, his self-respect, the woman he loved. But he'd saved the village and the seals. And he had Toro and Hanger to care for—to live for.

The water surged cool and silken around him, and he let his mind wander. He pictured the last time he'd seen her in that horrible chamber of death—Melissa with her horrendous pink hair leaning over him telling him he'd be all right, when he'd never be right again.

He was glad she'd left that day, run away from him. He hoped she'd finished her dissertation and was busy teaching, helping abused women, being the good person she was.

Something nudged him from the side. A furry head rolled under his hand. One of the monk seals come to welcome him. He slipped under the rock ledge and into the sea cavern. Seals glided around him. Mothers nuzzled their cubs on the rocks.

His feet scraped bottom. Pea gravel rolled and rubbed against his soles. He found his favorite spot on the tiny pebble beach and stretched out, let the lapping of the water against the stones lull him to oblivion.

Minutes or hours later he opened his eyes. A Nereida stood at the entrance to the cavern, her black hair long and flowing, her filmy linen dress floating about her in the sea breeze. Ari blinked, pushed up on his arms, blinked again. She was coming toward him.

"Little Bee? *Melissa?* How?"

"I came with Bella and Vernon."

She was real. Close enough to touch, close enough to feel her warmth, breathe in her scent. He took a step back.

She smoothed down her dress and glanced away. "I'm sorry I left—that day."

He shook his head. "You did the right thing."

"No—I should have stayed with you, trusted you."

She put out her arms. She was too brave for him. He backed farther away. "Don't touch me."

"Why? What's wrong?"

"I'm a beast—a murdering monster. I squeezed a man to death."

"You had to—he was going to kill us all."

"No. I didn't have to kill him. I let anger take over me, I let the beast out. I could have stopped, and I didn't."

"It was self-defense. The police said so." Melissa moved closer.

He shook his head. "I can't touch you. I am not safe to be around you or anyone." He waded into the water.

Her lips twisted. "Hanger and Toro seem safe enough—happy."

"Toro needed a quiet place to heal."

"Toro told me how you've cared for her. She says your heart is broken."

He bent down and picked up a gray banded murex shell. "You belong in New York. Studying."

"I finished my dissertation."

A pressure lifted from his chest. He studied the shell, turning it over and over. "I'm glad. You have a professorship?"

"I have a research grant."

"Good."

"To study traditional tattooing. Here in Greece. It seems in the Northern Pindos Mountains some women still wear tattoos."

"Do they?"

"I aim to find out. Will you come with me?" She smiled, and his heart thundered in his chest.

"Why?"

"I love you."

"Don't." He let the shell fall into the water. He didn't want to hurt her.

She stepped into the water. Tiny waves rippled outward casting aqua and gold flickers of light across the rock walls, across her. Water soaked into her dress, the thin fabric clinging to her in all the right places. He stared, his blood boiling hot, his cock rising.

Beneath the transparent linen, faint blue and green tattoos ran from her neck to her upper thigh. Spirals and swirls. Each one a replica of his brush strokes. She was his painting come to life.

She came up against him. "I thought I'd lost you." She took his broken hand and kissed each crushed finger, licked the palm, ran her tongue up his wrist, and sucked the small blue tattoo.

He rested his right hand on her shoulder. "Look at me. I'm ugly and useless. I'm a monster."

"No. You are a man—a kind, caring man. My man." She inhaled and whispered against his lips. "Didn't you say I have a gift for seeing what lies beneath the skin?"

And then she kissed him. And he kissed her back.

A word about the author...

Zara West loves all things dark, scary, and heart-stopping as long as they lead to true love. Born in Williamsburg, Brooklyn, Zara spends winters in New York where the streets hum with life, summers in the Maritimes where the sea can be cruel, and the rest of the year anywhere inspiration for tales of suspense, mystery, and romance are plentiful.

An accomplished artist by training and passion, she brings a love of art to every book she writes. When not marooned on an island or chasing after Greek shepherds, Zara tends her organic herb garden, collects hats and cats, and whips up ethnic dishes for friends and family.

A member of RWA, Zara West is an award-winning author of both fiction and non-fiction. This is her first romantic suspense.

www.zarawestsuspense.com

Thank you for purchasing
this publication of The Wild Rose Press, Inc.

If you enjoyed the story, we would appreciate your
letting others know by leaving a review.

For other wonderful stories,
please visit our on-line bookstore at
www.thewildroscpress.cum.

For questions or more information
contact us at
info@thewildrosepress.com.

The Wild Rose Press, Inc.
www.thewildrosepress.com

Stay current with The Wild Rose Press, Inc.

Like us on Facebook

https://www.facebook.com/TheWildRosePress

And Follow us on Twitter
https://twitter.com/WildRosePress